The Mystery of Metropolisville

Edward Eggleston

The Mystery of Metropolisville

ISBN: 978-1-63637-392-8

CONTENTS

PREFACE

A novel should be the truest of books. It partakes in a certain sense of the nature of both history and art. It needs to be true to human nature in its permanent and essential qualities, and it should truthfully represent some specific and temporary manifestation of human nature: that is, some form of society. It has been objected that I have copied life too closely, but it seems to me that the work to be done just now, is to represent the forms and spirit of our own life, and thus free ourselves from habitual imitation of that which is foreign. I have wished to make my stories of value as a contribution to the history of civilization in America. If it be urged that this is not the highest function, I reply that it is just now the most necessary function of this kind of literature. Of the value of these stories as works of art, others must judge; but I shall have the satisfaction of knowing that I have at least rendered one substantial though humble service to our literature, if I have portrayed correctly certain forms of American life and manners.

BROOKLYN, March, 1873

WORDS BEFOREHAND

Metropolisville is nothing but a memory now. If Jonah's gourd had not been a little too much used already, it would serve an excellent turn just here in the way of an apt figure of speech illustrating the growth, the wilting, and the withering of Metropolisville. The last time I saw the place the grass grew green where once stood the City Hall, the corn-stalks waved their banners on the very site of the old store—I ask pardon, the "Emporium"—of Jackson, Jones & Co., and what had been the square, staring white court-house—not a Temple but a Barn of Justice—had long since fallen to base uses. The walls which had echoed with forensic grandiloquence were now forced to hear only the bleating of silly sheep. The church, the school-house, and the City Hotel had been moved away bodily. The village grew, as hundreds of other frontier villages had grown, in the flush times; it died, as so many others died, of the financial crash which was the inevitable sequel and retribution of speculative madness. Its history resembles the history of other Western towns of the sort so strongly, that I should not take the trouble to write about it, nor ask you to take the trouble to read about it, if the history of the town did not involve also the history of certain human lives—of a tragedy that touched deeply more than one soul. And what is history worth but for its human interest? The history of Athens is not of value on account of its temples and statues, but on account of its men and women. And though the "Main street" of Metropolisville is now a country road where the dog-fennel blooms almost undisturbed by comers and goers, though the plowshare remorselessly turns over the earth in places where corner lots were once sold for a hundred dollars the front foot, and though the lot once sacredly set apart (on the map) as "Depot Ground" is now nothing but a potato-patch, yet there are hearts on which the brief history of Metropolisville has left traces ineffaceable by sunshine or storm, in time or eternity.

1

CHAPTER I

THE AUTOCRAT OF THE STAGECOACH

"Git up!"

No leader of a cavalry charge ever put more authority into his tones than did Whisky Jim, as he drew the lines over his four bay horses in the streets of Red Owl Landing, a village two years old, boasting three thousand inhabitants, and a certain prospect of having four thousand a month later.

Even ministers, poets, and writers of unworldly romances are sometimes influenced by mercenary considerations. But stage-drivers are entirely consecrated to their high calling. Here was Whisky Jim, in the very streets of Red Owl, in the spring of the year 1856, when money was worth five and six per cent a month on bond and mortgage, when corner lots doubled in value over night, when everybody was frantically trying to swindle everybody else—here was Whisky Jim, with the infatuation of a life-long devotion to horse-flesh, utterly oblivious to the chances of robbing green emigrants which a season of speculation affords. He was secure from the infection. You might have shown him a gold-mine under the very feet of his wheel-horses, and he could not have worked it twenty-four hours. He had an itching palm, which could be satisfied with nothing but the "ribbons" drawn over the backs of a four-in-hand.

"Git up!"

The coach moved away—slowly at first—from the front door of the large, rectangular, unpainted Red Owl Hotel, dragging its wheels heavily through the soft turf of a Main street from which the cotton-wood trees had been cut down, but in which the stumps were still standing, and which remained as innocent of all pavement as when, three years before, the chief whose name it bore, loaded his worldly goods upon the back of his oldest and ugliest wife, slung his gun over his shoulder, and started mournfully away from the home of his fathers, which he, shiftless fellow, had bargained away to the white man for an annuity of powder and blankets, and a little money, to be quickly spent for whisky. And yet, I might add digressively, there is comfort in the saddest situations. Even the venerable Red Owl bidding adieu to the home of his ancestors found solace in the sweet hope of returning under favorable circumstances to scalp the white man's wife and children.

"Git up, thair! G'lang!" The long whip swung round and

cracked threateningly over the haunches of the leaders, making them start suddenly as the coach went round a corner and dipped into a hole at the same instant, nearly throwing the driver, and the passenger who was enjoying the outride with him, from their seats.

"What a hole!" said the passenger, a studious-looking young man, with an entomologist's tin collecting-box slung over his shoulders.

The driver drew a long breath, moistened his lips, and said in a cool and aggravatingly deliberate fashion:

"That air blamed pollywog puddle sold las' week fer tew thaousand."

"Dollars?" asked the young man.

Jim gave him an annihilating look, and queried: "Didn' think I meant tew thaousand acorns, did ye?"

"It's an awful price," said the abashed passenger, speaking as one might in the presence of a superior being.

Jim was silent awhile, and then resumed in the same slow tone, but with something of condescension mixed with it:

"Think so, do ye? Mebbe so, stranger. Fool what bought that tadpole lake done middlin' well in disposin' of it, how-sumdever."

Here the Superior Being came to a dead pause, and waited to be questioned.

"How's that?" asked the young man.

After a proper interval of meditation, Jim said: "Sol' it this week. Tuck jest twice what he invested in his frog-fishery."

"Four thousand?" said the passenger with an inquisitive and surprised rising inflection.

"Hey?" said Jim, looking at him solemnly. "Tew times tew use to be four when I larnt the rewl of three in old Varmount. Mebbe 'taint so in the country you come from, where they call a pail a bucket."

The passenger kept still awhile. The manner of the Superior Being chilled him a little. But Whisky Jim graciously broke the silence himself.

"Sell nex' week fer six."

The young man's mind had already left the subject under discussion, and it took some little effort of recollection to bring it back.

"How long will it keep on going up?" he asked.

"Tell it teches the top. Come daown then like a spile-driver in a hurry. Higher it goes, the wuss it'll mash anybody what happens to stan' percisely under it."

"When will it reach the top?"

3

The Superior Being turned his eyes full upon the student, who blushed a little under the half-sneer of his look.

"Yaou tell! Thunder, stranger, that's jest what everybody'd pay money tew find out. Everybody means to git aout in time, but—thunder!—every piece of perrary in this territory's a deadfall. Somebody'll git catched in every one of them air traps. Gee up! G'lang! Git up, won't you? Hey?" And this last sentence was ornamented with another magnificent writing-master flourish of the whip-lash, and emphasized by an explosive crack at the end, which started the four horses off in a swinging gallop, from which Jim did not allow them to settle back into a walk until they had reached the high prairie land in the rear of the town.

"What are those people living in tents for?" asked the student as he pointed back to Red Owl, now considerably below them, and which presented a panorama of balloon-frame houses, mostly innocent of paint, with a sprinkling of tents pitched here and there among the trees; on lots not yet redeemed from virgin wildness, but which possessed the remarkable quality of "fetching" prices that would have done honor to well-located land in Philadelphia.

"What they live that a-way fer? Hey? Mos'ly 'cause they can't live no other." Then, after a long pause, the Superior Being resumed in a tone of half-soliloquy: "A'n't a bed nur a board in the hull city of Red Owl to be had for payin' nur coaxin'. Beds is aces. Houses is trumps. Landlords is got high, low, Jack, and the game in ther hands. Looky there! A bran-new lot of fools fresh from the factory." And he pointed to the old steamboat "Ben Bolt," which was just coming up to the landing with deck and guards black with eager immigrants of all classes.

But Albert Charlton, the student, did not look back any longer. It marks an epoch in a man's life when he first catches sight of a prairie landscape, especially if that landscape be one of those great rolling ones to be seen nowhere so well as in Minnesota. Charlton had crossed Illinois from Chicago to Dunleith in the night-time, and so had missed the flat prairies. His sense of sublimity was keen, and, besides his natural love for such scenes, he had a hobbyist passion for virgin nature superadded.

"What a magnificent country!" he cried.

"Talkin' sense!" muttered Jim. "Never seed so good a place fer stagin' in my day."

For every man sees through his own eyes. To the emigrants whose white-top "prairie schooners" wound slowly along the road, these grass-grown hills and those far-away meadowy valleys were only so many places where good farms could be opened without the trouble of cutting off the trees. It was not landscape, but simply land

4

where one might raise thirty or forty bushels of spring wheat to the acre, without any danger of "fevernager;" to the keen-witted speculator looking sharply after corner stakes, at a little distance from the road, it was just so many quarter sections, "eighties," and "forties," to be bought low and sold high whenever opportunity offered; to Jim it was a good country for staging, except a few "blamed sloughs where the bottom had fell out." But the enthusiastic eyes of young Albert Charlton despised all sordid and "culinary uses" of the earth; to him this limitless vista of waving wild grass, these green meadows and treeless hills dotted everywhere with purple and yellow flowers, was a sight of Nature in her noblest mood. Such rolling hills behind hills! If those rolls could be called hills! After an hour the coach had gradually ascended to the summit of the "divide" between Purple River on the one side and Big Gun River on the other, and the rows of willows and cotton-woods that hung over the water's edge—the only trees under the whole sky—marked distinctly the meandering lines of the two streams. Albert Charlton shouted and laughed; he stood up beside Jim, and cried out that it was a paradise.

"Mebbe 'tis," sneered Jim, "Anyway, it's got more'n one devil into it. Gil—lang!"

And under the inspiration of the scenery, Albert, with the impulsiveness of a young man, unfolded to Whisky Jim all the beauties of his own theories: how a man should live naturally and let other creatures live; how much better a man was without flesh-eating; how wrong it was to speculate, and that a speculator gave nothing in return; and that it was not best to wear flannels, seeing one should harden his body to endure cold and all that; and how a man should let his beard grow, not use tobacco nor coffee nor whisky, should get up at four o'clock in the morning and go to bed early.

"Looky here, mister!" said the Superior Being, after a while. "I wouldn't naow, ef I was you!"

"Wouldn't what?"

"Wouldn't fetch no sich notions into this ked'ntry. Can't afford tew. 'Taint no land of ideas. It's the ked'ntry of corner lots. Ideas is in the way—don't pay no interest. Haint had time to build a 'sylum fer people with idees yet, in this territory. Ef you must have 'em, why let me rec-ommend Bost'n. Drove hack there wunst, myself." Then after a pause he proceeded with the deliberation of a judge: "It's the best village I ever lay eyes on fer idees, is Bost'n. Thicker'n hops! Grow single and in bunches. Have s'cieties there fer idees. Used to make money outen the fellows with idees, cartin 'em round to anniversaries and sich. Ef you only wear a nice slick plug-hat

5

there, you kin believe anything you choose or not, and be a gentleman all the same. The more you believe or don't believe in Bost'n, the more gentleman you be. The don't-believers is just as good as the believers. Idees inside the head, and plug-hats outside. But idees out here! I tell you, here it's nothin' but per-cent." The Superior Being puckered his lips and whistled. "Git up, will you! G'lang! Better try Bost'n."

Perhaps Albert Charlton, the student passenger, was a little offended with the liberty the driver had taken in rebuking his theories. He was full of "idees," and his fundamental idea was of course his belief in the equality and universal brotherhood of men. In theory he recognized no social distinctions. But the most democratic of democrats in theory is just a little bit of an aristocrat in feeling—he doesn't like to be patted on the back by the hostler; much less does he like to be reprimanded by a stage-driver. And Charlton was all the more sensitive from a certain vague consciousness that he himself had let down the bars of his dignity by unfolding his theories so gushingly to Whisky Jim. What did Jim know—what could a man who said "idees" know—about the great world-reforming thoughts that engaged his attention? But when dignity is once fallen, all the king's oxen and all the king's men can't stand it on its legs again. In such a strait, one must flee from him who saw the fall.

Albert Charlton therefore determined that he would change to the inside of the coach when an opportunity should offer, and leave the Superior Being to sit "wrapped in the solitude of his own originality."

CHAPTER II

THE SOD TAVERN

Here and there Charlton noticed the little claim-shanties, built in every sort of fashion, mere excuses for pre-emption. Some were even constructed of brush. What was lacking in the house was amply atoned for by the perjury of the claimant who, in pre-empting, would swear to any necessary number of good qualities in his habitation. On a little knoll ahead of the stage he saw what seemed to be a heap of earth. There must have been some inspiration in this mound, for, as soon as it came in sight, Whisky Jim began to chirrup and swear at his horses, and to crack his long whip threateningly until he had sent them off up the hill at a splendid pace. Just by this mound of earth he reined up with an air that said the forenoon route was finished. For this was nothing less than the "Sod Tavern," a house built of cakes of the tenacious prairiesod. No other material was used except the popple-poles, which served for supports to the sod-roof. The tavern was not over ten feet high at the apex of the roof; it had been built for two or three years, and the grass was now growing on top. A red-shirted publican sallied out of this artificial grotto, and invited the ladies and gentlemen to dinner.

It appeared, from a beautifully-engraved map hanging on the walls of the Sod Tavern, that this earthly tabernacle stood in the midst of an ideal town. The map had probably been constructed by a poet, for it was quite superior to the limitations of sense and matter-of-fact. According to the map, this solitary burrow was surrounded by Seminary, Depôt, Court-House, Woolen Factory, and a variety of other potential institutions, which composed the flourishing city of New Cincinnati. But the map was meant chiefly for Eastern circulation.

Charlton's dietetic theories were put to the severest test at the table. He had a good appetite. A ride in the open air in Minnesota is apt to make one hungry. But the first thing that disgusted Mr. Charlton was the coffee, already poured out, and steaming under his nose. He hated coffee because he liked it; and the look of disgust with which he shoved it away was the exact measure of his physical craving for it. The solid food on the table consisted of waterlogged potatoes, half-baked salt-rising bread, and salt-pork. Now, young Charlton was a reader of the Water-Cure Journal of that day, and despised meat of all things, and of all meat despised swine's flesh, as not even fit for Jews; and of all forms of hog, hated fat salt-pork as poisonously indigestible. So with a dyspeptic self-consciousness he rejected the pork, picked off the periphery of the bread near the crust, cautiously avoiding the dough-bogs in the middle; but then he revenged himself by falling furiously upon the aquatic potatoes, out of which most of the nutriment had been soaked.

Jim, who sat alongside him, doing cordial justice to the badness of the meal, muttered that it wouldn't do to eat by idees in Minnesoty. And with the freedom that belongs to the frontier, the company begun to discuss dietetics, the fat gentleman roundly abusing the food for the express purpose, as Charlton thought, of diverting attention from his voracious eating of it.

"Simply despicable," grunted the fat man, as he took a third slice of the greasy pork. "I do despise such food."

"Eats it like he was mad at it," said Driver Jim in an undertone.

But as Charlton's vegetarianism was noticed, all fell to denouncing it. Couldn't live in a cold climate without meat. Cadaverous Mr. Minorkey, the broad-shouldered, sad-looking man with side-whiskers, who complained incessantly of a complication of disorders, which included dyspepsia, consumption, liver-disease, organic disease of the heart, rheumatism, neuralgia, and entire nervous prostration, and who was never entirely happy except in telling over the oft-repeated catalogue of his disgusting symptoms— Mr. Minorkey, as he sat by his daughter, inveighed, in an earnest crab-apple voice, against Grahamism. He would have been in his grave twenty years ago if it hadn't been for good meat. And then he recited in detail the many desperate attacks from which he had been saved by beefsteak. But this pork he felt sure would make him sick. It might kill him. And he evidently meant to sell his life as dearly as possible, for, as Jim muttered to Charlton, he was "goin' the whole hog anyhow."

"Miss Minorkey," said the fat gentleman checking a piece of pork in the middle of its mad career toward his lips, "Miss Minorkey, we should like to hear from you on this subject." In truth, the fat gentleman was very weary of Mr. Minorkey's pitiful succession of diagnoses of the awful symptoms and fatal complications of which he had been cured by very allopathic doses of animal food. So he appealed to Miss Minorkey for relief at a moment when her father had checked and choked his utterance with coffee.

Miss Minorkey was quite a different affair from her father. She was thoroughly but not obtrusively healthy. She had a high, white forehead, a fresh complexion, and a mouth which, if it was

8

deficient in sweetness and warmth of expression, was also free from all bitterness and aggressiveness. Miss Minorkey was an eminently well-educated young lady as education goes. She was more—she was a young lady of reading and of ideas. She did not exactly defend Charlton's theory in her reply, but she presented both sides of the controversy, and quoted some scientific authorities in such a way as to make it apparent that there were two sides. This unexpected and rather judicial assistance called forth from Charlton a warm acknowledgment, his pale face flushed with modest pleasure, and as he noted the intellectuality of Miss Minorkey's forehead he inwardly comforted himself that the only person of ideas in the whole company was not wholly against him.

Albert Charlton was far from being a "ladies' man;" indeed, nothing was more despicable in his eyes than men who frittered away life in ladies' company. But this did not at all prevent him from being very human himself in his regard for ladies. All the more that he had lived out of society all his life, did his heart flutter when he took his seat in the stage after dinner. For Miss Minorkey's father and the fat gentleman felt that they must have the back seat; there were two other gentlemen on the middle seat; and Albert Charlton, all unused to the presence of ladies, must needs sit on the front seat, alongside the gray traveling-dress of the intellectual Miss Minorkey, who, for her part, was not in the least bit nervous. Young Charlton might have liked her better if she had been.

But if she was not shy, neither was she obtrusive. When Mr. Charlton had grown weary of hearing Mr. Minorkey pity himself, and of hearing the fat gentleman boast of the excellence of the Minnesota climate, the dryness of the air, and the wonderful excess of its oxygen, and the entire absence of wintry winds, and the rapid development of the country, and when he had grown weary of discussions of investments at five per cent a month, he ventured to interrupt Miss Minorkey's reverie by a remark to which she responded. And he was soon in a current of delightful talk. The young gentleman spoke with great enthusiasm; the young woman without warmth, but with a clear intellectual interest in literary subjects, that charmed her interlocutor. I say literary subjects, though the range of the conversation was not very wide. It was a great surprise to Charlton, however, to find in a new country a young woman so well informed.

Did he fall in love? Gentle reader, be patient. You want a love-story, and I don't blame you. For my part, I should not take the trouble to record this history if there were no love in it. Love is the universal bond of human sympathy. But you must give people time. What we call falling in love is not half so simple an affair as you

9

think, though it often looks simple enough to the spectator. Albert Charlton was pleased, he was full of enthusiasm, and I will not deny that he several times reflected in a general way that so clear a talker and so fine a thinker would make a charming wife for some man— some intellectual man—some man like himself, for instance. He admired Miss Minorkey. He liked her. With an enthusiastic young man, admiring and liking are, to say the least, steps that lead easily to something else. But you must remember how complex a thing love is. Charlton—I have to confess it—was a little conceited, as every young man is at twenty. He flattered himself that the most intelligent woman he could find would be a good match for him. He loved ideas, and a woman of ideas pleased his fancy. Add to this that he had come to a time of life when he was very liable to fall in love with somebody, and that he was in the best of spirits from the influence of air and scenery and motion and novelty, and you render it quite probable that he could not be tossed for half a day on the same seat in a coach with such a girl as Helen Minorkey was—that, above all, he could not discuss Hugh Miller and the "Vestiges of Creation" with her, without imminent peril of experiencing an admiration for her and an admiration for himself, and a liking and a palpitating and a castle-building that under favorable conditions might somehow grow into that complex and inexplicable feeling which we call love.

In fact, Jim, who drove both routes on this day, and who peeped into the coach whenever he stopped to water, soliloquized that two fools with idees would make a quare span ef they had a neck-yoke on.

10

CHAPTER III

LAND AND LOVE

Mr. Minorkey and the fat gentleman found much to interest them as the coach rolled over the smooth prairie road, now and then crossing a slough. Not that Mr. Minorkey or his fat friend had any particular interest in the beautiful outline of the grassy knolls, the gracefulness of the water-willows that grew along the river edge, and whose paler green was the prominent feature of the landscape, or in the sweet contrast at the horizon where grass-green earth met the light blue northern sky. But the scenery none the less suggested fruitful themes for talk to the two gentlemen on the back-seat.

"I've got money loaned on that quarter at three per cent a month and five after due. The mortgage has a waiver in it too. You see, the security was unusually good, and that was why I let him have it so low." This was what Mr. Minorkey said at intervals and with some variations, generally adding something like this: "The day I went to look at that claim, to see whether the security was good or not, I got caught in the rain. I expected it would kill me. Well, sir, I was taken that night with a pain—just here—and it ran through the lung to the point of the shoulder-blade—here. I had to get my feet into a tub of water and take some brandy. I'd a had pleurisy if I'd been in any other country but this. I tell you, nothing saved me but the oxygen in this air. There! there's a forty that I lent a hundred dollars on at five per cent a month and six per cent after maturity, with a waiver in the mortgage. The day I came here to see this I was nearly dead. I had a—"

Just here the fat gentleman would get desperate, and, by way of preventing the completion of the dolorous account, would break out with: "That's Sokaska, the new town laid out by Johnson—that hill over there, where you see those stakes. I bought a corner-lot fronting the public square, and a block opposite where they hope to get a factory. There's a brook runs through the town, and they think it has water enough and fall enough to furnish a water-power part of the day, during part of the year, and they hope to get a factory located there. There'll be a territorial road run through from St. Paul next spring if they can get a bill through the legislature this winter. You'd best buy there."

"I never buy town lots," said Minorkey, coughing despairingly, "never! I run no risks. I take my interest at three and five per cent a month on a good mortgage, with a waiver, and let other folks take risks."

But the hopeful fat gentleman evidently took risks and slept soundly. There was no hypothetical town, laid out hypothetically on paper, in whose hypothetical advantages he did not covet a share.

"You see," he resumed, "I buy low—cheap as dirt—and get the rise. Some towns must get to be cities. I have a little all round, scattered here and there. I am sure to have a lucky ticket in some of these lotteries."

Mr. Minorkey only coughed and shook his head despondently, and said that "there was nothing so good as a mortgage with a waiver in it. Shut down in short order if you don't get your interest, if you've only got a waiver. I always shut down unless I've got five per cent after maturity. But I have the waiver in the mortgage anyhow."

As the stage drove on, up one grassy slope and down another, there was quite a different sort of a conversation going on in the other end of the coach. Charlton found many things which suggested subjects about which he and Miss Minorkey could converse, notwithstanding the strange contrast in their way of expressing themselves. He was full of eagerness, positiveness, and a fresh-hearted egoism. He had an opinion on everything; he liked or disliked everything; and when he disliked anything, he never spared invective in giving expression to his antipathy. His moral convictions were not simply strong—they were vehement. His intellectual opinions were hobbies that he rode under whip and spur. A theory for everything, a solution of every difficulty, a "high moral" view of politics, a sharp skepticism in religion, but a skepticism that took hold of him as strongly as if it had been a faith. He held to his non credo with as much vigor as a religionist holds to his creed.

Miss Minorkey was just a little irritating to one so enthusiastic. She neither believed nor disbelieved anything in particular. She liked to talk about everything in a cool and objective fashion; and Charlton was provoked to find that, with all her intellectual interest in things, she had no sort of personal interest in anything. If she had been a disinterested spectator, dropped down from another sphere, she could not have discussed the affairs of this planet with more complete impartiality, not to say indifference. Theories, doctrines, faiths, and even moral duties, she treated as Charlton did beetles; ran pins through them and held them up where she could get a good view of them—put them away as curiosities. She listened with an attention that was surely flattering enough, but Charlton felt that he had not made much impression on her. There was a sort of attraction in this repulsion. There was an excitement in his ambition to impress this impartial and judicial mind with the truth and importance of the glorious and regenerating views he had embraced. His self-esteem was pleased at the thought that he should yet conquer this cool and open-minded girl by the force of his own intelligence. He admired her intellectual self-possession all the more that it was a quality which he lacked. Before that afternoon ride was over, he was convinced that he sat by the supreme woman of all he had ever known. And who was so fit to marry the supreme woman as he, Albert Charlton, who was to do so much by advocating all sorts of reforms to help the world forward to its goal?

He liked that word goal. A man's pet words are the key to his character. A man who talks of "vocation," of "goal," and all that, may be laughed at while he is in the period of intellectual fermentation. The time is sure to come, however, when such a man can excite other emotions than mirth.

And so Charlton, full of thoughts of his "vocation" and the world's "goal," was slipping into an attachment for a woman to whom both words were Choctaw. Do you wonder at it? If she had had a vocation also, and had talked about goals, they would mutually have repelled each other, like two bodies charged with the same kind of electricity. People with vocations can hardly fall in love with other people with vocations.

But now Metropolisville was coming in sight, and Albert's attention was attracted by the conversation of Mr. Minorkey and the fat gentleman.

"Mr. Plausaby has selected an admirable site," Charlton heard the fat gentleman remark, and as Mr. Plausaby was his own step-father, he began to listen. "Pretty sharp! pretty sharp!" continued the fat gentleman. "I tell you what, Mr. Minorkey, that man Plausaby sees through a millstone with a hole in it. I mean to buy some lots in this place. It'll be the county-seat and a railroad junction, as sure as you're alive. And Plausaby has saved some of his best lots for me."

"Yes, it's a nice town, or will be. I hold a mortgage on the best eighty—the one this way—at three per cent and five after maturity, with a waiver. I liked to have died here one night last summer. I was taken just after supper with a violent—"

"What a beauty of a girl that is," broke in the fat gentleman, "little Katy Charlton, Plausaby's step-daughter!" And instantly Mr. Albert Charlton thrust his head out of the coach and shouted "Hello, Katy!" to a girl of fifteen, who ran to intercept the coach at the hotel steps.

"Hurrah, Katy!" said the young man, as she kissed him impulsively as soon as he had alighted.

"P'int out your baggage, mister," said Jim, interrupting Katy's raptures with a tone that befitted a Superior Being.

In a few moments the coach, having deposited Charlton and the fat gentleman, was starting away for its destination at Perritaut, eight miles farther on, when Charlton, remembering again his companion on the front seat, lifted his hat and bowed, and Miss Minorkey was kind enough to return the bow. Albert tried to analyze her bow as he lay awake in bed that night. Miss Minorkey doubtless slept soundly. She always did.

CHAPTER IV

ALBERT AND KATY

All that day in which Albert Charlton had been riding from Red Owl Landing to Metropolisville, sweet Little Katy Charlton had been expecting him. Everybody called her sweet, and I suppose there was no word in the dictionary that so perfectly described her. She was not well-read, like Miss Minorkey; she was not even very smart at her lessons: but she was sweet. Sweetness is a quality that covers a multitude of defects. Katy's heart had love in it for everybody. She loved her mother; she loved Squire Plausaby, her step-father; she loved cousin Isa, as she called her step-father's niece; she loved—well, no matter, she would have told you that she loved nobody more than Brother Albert.

And now that Brother Albert was coming to the new home in the new land he had never seen before, Katy's heart was in her eyes. She would show him so many things he had never seen, explain how the pocket-gophers built their mounds, show him the nestful of flying-squirrels—had he ever seen flying-squirrels? And she would show him Diamond Lake, and the speckled pickerel among the water-plants. And she would point out the people, and entertain Albert with telling him their names and the curious gossip about them. It was so fine to know something that even Albert, with all his learning, did not know. And she would introduce Albert to him. Would Albert like him? Of course he would. They were both such dear men.

And as the hours wore on, Katy grew more and more excited and nervous. She talked about Albert to her mother till she wearied that worthy woman, to whom the arrival of any one was an excuse for dressing if possible in worse taste than usual, or at least for tying an extra ribbon in her hair, and the extra ribbon was sure to be of a hue entirely discordant with the mutually discordant ones that preceded it. Tired of talking to her mother, she readily found an excuse to buy something—ribbons, or candles, or hair-pins, or dried apples—something kept in the very miscellaneous stock of the "Emporium," and she knew who would wait upon her, and who would kindly prolong the small transaction by every artifice in his power, and thus give her time to tell him about her Brother Albert. He would be so glad to hear about Albert. He was always glad to hear her tell about anybody or anything.

And when the talk over the counter at the Emporium could

not be farther prolonged, she had even stopped on her way home at Mrs. Ferret's, and told her about Albert, though she did not much like to talk to her—she looked so penetratingly at her out of her round, near-sighted eyes, which seemed always keeping a watch on the tip of her nose. And Mrs. Ferret, with her jerky voice, and a smile that was meant to be an expression of mingled cheerfulness and intelligence, but which expressed neither, said: "Is your brother a Christian?"

And Katy said he was a dear, dear fellow, but she didn't know as he was a church-member.

"Does he hold scriptural views? You know so many people in colleges are not evangelical."

Mrs. Ferret had a provoking way of pronouncing certain words unctuously—she said "Chrishchen" "shcripcherral," and even in the word evangelical she made the first e very hard and long.

And when little Katy could not tell whether Albert held "shcripcherral" views or not, and was thoroughly tired of being quizzed as to whether she "really thought Albert had a personal interest in religion," she made an excuse to run away into the chamber of Mrs. Morrow, Mrs. Ferret's mother, who was an invalid—Mrs. Ferret said "inva_leed_," for the sake of emphasis. The old lady never asked impertinent questions, never talked about "shcripcherral" or "ee-vangelical" views, but nevertheless breathed an atmosphere of scriptural patience and evangelical fortitude and Christian victory over the world's tribulations. Little Katy couldn't have defined, the difference between the two in words; she never attempted it but once, and then she said that Mrs. Ferret was like a crabapple, and her mother like a Bartlett pear.

But she was too much excited to stay long in one place, and so she hurried home and went to talking to Cousin Isa, who was sewing by the west window. And to her she poured forth praises of Albert without stint; of his immense knowledge of everything, of his goodness and his beauty and his strength, and his voice, and his eyes.

"And you'll love him better'n you ever loved anybody," she wound up.

And Cousin Isa said she didn't know about that.

After all this weary waiting Albert had come. He had not been at home for two years. It was during his absence that his mother had married Squire Plausaby, and had moved to Minnesota. He wanted to see everybody at home. His sister had written him favorable accounts of his step-father; he had heard other accounts, not quite so favorable, perhaps. He persuaded himself that like a dutiful son he wanted most to see his mother, who was really very

16

fond of him. But in truth he spent his spare time in thinking about Katy. He sincerely believed that he loved his mother better than anybody in the world. All his college cronies knew that the idol of his heart was Katy, whose daguerreotype he carried in the inside pocket of his vest, and whose letters he looked for with the eagerness of a lover.

At last he had come, and Katy had carried him off into the house in triumph, showing him—showing is the word, I think—showing him to her mother, whom he kissed tenderly, and to her step-father, and most triumphantly to Isa, with an air that said, "Now, isn't he just the finest fellow in the world!" And she was not a little indignant that Isa was so quiet in her treatment of the big brother. Couldn't she see what a forehead and eyes he had?

And the mother, with one shade of scarlet and two of pink in her hair-ribbons, was rather proud of her son, but not satisfied.

"Why didn't you graduate?" she queried as she poured the coffee at supper.

"Because there were so many studies in the course which were a dead waste of time. I learned six times as much as some of the dunderheads that got sheepskins, and the professors knew it, but they do not dare to put their seal on anybody's education unless it is mixed in exact proportions—so much Latin, so much Greek, so much mathematics. The professors don't like a man to travel any road but theirs. It is a reflection on their own education. Why, I learned more out of some of the old German books in the library than out of all their teaching."

"But why didn't you graduate? It would have sounded so nice to be able to say that you had graduated. That's what I sent you for, you know, and I don't see what you got by going if you haven't graduated."

"Why, mother, I got an education. I thought that was what a college was for."

"But how will anybody know that you're well-educated, I'd like to know, when you can't say that you've graduated?" answered the mother petulantly.

"Whether they know it or not, I am."

"I should think they'd know it just to look at him," said Katy, who thought that Albert's erudition must be as apparent to everybody as to herself.

Mr. Plausaby quietly remarked that he had no doubt Albert had improved his time at school, a remark which for some undefined reason vexed Albert more than his mother's censures.

"Well," said his mother, "a body never has any satisfaction with boys that have got notions. Deliver me from notions. Your father had notions. If it hadn't been for that, we might all of us have been rich to-day. But notions kept us down. That's what I like about Mr. Plausaby. He hasn't a single notion to bother a body with. But, I think, notions run in the blood, and, I suppose, you'll always be putting some fool notion or other in your own way. I meant you to be a lawyer, but I s'pose you've got something against that, though it was your own father's calling."

"I'd about as soon be a thief as a lawyer," Albert broke out in his irritation.

"Well, that's a nice way to speak about your father's profession, I'm sure," said his mother. "But that's what comes of notions. I don't care much, though, if you a'n't a lawyer. Doctors make more than lawyers do, and you can't have any notions against being a doctor."

"What, and drug people? Doctors are quacks. They know that drugs are good for nothing, and yet they go on dosing everybody to make money. It people would bathe, and live in the open air, and get up early, and harden themselves to endure changes of climate, and not violate God's decalogue written in their own muscles and nerves and head and stomach, they wouldn't want to swallow an apothecary-shop every year."

"Did you ever!" said Mrs. Plausaby, looking at her husband, who smiled knowingly (as much as to reply that he had often), and at Cousin Isa, who looked perplexed between her admiration at a certain chivalrous courage in Albert's devotion to his ideas, and her surprise at the ultraism of his opinions.

"Did you ever!" said the mother again. "That's carrying notions further than your father did. You'll never be anything, Albert. Well, well, what comfort can I take in a boy that'll turn his back on all his chances, and never be anything but a poor preacher, without money enough to make your mother a Christmas present of a—a piece of ribbon?"

"Why, ma, you've got ribbons enough now, I'm sure," said Katy, looking at the queer tri-color which her mother was flying in revolutionary defiance of the despotism of good taste. "I'm sure I'm glad Albert's going to be a minister. He'll look so splendid in the pulpit! What kind of a preacher will you be, Albert?"

"I hope it'll be Episcopal, or any way Presbyterian," said Mrs. Plausaby, "for they get paid better than Methodist or Baptist. And besides, it's genteel to be Episcopal. But, I suppose, some notion'll keep you out of being Episcopal too. You'll try to be just as poor and ungenteel as you can. Folks with notions always do."

"If I was going to be a minister, I would find out the poorest sect in the country, the one that all your genteel folks turned up

18

their noses at—the Winnebrenarians, or the Mennonites, or the Albrights, or something of that sort. I would join such a sect, and live and work for the poor—"

"Yes, I'll be bound!" said Mrs. Plausaby, feeling of her breastpin to be sure it was in the right place.

"But I'll never be a parson. I hope I'm too honest. Half the preachers are dishonest."

Then, seeing Isa's look of horrified surprise, Albert added: "Not in money matters, but in matters of opinion. They do not deal honestly with themselves or other people. Ministers are about as unfair as pettifoggers in their way of arguing, and not more than one in twenty of them is brave enough to tell the whole truth."

"Such notions! such notions!" cried Mrs. Plausaby.

And Cousin Isa—Miss Isabel Marlay, I should say for she was only a cousin by brevet—here joined valiant battle in favor of the clergy. And poor little Katy, who dearly loved to take sides with her friends, found her sympathies sadly split in two in a contest between her dear, dear brother and her dear, dear Cousin Isa, and she did wish they would quit talking about such disagreeable things. I do not think either of the combatants convinced the other, but as each fought fairly they did not offend one another, and when the battle was over, Albert bluntly confessed that he had spoken too strongly, and though Isa made no confession, she felt that after all ministers were not impeccable, and that Albert was a brave fellow.

And Mrs. Plausaby said that she hoped Isabel would beat some sense into the boy, for she was really afraid that he never would have anything but notions. She pitied the woman that married him. She wouldn't get many silk-dresses, and she'd have to fix her old bonnets over two or three years hand-running.

CHAPTER V

CORNER LOTS

Mr. Plausaby was one of those men who speak upon a level pitch, in a gentle and winsome monotony. His voice was never broken by impulse, never shaken by feeling. He was courteous without ostentation, treating everybody kindly without exactly seeming to intend it. He let fall pleasant remarks incidentally or accidentally, so that one was always fortuitously overhearing his good opinion of one's self. He did not have any conscious intent to flatter each person with some ulterior design in view, but only a general disposition to keep everybody cheerful, and an impression that it was quite profitable as a rule to stand well with one's neighbors.

The morning after Charlton's arrival the fat passenger called, eager as usual to buy lots. To his lively imagination, every piece of ground staked off into town lots had infinite possibilities. It seemed that the law of probabilities had been no part of the sanguine gentleman's education, but the gloriousness of possibilities was a thing that he appreciated naturally; hopefulness was in his very fiber.

Mr. Plausaby spread his "Map of Metropolisville" on the table, let his hand slip gently down past the "Depot Ground," so that the fat gentleman saw it without seeming to have had his attention called to it; then Plausaby, Esq., looked meditatively at the ground set apart for "College," and seemed to be making a mental calculation. Then Plausaby proceeded to unfold the many advantages of the place, and Albert was a pleased listener; he had never before suspected that Metropolisville had prospects so entirely dazzling. He could not doubt the statements of the bland Plausaby, who said these things in a confidential and reserved way to the fat gentleman. Charlton did not understand, but Plausaby did, that what is told in a corner to a fat gentleman with curly hair and a hopeful nose is sure to be repeated from the house-tops.

"You are an Episcopalian, I believe?" said Plausaby, Esq. The fat gentleman replied that he was a Baptist.

"Oh! well, I might have known it from your cordial way of talking. Baptist myself, in principle. In principle, at least Not a member of any church, sorry to say. Very sorry. My mother and my first Wife were both Baptists. Both of them. I have a very warm side for the good old Baptist church. Very warm side. And a warm side for every Baptist. Every Baptist. To say nothing of the feeling I have always had for you—well, well, let us not pass compliments. Business is business in this country. In this country, you know. But I will tell you one thing. The lot there marked 'College' I am just about transferring to trustees for a Baptist university. There are two or three parties, members of Dr. Armitage's church in New York City, that are going to give us a hundred thousand dollars endowment. A hundred thousand dollars. Don't say anything about it. There are people who—well, who would spoil the thing if they could. We have neighbors, you know. Not very friendly ones. Not very friendly. Perritaut, for instance. It isn't best to tell one's neighbor all one's good luck. Not all one's good luck," and Plausaby, Esq., smiled knowingly at the fat man, who did his best to screw his very transparent face into a crafty smile in return. "Besides," continued Squire Plausaby, "once let it get out that the Baptist University is going to occupy that block, and there'll be a great demand—"

"For all the blocks around," said the eager fat gentleman, growing impatient at Plausaby's long-windedness.

"Precisely. For all the blocks around," went on Plausaby. "And I want to hold on to as much of the property in this quarter as—"

"As you can, of course," said the other.

"As I can, of course. As much as I can, of course. But I'd like to have you interested. You are a man of influence. A man of weight. Of weight of character. You will bring other Baptists. And the more Baptists, the better for—the better for—"

"For the college, of course."

"Exactly. Precisely. For the college, of course. The more, the better. And I should like your name on the board of trustees of—of"

"The college?"

"The university, of course. I should like your name."

The fat gentleman was pleased at the prospect of owning land near the Baptist University, and doubly pleased at the prospect of seeing his name in print as one of the guardians of the destiny of the infant institution. He thought he would like to buy half of block 26.

"Well, no. I couldn't sell in 26 to you or any man. Couldn't sell to any man. I want to hold that block because of its slope. I'll sell in 28 to you, and the lots there are just about as good. Quite as good, indeed. But I want to build on 26."

The fat gentleman declared that he wouldn't have anything but lots in 26. That block suited his fancy, and he didn't care to buy if he could not have a pick.

"Well, you're an experienced buyer, I see," said Plausaby, Esq. "An experienced buyer. Any other man would have preferred 28 to

21

26. But you're a little hard to insist on that particular block. I want you here, and I'll give half of 28 rather than sell you out of 26."

"Well, now, my friend, I am sorry to seem hard. But I fastened my eye on 26. I have a fine eye for direction and distance. One, two, three, four blocks from the public square. That's the block with the solitary oak-tree in it, if I'm right. Yes? Well, I must have lots in that very block. When I take a whim of that kind, heaven and earth can't turn me, Mr. Plausaby. So you'd just as well let me have them."

Plausaby, Esq., at last concluded that he would sell to the plump gentleman any part of block 26 except the two lots on the south-east corner. But that gentleman said that those were the very two he had fixed his eyes upon. He would not buy if there were any reserves. He always took his very pick out of each town.

"Well," said Mr. Plausaby coaxingly, "you see I have selected those two lots for my step-daughter. For little Katy. She is going to get married next spring, I suppose, and I have promised her the two best in the town, and I had marked off these two. Marked them off for her. I'll sell you lots alongside, nearly as good, for half-price. Just half-price."

But the fat gentleman was inexorable. Mr. Plausaby complained that the fat gentleman was hard, and the fat gentleman was pleased with the compliment. Having been frequently lectured by his wife for being so easy and gullible, he was now eager to believe himself a very Shylock. Did not like to rob little Kate of her marriage portion, he said, but he must have the best or none. He wanted the whole south half of 26.

And so Mr. Plausaby sold him the corner-lot and the one next to it for ever so much more than their value, pathetically remarking that he'd have to hunt up some other lots for Kate. And then Mr. Plausaby took the fat gentleman out and showed him the identical corner, with the little oak and the slope to the south.

"Mother," said Albert, when they were gone, "is Katy going to be married in the spring?"

"Why, how should I know?" queried Mrs. Plausaby, as she adjusted her collar, the wide collar of that day, and set her breastpin before the glass. "How should I know? Katy has never told me. There's a young man hangs round here Sundays, and goes boating and riding with her, and makes her presents, and walks with her of evenings, and calls her his pet and his darling and all that kind of nonsense, and I half-suspect"—here she took out her breastpin entirely and began over again—"I half-suspect he's in earnest. But what have I got to do with it? Kate must marry for herself. I did twice, and done pretty well both times. But I can't see to Kate's beaux. Marrying, my son, is a thing everybody must attend to personally for themselves. At least, so it seems to me." And having succeeded in getting her ribbon adjusted as she wanted it, Mrs. Plausaby looked at herself in the glass with an approving conscience.

"But is Kate going to be married in the spring?" asked Albert.

"I don't know whether she will have her wedding in the spring or summer. I can't bother myself about Kate's affairs. Marrying is a thing that everybody must attend to personally for themselves, Albert. If Kate gets married, I can't help it; and I don't know as there's any great sin in it. You'll get married yourself some day."

"Did fa—did Mr. Plausaby promise Katy some lots?"

"Law, no! Every lot he sells 'most is sold for Kate's lot. It's a way he has. He knows how to deal with these sharks. If you want any trading done, Albert, you let Mr. Plausaby do it for you."

"But, mother, that isn't right."

"You've got queer notions, Albert. You'll want us all to quit eating meat, I suppose. Mr. Plausaby said last night you'd be cheated out of your eyes before you'd been here a month, if you stuck to your ideas of things. You see, you don't understand sharks. Plausaby does. But then that is not my lookout. I have all I can do to attend to myself. But Mr. Plausaby does know how to manage sharks."

The more Albert thought the matter over, the more he was convinced that Mr. Plausaby did know how to manage sharks. He went out and examined the stakes, and found that block 26 did not contain the oak, but was much farther down in the slough, and that the corner lots that were to have been Katy's wedding portion stretched quite into the peat bog, and further that if the Baptist University should stand on block 27, it would have a baptistery all around it.

CHAPTER VI

LITTLE KATY'S LOVER

Katy was fifteen and a half, according to the family Bible. Katy was a woman grown in the depth and tenderness of her feeling. But Katy wasn't twelve years of age, if measured by the development of her discretionary powers. The phenomenon of a girl in intellect with a woman's passion is not an uncommon one. Such girls are always attractive—feeling in woman goes for so much more than thought. And such a girl-woman as Kate has a twofold hold on other people— she is loved as a woman and petted as a child.

Albert Charlton knew that for her to love was for her to give herself away without thought, without reserve, almost without the possibility of revocation. Because he was so oppressed with dread in regard to the young man who walked and boated with Katy, courted and caressed her, but about the seriousness of whose intentions the mother seemed to have some doubt—because of the very awfulness of his apprehensions, he dared not ask Kate anything.

The suspense was not for long. On the second evening after Albert's return, Smith Westcott, the chief clerk, the agent in charge of the branch store of Jackson, Jones & Co., in Metropolisville, called at the house of Plausaby. Mr. Smith Westcott was apparently more than twenty-six, but not more than thirty years of age, very well-dressed, rather fast-looking, and decidedly blasé. His history was written in general but not-to-be-misunderstood terms all over his face. It was not the face of a drunkard, but there was the redness of many glasses of wine in his complexion, and a nose that expressed nothing so much as pampered self-indulgence. He had the reputation of being a good, sharp business man, with his "eye-teeth cut," but his conversation was:

"Well—ha! ha!—and how's Katy? Divine as ever! he! he!" rattling the keys and coins in his pocket and frisking about. "Beautiful evening! And how does my sweet Katy? The loveliest maiden in the town! He! he! ha! ha! I declare!"

Then, as Albert came in and was introduced, he broke out with:

"Glad to see you! By George! He! he! Brother, eh? Always glad to see anybody related to Kate. Look like her a little. That's a compliment to you, Mr. Charlton, he! he! You aren't quite so handsome though, by George! Confound the cigar"—throwing it away; "I ordered a box in Red Owl last week—generally get 'em in

Chicago. If there's anything I like it's a good cigar, he! he! Next to a purty girl, ha! ha! But this last box is stronger'n pison. That sort of a cigar floors me. Can't go entirely without, you know, so I smoke half a one, and by that time I get so confounded mad I throw it away. Ha! ha! Smoke, Mr. Charlton? No! No small vices, I s'pose. Couldn't live without my cigar. I'm glad smoking isn't offensive to Kate. Ah! this window's nice, I do like fresh air. Kate knows my habits pretty well by this time. By George, I must try another cigar. I get so nervous when trade's dull and I don't have much to do. Wish you smoked, Mr. Charlton. Keep a man company, ha! ha! Ever been here before? No? By George, must seem strange, he! he! It's a confounded country. Can't get anything to eat. Nor to drink neither, for that matter. By cracky! what nights we used to have at the Elysian Club in New York! Ever go to the Elysian? No? Well, we did have a confounded time there. And headaches in the morning. Punch was too sweet, you see. Sweet punch is sure to make your headache. He! he! But I'm done with clubs and Delmonico's, you know. I'm going to settle down and be a steady family man." Walking to the door, he sang in capital minstrel style:

"When de preacher took his text
He looked so berry much perplext,
Fer nothin' come acrost his mine
But Dandy Jim from Caroline!

"Yah! yah! Plague take it! Come, Kate, stick on a sun-bonnet or a hat, and let's walk. It's too nice a night to stay in the house, by George! You'll excuse, Mr. Charlton? All right; come on, Kate."

And Katy hesitated, and said in a deprecating tone: "You won't mind, will you, Brother Albert?"

And Albert said no, that he wouldn't mind, with a calmness that astonished himself; for he was aching to fall foul of Katy's lover, and beat the coxcombry out of him, or kill him.

"By-by!" said Westcott to Albert, as he went out, and young Charlton went out another door, and strode off toward Diamond Lake. On the high knoll overlooking the lake he stopped and looked away to the east, where the darkness was slowly gathering over the prairie. Night never looks so strange as when it creeps over a prairie, seeming to rise, like a shadowy Old Man of the Sea, out of the grass. The images become more and more confused, and the landscape vanishes by degrees. Away to the west Charlton saw the groves that grew on the banks of the Big Gun River, and then the smooth prairie knolls beyond, and in the dim horizon the "Big Woods." Despite ail his anxiety, Charlton could not help feeling the influence of such a landscape. The greatness, the majesty of God, came to him for a moment. Then the thought of Kate's unhappy love came over him more bitterly from the contrast with the feelings excited by the landscape. He went rapidly over the possible remedies. To remonstrate with Katy seemed out of the question. If she had any power of reason, he might argue. Bat one can not reason with feeling. It was so hard that a soul so sweet, so free from the all but universal human taint of egoism, a soul so loving, self-sacrificing, and self-consecrating, should throw itself away.

"O God!" he cried, between praying and swearing, "must this alabaster-box of precious ointment be broken upon the head of an infernal coxcomb?"

And then, as he remembered how many alabaster-boxes of precious womanly love were thus wasted, and as he looked abroad at the night settling down so inevitably on trees and grass and placid lake, it seemed to him that there could be no Benevolent Intelligence in the universe. Things rolled on as they would, and all his praying would no more drive away the threatened darkness from Kate's life than any cry of his would avail to drive back the all-pervading, awesome presence of night, which was putting out the features of the landscape one after another.

Albert thought to go to his mother. But then with bitterness he confessed to himself, for the first time, that his mother was less wise than Katy herself. He almost called her a fool. And he at once rejected the thought of appealing to his step-father. He felt, also, that this was an emergency in which all his own knowledge and intelligence were of no account. In a matter of affection, a conceited coxcomb, full of flattering speeches, was too strong for him.

The landscape was almost swallowed up. The glassy little lake was at his feet, smooth and quiet. It seemed to him that God was as unresponsive to his distress as the lake. Was there any God?

There was one hope. Westcott might die. He wished he might. But Charlton had lived long enough to observe that people who ought to die, hardly ever do. You, reader, can recall many instances of this general principle, which, however, I do not remember to have seen stated in any discussions of mortality tables.

After all, Albert reflected that he ought not to expect Kate's lover to satisfy him. For he flattered himself that he was a somewhat peculiar man—a man of ideas, a man of the future—and he must not expect to conform everybody to his own standard. Smith Westcott was a man of fine business qualities, he had heard; and most commercial men were, in Albert's estimation, a little weak, morally. He might be a man of deep feeling, and, as Albert walked home, he

26

made up his mind to be charitable. But just then he heard that rattling voice:

"Purty night! By George! Katy, you're divine, by George! Sweeter'n honey and a fine-tooth comb! Dearer to my heart than a gold dollar! Beautiful as a dew-drop and better than a good cigar! He! he! he!"

At such wit and such a giggle Charlton's charity vanished. To him this idiotic giggle at idiotic jokes was a capital offense, and he was seized with a murderous desire to choke his sister's lover. Kate should not marry that fellow if he could help it. He would kill him. But then to kill Westcott would be to kill Katy, to say nothing of hanging himself. Killing has so many sequels. But Charlton was at the fiercely executive stage of his development, and such a man must act. And so he lingered about until Westcott kissed Katy and Katy kissed Westcott back again, and Westcott cried back from the gate, "Dood night! dood night, 'ittle girl! By-by! He! he! By George!" and passed out rattling the keys and coins in his pocket and singing:

"O dear Miss Lucy Neal!" etc.

Then Albert went in, determined to have it all out with Katy. But one sight of her happy, helpless face disarmed him. What an overturning of the heaven of her dreams would he produce by a word! And what could be more useless than remonstrance with one so infatuated! How would she receive his bitter words about one she loved to idolatry?

He kissed her and went to bed.

As Albert Charlton lay awake in his unplastered room in the house of Plausaby, Esq., on the night after he had made the acquaintance of the dear, dear fellow whom his sister loved, he busied himself with various calculations. Notwithstanding his father's "notions," as his mother styled them, he had been able to leave his widow ten thousand dollars, besides a fund for the education of his children. And, as Albert phrased it to himself that night, the ten thousand dollars was every cent clean money, for his father had been a man of integrity. On this ten thousand, he felt sure, Plausaby, Esq., was speculating in a way that might make him rich and respected, or send him to State's-prison, as the chance fell out, but at any rate in a way that was not promotive of the interests of those who traded with him. Of the thousand set apart for Katy's education Plausaby was guardian, and Kate's education was not likely to be greatly advanced by any efforts of his to invest the money in her intellectual development. It would not be hard to persuade the rather indolent and altogether confiding Katy that she was now old enough to cease bothering herself with the rules of syntax, and to devote herself to the happiness and comfort of Smith

27

Westcott, who seemed, poor fellow, entirely unable to exist out of sight of her eyes, which he often complimented by singing, as he cut a double-shuffle on the piazza,

"Her eyes so bright Dey shine at night When de moon am far away!"

generally adding, "Ya! ya! dat am a fack, Brudder Bones! He! he! By George!"

As Charlton's thoughts forecast his sister's future, it seemed to him darker than before. He had little hope of changing her, for it was clear that all the household authority was against him, and that Katy was hopelessly in love. If he should succeed in breaking the engagement, it would cost her untold suffering, and Albert was tender-hearted enough to shrink from inflicting suffering on any one, and especially on Kate. But when that heartless "he! he!" returned to his memory, and he thought of all the consequences of such a marriage, he nerved himself for a sharp and strong interference. It was his habit to plunge into every conflict with a radical's recklessness, and his present impulse was to attempt to carry his point by storm. If there had been opportunity, he would have moved on Katy's slender reasoning faculties at once. But as the night of sleeplessness wore on, the substratum of practical sense in his character made itself felt. To attack the difficulty in this way was to insure a great many tears from Katy, a great quarrel with a coxcomb, a difficulty with his mother, an interference in favor of Kate's marriage on the part of Plausaby, and a general success in precipitating what he desired to prevent.

And so for the first time this opinionated young man, who had always taken responsibility, and fought his battles alone and by the most direct methods, began to look round for a possible ally or an indirect approach. He went over the ground several times without finding any one on whom he could depend, or any device that offered the remotest chance of success, until he happened to think of Isabel Marlay—Cousin Isa, as Katy called her. He remembered how much surprised he had been a few days before, when the quiet girl, whom he had thought a sort of animated sewing-machine, suddenly developed so much force of thought in her defense of the clergy. Why not get her strong sense on his side?

CHAPTER VII

CATCHING AND GETTING CAUGHT

Did you never notice how many reasons, never thought of before, against having an aching tooth drawn, occur to you when once you stand on the dentist's door-stone ready to ring the bell? Albert Charlton was full of doubts of what Miss Isabel Marlay's opinion of his sister might be, and of what Miss Isabel Marlay might think of him after his intemperate denunciation of ministers and all other men of the learned professions. It was quite a difficult thing for him to speak to her on the subject of his sister's love-affair, and so, whenever an opportunity presented itself, he found reason to apprehend interruption. On one plea or another he deferred the matter until afternoon, and when afternoon came, Isa had gone out. So that what had seemed to him in the watchfulness of the night an affair for prompt action, was now deferred till evening. But in his indecision and impatience Charlton found it impossible to remain quiet. He must do something, and so he betook himself to his old recreation of catching insects. He would have scorned to amuse himself with so cruel a sport as fishing; he would not eat a fish when it was caught. But though he did not think it right for man to be a beast of prey, slaughtering other animals to gratify his appetites, he did not hesitate to sacrifice the lives of creeping things to satisfy the intellectual needs of humanity. Even this he did with characteristic tenderness, never leaving a grasshopper to writhe on a pin for two days, but kindly giving him a drop of chloroform to pass him into the Buddhist's heaven of eternal repose. In the course of an hour or two he had adorned his hat with a variety of orthoptera, coleoptera, and all the other opteras known to the insect-catching profession. A large Cecropia spread its bright wings across the crown of his hat, and several green Katydids appeared to be climbing up the sides for an introduction to the brilliant moth; three dragon-flies sat on the brim, and two or three ugly beetles kept watch between them. As for grasshoppers, they hung by threads from the hat-brim, and made unique pendants, which flew and flopped about his face as he ran hither and thither with his net, sweeping the air for new victims. Hurrying with long strides after a large locust which he suspected of belonging to a new species, and which flew high and far, his eyes were so uplifted to his game that he did not see anything else, and he ran down a hill and fairly against a lady, and then drew back in startled surprise and apologized. But before his hasty apology was

29

half-uttered he lifted his eyes to the face of the lady and saw that it was Miss Minorkey, walking with her father. Albert was still more confused when he recognized her, and his confusion was not relieved by her laughter. For the picturesque figure of Charlton and his portable museum was too much for her gravity, and as the French ladies of two centuries ago used to say, she "lost her serious." Guessing the cause of her merriment, Charlton lifted his hat off his head, held it up, and laughed with her.

"Well, Miss Minorkey, no wonder you laugh. This is a queer hat-buggery and dangling grasshoppery."

"That's a beautiful Cecropia," said Helen Minorkey, recovering a little, and winning on Albert at once by showing a little knowledge of his pet science, if it was only the name of a single specimen. "I wouldn't mind being an entomologist myself if there were many such as this and that green beetle to be had. I am gathering botanical specimens," and she opened her portfolio.

"But how did you come to be in Metropolisville?"

"Why," interrupted Mr. Minorkey, "I couldn't stand the climate at Perritaut. The malaria of the Big Gun River affected my health seriously. I had a fever night before last, and I thought I'd get away at once, and I made up my mind there was more oxygen in this air than in that at Perritaut. So I came up here this morning. But I'm nearly dead," and here Mr. Minorkey coughed and sighed, and put his hand on his breast in a self-pitying fashion.

As Mr. Minorkey wanted to inspect an eighty across the slough, on which he had been asked to lend four hundred dollars at three per cent a month, and five after maturity, with a waiver in the mortgage, he suggested that Helen should walk back, leaving him to go on slowly, as the rheumatism in his left knee would permit. It was quite necessary that Miss Minorkey should go back; her boots were not thick enough for the passage of the slough. Mr. Charlton kindly offered to accompany her.

Albert Charlton thought that Helen Minorkey looked finer than ever, for sun and wind had put more color into her cheeks, and he, warm with running, pushed back his long light hair, and looked side-wise at the white forehead and the delicate but fresh cheeks below.

"So you like Cecropias and bright-green beetles, do you?" he said, and he gallantly unpinned the wide-winged moth from his hat-crown and stuck it on the cover of Miss Minorkey's portfolio, and then added the green beetle. Helen thanked him in her quiet way, but with pleased eyes.

"Excuse me, Miss Minorkey," said Albert, blushing, as they approached the hotel, "I should like very much to accompany you to the parlor of the hotel, but people generally see nothing but the ludicrous side of scientific pursuits, and I should only make you ridiculous."

"I should be very glad to have you come," said Helen. "I don't mind being laughed at in good company, and it is such a relief to meet a gentleman who can talk about something besides corner lots and five per cent a month, and," with a wicked look at the figure of her father in the distance, "and mortgages with waivers in them!"

Our cynic philosopher found his cynicism melting away like an iceberg in the Gulf-stream. An hour before he would have told you that a woman's flattery could have no effect on an intellectual man; now he felt a tremor of pleasure, an indescribable something, as he shortened his steps to keep time with the little boots with which Miss Minorkey trod down the prairie grass, and he who had laughed at awkward boys for seeking the aid of dancing-masters to improve their gait, wished himself less awkward, and actually blushed with pleasure when this self-possessed young lady praised his conversation. He walked with her to the hotel, though he took the precaution to take his hat off his head and hang it on his finger, and twirl it round, as if laughing at it himself—back-firing against the ridicule of others. He who thought himself sublimely indifferent to the laughter of ignoramuses, now fencing against it!

The parlor of the huge pine hotel (a huge unfinished pine hotel is the starting point of speculative cities), the parlor of the Metropolisville City Hotel was a large room, the floor of which was covered with a very cheap but bright-colored ingrain carpet; the furniture consisted of six wooden-bottomed chairs, very bright and new, with a very yellow rose painted on the upper slat of the back of each, a badly tattered hair-cloth sofa, of a very antiquated pattern, and a small old piano, whose tinny tones were only matched by its entire lack of tune. The last two valuable articles had been bought at auction, and some of the keys of the piano had been permanently silenced by its ride in an ox-cart from Red Owl to Metropolisville.

But intellect and culture are always superior to external circumstances, and Mr. Charlton was soon sublimely oblivious to the tattered hair-cloth of the sofa on which he sat, and he utterly failed to notice the stiff wooden chair on which Miss Minorkey reposed. Both were too much interested in science to observe furniture; She admired the wonders of his dragon-flies, always in her quiet and intelligent fashion; he returned the compliment by praising her flowers in his eager, hearty, enthusiastic way. Her coolness made her seem to him very superior; his enthusiasm made him very piquant and delightful to her. And when he got upon his hobby and told her how grand a vocation the teacher's profession

31

was, and recited stories of the self-denial of Pestalozzi and Froebel, and the great schemes of Basedow, and told how he meant here in this new country to build a great Institute on rational principles, Helen Minorkey found him more interesting than ever. Like you and me, she loved philanthropy at other people's expense. She admired great reformers, though she herself never dreamed of putting a little finger to anybody's burden.

It took so long to explain fully this great project that Albert staid until nearly supper-time, forgetting the burden of his sister's unhappy future in the interest of science and philanthropy. And even when he rose to go, Charlton turned back to look again at a "prairie sun-flower" which Helen Minorkey had dissected while he spoke, and, finding something curious, perhaps in the fiber, he proposed to bring his microscope over in the evening and examine it—a proposition very grateful to Helen, who had nothing but ennui to expect in Metropolisville, and who was therefore delighted. Delighted is a strong word for one so cool: perhaps it would be better to say that she was relieved and pleased at the prospect of passing an evening with so curious and interesting a companion. For Charlton was both curious and interesting to her. She sympathized with his intellectual activity, and she was full of wonder at his intense moral earnestness.

As for Albert, botany suddenly took on a new interest in his eyes. He had hitherto regarded it as a science for girls. But now he was so profoundly desirous of discovering the true character of the tissue in the plant which Miss Minorkey had dissected, that it seemed to him of the utmost importance to settle it that very evening. His mother for the first time complained of his going out, and seemed not very well satisfied about something. He found that he was likely to have a good opportunity, after supper, to speak to Isabel Marlay in regard to his sister and her lover, but somehow the matter did not seem so exigent as it had. The night before, he had determined that it was needful to check the intimacy before it went farther, that every day of delay increased the peril; but things often look differently under different circumstances, and now the most important duty in life for Albert Charlton was the immediate settlement of a question in structural botany by means of microscopic investigation. Albert was at this moment a curious illustration of the influence of scientific enthusiasm, for he hurriedly relieved his hat of its little museum, ate his supper, got out his microscope, and returned to the hotel. He placed the instrument on the old piano, adjusted the object, and pedagogically expounded to Miss Minorkey the true method of observing. Microscopy proved very entertaining to both. Albert did not feel sure that it might not

32

become a life-work with him. It would be a delightful thing to study microscopic botany forever, if he could have Helen Minorkey to listen to his enthusiastic expositions. From her science the transition to his was easy, and they studied under every combination of glasses the beautiful lace of a dragon-fly's wing, and the irregular spots on a drab grasshopper which ran by chance half-across one of his eyes. The thrifty landlord had twice looked in at the door in hope of finding the parlor empty, intending in which case to put out the lamp. But I can not tell how long this enthusiastic pursuit of scientific knowledge might have lasted had not Mr. Minorkey been seized with one of his dying spells. When the message was brought by a Norwegian servant-girl, whose white hair fairly stood up with fright, Mr. Charlton was very much shocked, but Miss Minorkey did not for a moment lose her self-possession. Besides having the advantage of quiet nerves, she had become inured to the presence of Death in all his protean forms—it was impossible that her father should be threatened in a way with which she was not already familiar.

Emotions may be suspended by being superseded for a time by stronger ones. In such case, they are likely to return with great force, when revived by some association. Charlton stepped out on the piazza with his microscope in his hand and stopped a moment to take in the scene—the rawness and newness and flimsiness of the mushroom village, with its hundred unpainted bass-wood houses, the sweetness, peacefulness, and freshness of the unfurrowed prairie beyond, the calmness and immutability of the clear, star-lit sky above—when he heard a voice round the corner of the building that put out his eyes and opened his ears, if I may so speak. Somebody was reproaching somebody else with being "spooney on the little girl."

"He! he!"—the reply began with that hateful giggle—"I know my business, gentlemen. Not such a fool as you think." Here there was a shuffling of feet, and Charlton's imagination easily supplied the image of Smith Westcott cutting a "pigeon-wing."

"Don't I know the ways of this wicked world? Haven't I had all the silly sentiment took out of me? He! he! I've seen the world," and then he danced again and sang:

> "Can't you come out to-night,
> Can't you come out to-night,
> And dance by the light of the moon?"

"Now, boys," he began, again rattling his coins and keys, "I learnt too much about New York. I had to leave. They didn't want a

33

man there that knew all the ropes so well, and so I called a meeting of the mayor and told him good-by. He! he! By George! 'S a fack! I drank too much and I lived two-forty on the plank-road, till the devil sent me word he didn't want to lose his best friend, and he wished I'd just put out from New York. 'Twas leave New York or die. That's what brought me here. It I'd lived in New York I wouldn't never 've married. Not much, Mary Ann or Sukey Jane. He! he!" And then he sang again:

> "If I was young and in my prime,
> I'd lead a different life,
> I'd spend my money—

"but I'd be hanged if I'd marry a wife to save her from the Tower of London, you know. As long as I could live at the Elysian Club, didn' want a wife. But this country! Psha! this is a-going to be a land of Sunday-schools and sewing-societies. A fellow can't live here without a wife:

> "'Den lay down de shubble and de hoe,
> Den hang up de fiddle and de bow—
> For poor old Ned—'

"Yah! Can't sing! Out of practice! Got a cold! Instrument needs tuning! Excuse me! He! he!"

There was some other talk, in a voice too low for Albert to hear, though he listened with both ears, waiving all sense of delicacy about eavesdropping in his anger and his desire to rescue Katy. Then Westcott, who had evidently been drinking and was vinously frank, burst out with:

"Think I'd marry an old girl! Think I'd marry a smart one! I want a sweet little thing that would love me and worship me and believe everything I said. I know! By George! He! he! That Miss Minorkey at the table! She'd see through a fellow! Now, looky here, boys, I'm goin' to be serious for once. I want a girl that'll exert a moral influence over me, you know! But I'll be confounded if I want too much moral influence, by George, he! he! A little spree now and then all smoothed over! I need moral influence, but in small doses. Weak constitution, you know! Can't stand too much moral influence. Head's level. A little girl! Educate her yourself, you know! He! he! By George! And do as you please.

> "'O Jinny! git yer hoe-cake done, my dear!
> O Jinny! git yer hoe-cake done!'

34

"Yah! yah! He! he! he!"

It is not strange that Charlton did not sleep that night, that he was a prey to conflicting emotions, blessing the cool, intellectual, self-possessed face of Miss Minorkey, who knew botany, and inwardly cursing the fate that had handed little Katy over to be the prey of such a man as Smith Westcott.

CHAPTER VIII

ISABEL MARLAY

Isabel Marlay was not the niece of our friend Squire Plausaby, but of his first wife. Plausaby, Esq., had been the guardian of her small inheritance in her childhood, and the property had quite mysteriously suffered from a series of curious misfortunes: the investments were unlucky; those who borrowed of the guardian proved worthless, and so did their securities. Of course the guardian was not to blame, and of course he handled the money honestly. But people will be suspicious even of the kindest and most smoothly-speaking men; and the bland manner and innocent, open countenance of Plausaby, Esq., could not save him from the reproaches of uncharitable people. As he could not prove his innocence, he had no consolation but that which is ever to be derived from a conscience void of offense.

Isabel Marlay found herself at an early age without means. But she had never seen a day of dependence. Deft hands, infallible taste in matters of dress, invincible cheerfulness, and swift industry made her always valuable. She had not been content to live in the house of her aunt, the first Mrs. Plausaby, as a dependent, and she even refused to remain in the undefined relation of a member of the family whose general utility, in some sort, roughly squares the account of board and clothes at the year's end. Whether or not she had any suspicions in regard to the transactions of Plausaby, Esq., in the matter of her patrimony, I do not know. She may have been actuated by nothing but a desire to have her independence apparent. Or, she may have enjoyed—as who would not?—having her own money to spend. At any rate, she made a definite bargain with her uncle-in-law, by which she took charge of the sewing in his house, and received each year a hundred dollars in cash and her board. It was not large pay for such service as she rendered, but then she preferred the house of a relative to that of a stranger. When the second Mrs. Plausaby had come into the house, Mr. Plausaby had been glad to continue the arrangement, in the hope, perhaps, that Isa's good taste might modify that lady's love for discordant gauds.

To Albert Charlton, Isa's life seemed not to be on a very high key. She had only a common-school education, and the leisure she had been able to command for general reading was not very great, nor had the library in the house of Plausaby been very extensive.

She had read a good deal of Matthew Henry, the "Life and Labors of Mary Lyon" and the "Life of Isabella Graham," the "Works of Josephus," "Hume's History of England," and Milton's "Paradise Lost." She had tried to read Mrs. Sigourney's "Poems" and Pollok's "Course of Time," but had not enjoyed them much. She was not imaginative. She had plenty of feeling, but no sentiment, for sentiment is feeling that has been thought over; and her life was too entirely objective to allow her to think of her own feelings. Her highest qualities, as Albert inventoried them, were good sense, good taste, and absolute truthfulness and simplicity of character. These were the qualities that he saw in her after a brief acquaintance. They were not striking, and yet they were qualities that commanded respect. But he looked in vain for those high ideals of a vocation and a goal that so filled his own soul. If she read of Mary Lyon, she had no aspiration to imitate her. Her whole mind seemed full of the ordinary cares of life. Albert could not abide that anybody should expend even such abilities as Isa possessed on affairs of raiment and domestic economy. The very tokens of good taste and refined feeling in her dress were to him evidences of over-careful vanity.

But when his mother and Katy had gone out on the morning after he had overheard Smith Westcott expound his views on the matter of marriage, Charlton sought Isa Marlay. She sat sewing in the parlor, as it was called—the common sitting-room of the house— by the west window. The whole arrangement of the room was hers; and though Albert was neither an artist nor a critic in matters of taste, he was, as I have already indicated, a man of fine susceptibility. He rejoiced in this susceptibility when it enabled him to appreciate nature. He repressed it when he found himself vibrating in sympathy with those arts that had, as he thought, relations with human weakness and vanity; as, for instance, the arts of music and dress. But, resist as one may, a man can not fight against his susceptibilities. And those who can feel the effect of any art are very many more than those who can practice it or criticise it. It does not matter that my Bohemian friend's musical abilities are slender. No man in the great Boston Jubilee got more out of Johann Strauss, in his "Kunstleben," that inimitable expression of inspired vagabondage, than he did. And so, though Albert Charlton could not have told you what colors would "go together," as the ladies say, he could, none the less, always feel the discord of his mother's dress, as now he felt the beauty of the room and appreciated the genius of Isa, that had made so much out of resources so slender. For there were only a few touch-me-nots in the two vases on the mantel-piece; there were wild-flowers and prairie-grasses over the picture-frames; there were asparagus-stalks in the fireplace; there was—well, there

37

was a tout-ensemble of coolness and delightfulness, of freshness and repose. There was the graceful figure of Isabel by the window, with the yet dewy grass and the distant rolling, boundless meadow for a background. And there was in Isabel's brown calico dress a faultlessness of fit, and a suitableness of color—a perfect harmony, like that of music. There was real art, pure and refined, in her dress, as in the arrangement of the room. Albert was angry with it, while he felt its effect; it was as though she had set herself there to be admired. But nothing was further from her thought. The artist works not for the eyes of others, but for his own, and Isabel Marlay would have taken not one whit less of pains if she could have been assured that no eye in the universe would look in upon that frontier-village parlor.

I said that Charlton was vexed. He was vexed because he felt a weakness in himself that admired such "gewgaws," as he called everything relating to dress or artistic housekeeping. He rejoiced mentally in the superiority of Helen Minorkey, who gave her talents to higher themes. And yet he felt a sense of restfulness in this cool room, where every color was tuned to harmony with every other. He was struck, too, with the gracefulness of Isa's figure. Her face was not handsome, but the good genius that gave her the feeling of an artist must have molded her own form, and every lithe motion was full of poetry. You have seen some people who made upon you the impression that they were beautiful, and yet the beauty was all in a statuesque figure and a graceful carriage. For it makes every difference how a face is carried.

The conversation between Charlton and Miss Marlay had not gone far in the matter of Katy and Smith Westcott until Albert found that her instincts had set more against the man than even his convictions. A woman like Isabel Marlay is never so fine as in her indignation, and there never was any indignation finer than Isa Marlay's when she spoke of the sacrifice of such a girl as Katy to such a man as Westcott. In his admiration of her thorough-going earnestness, Albert forgave her devotion to domestic pursuits and the arts of dress and ornamentation. He found sailing with her earnestness much pleasanter than he had found rowing against it on the occasion of his battle about the clergy.

"What can I do, Miss Marlay?" Albert did not ask her what she could do. A self-reliant man at his time of life always asks first what he himself can do.

"I can not think of anything that anybody can do, with any hope of success." Isa's good sense penetrated entirely through the subject, she saw all the difficulties, she had not imagination or sentiment enough to delude her practical faculty with false lights.

38

"Can not you do something?" asked Charlton, almost begging.

"I have tried everything. I have spoken to your mother. I have spoken to Uncle Plausaby. I have begged Katy to listen to me, but Katy would only feel sorry for him if she believed he was bad. She can love, but she can't think, and if she knew him to be the worst man in the Territory she would marry him to reform him. I did hope that you would have some influence over her."

"But Katy is such a child. She won't listen if I talk to her. Any opposition would only hurry the matter. I wish it were right to blow out his brains, if he has any, and I suppose the monkey has."

"It is a great deal better, Mr. Charlton, to trust in Providence where we can't do anything without doing wrong."

"Well, Miss Marlay, I didn't look for cant from you. I don't believe that God cares. Everything goes on by the almanac and natural law. The sun sets when the time comes, no matter who is belated. Girls that are sweet and loving and trusting, like Katy, have always been and will always be victims of rakish fools like Smith Westcott. I wish I were an Indian, and then I could be my own Providence. I would cut short his career, and make what David said about wicked men being cut off come true in this case, in the same way as I suppose David did in the case of the wicked of his day, by cutting them off himself."

Isabel was thoroughly shocked with this speech. What good religious girl would not have been? She told Mr. Charlton with much plainness of speech that she thought common modesty might keep him from making such criticisms on God. She for her part doubted whether all the facts of the case were known to him. She intimated that there were many things in God's administration not set down in almanacs, and she thought that, whatever God might be, a young man should not be in too great a hurry about arraigning Him for neglect of duty. I fear it would not contribute much to the settlement of the very ancient controversy if I should record all the arguments, which were not fresh or profound. It is enough that Albert replied sturdily, and that he went away presently with his vanity piqued by her censures. Not that he could not answer her reasoning, if it were worthy to be called reasoning. But he had lost ground in the estimation of a person whose good sense he could not help respecting, and the consciousness of this wounded his vanity. And whilst all she said was courteous, it was vehement as any defense of the faith is likely to be; he felt, besides, that he had spoken with rather more of the ex cathedra tone than was proper. A young man of opinions generally finds it so much easier to impress people with his tone than with his arguments! But he consoled himself with the reflection that the average woman—that word

39

average was a balm for every wound—that the average woman is always tied to her religion, and intolerant of any doubts. He was pleased to think that Helen Minorkey was not intolerant. Of that he felt sure. He did not carry the analysis any farther, however; he did not ask why Helen was not intolerant, nor ask whether even intolerance may not sometimes be more tolerable than indifference. And in spite of his unpleasant irritation at finding this "average" woman not overawed by his oracular utterances, nor easily beaten in a controversy, Albert had a respect for her deeper than ever. There was something in her anger at Westcott that for a moment had seemed finer than anything he had seen in the self-possessed Miss Minorkey. But then she was so weak as to allow her intellectual conclusions to be influenced by her feelings, and to be intolerant.

I have said that this thing of falling in love is a very complex catastrophe. I might say that it is also a very uncertain one. Since we all of us "rub clothes with fate along the street," who knows whether Charlton would not, by this time, have been in love with Miss Marlay if he had not seen Miss Minorkey in the stage? If he had not run against her, while madly chasing a grasshopper? If he had not had a great curiosity about a question in botany which he could only settle in her company? And even yet, if he had not had collision with Isa on the question of Divine Providence? And even after that collision I will not be sure that the scale might not have been turned, had it not been that while he was holding this conversation with Isa Marlay, his mother and sister had come into the next room. For when he went out they showed unmistakable pleasure in their faces, and Mrs. Plausaby even ventured to ask: "Don't you like her, Albert?"

And when the mother tried to persuade him to forego his visit to the hotel in the evening, he put this and that together. And when this and that were put together, they combined to produce a soliloquy:

"Mother and Katy want to make a match for me. As if they understood me! They want me to marry an average woman, of course. Pshaw! Isabel Marlay only understands the 'culinary use' of things. My mother knows that she has a 'knack,' and thinks it would be nice for me to have a wife with a knack. But mother can't judge for me. I ought to have a wife with ideas. And I don't doubt Plausaby has a hand in trying to marry off his ward to somebody that won't make too much fuss about his accounts."

And so Charlton was put upon studying all the evening, to find points in which Miss Minorkey's conversation was superior to Miss Marlay's. And judged as he judged it—as a literary product—it was not difficult to find an abundant advantage on her side.

40

CHAPTER IX

LOVERS AND LOVERS

Albert Charlton had little money, and he was not a man to remain idle. He was good in mathematics, and did a little surveying now and then; in fact, with true democratic courage, he turned his hand to any useful employment. He did not regard these things as having any bearing on his career. He was only waiting for the time to come when he could found his Great Educational Institution on the virgin soil of Minnesota. Then he would give his life to training boys to live without meat or practical jokes, to love truth, honesty, and hard lessons; he would teach girls to forego jewelry and cucumber-pickles, to study physiology, and to abhor flirtations. Visionary, was he? You can not help smiling at a man who has a "vocation," and who wants to give the world a good send-off toward its "goal." But there is something noble about it after all. Something to make you and me ashamed of our selfishness. Let us not judge Charlton by his green flavor. When these discordant acids shall have ripened in the sunshine and the rain, who shall tell how good the fruit may be? We may laugh, however, at Albert, and his school that was to be. I do not doubt that even that visionary street-loafer known to the Athenians as Sokrates, was funny to those who looked at him from a great distance below.

During the time in which Charlton waited, and meditated his plans for the world's advancement by means of a school that should be so admirable as to modify the whole system of education by the sheer force of its example, he found it of very great advantage to unfold his plans to Miss Helen Minorkey. Miss Helen loved to hear him talk. His enthusiasm was the finest thing she had found, out of books. It was like a heroic poem, as she often remarked, this fine philanthropy of his, and he seemed to her like King Arthur preparing his Table Round to regenerate the earth. This compliment, uttered with the coolness of a literary criticism—and nothing could be cooler than a certain sort of literary criticism—this deliberate and oft-repeated compliment of Miss Minorkey always set Charlton's enthusiastic blood afire with love and admiration for the one Being, as he declared, born to appreciate his great purposes. And the Being was pleased to be made the partner of such dreams and hopes. In an intellectual and ideal fashion she did appreciate them. If Albert had carried out his great plans, she, as a disinterested spectator, would have written a critical analysis of them much as she would have described a new plant.

But whenever Charlton tried to excite in her an enthusiasm similar to his own, he was completely foiled. She shrunk from everything like self-denial or labor of any sort. She was not adapted to it, she assured him. And he who made fierce war on the uselessness of woman in general came to reconcile himself to the uselessness of woman in particular, to apologize for it, to justify it, to admire it. Love is the mother of invention, and Charlton persuaded himself that it was quite becoming in such a woman as the most remarkably cultivated, refined, and intellectual Helen Minorkey, to shrink from the drudgery of life. She was not intended for it. Her susceptibilities were too keen, according to him, though Helen Minorkey's susceptibilities were indeed of a very quiet sort. I believe that Charlton, the sweeping radical, who thought, when thinking on general principles, that every human-creature should live wholly for every other human creature, actually addressed some "Lines to H.M.," through the columns of the St. Paul Advertiser of that day, in which he promulgated the startling doctrine that a Being such as was the aforesaid H.M., could not be expected to come into contact with the hard realities of life. She must content herself with being the Inspiration of the life of Another, who would work out plans that should inure to the good of man and the honor of the Being, who would inspire and sustain the Toiler. The poem was considered very fine by H.M., though the thoughts were a little too obscure for the general public and the meter was not very smooth. You have doubtless had occasion to notice that poems which deal with Beings and Inspirations are usually of very imperfect fluidity.

Charlton worked at surveying and such other employments as offered themselves, wrote poems to Helen Minorkey, and plotted and planned how he might break up little Katy's engagement. He plotted and planned sometimes with a breaking heart, for the more he saw of Smith Westcott, the more entirely detestable he seemed. But he did not get much co-operation from Isabel Marlay. If he resented any effort to make a match between him and "Cousin Isa," she resented it ten times more vehemently, and all the more that she, in her unselfishness of spirit, admired sincerely the unselfishness of Charlton, and in her practical and unimaginative life felt drawn toward the idealist young man who planned and dreamed in a way quite wonderful to her. All her woman's pride made her resent the effort to marry her to a man in love with another, a man who had not sought her.

42

"Albert is smart," said Mrs. Plausaby to her significantly one day; "he would be just the man for you, Isa."

"Why, Mrs. Plausaby, I heard you say yourself that his wife would have to do without silk dresses and new bonnets. For my part, I don't think much of that kind of smartness that can't get a living. I wouldn't have a man like Mr. Charlton on any, terms."

And she believed that she spoke the truth; having never learned to analyze her own feelings, she did not know that all her dislike for Charlton had its root in a secret liking for him, and that having practical ability herself, the kind of ability that did not make a living was just the sort that she admired most.

It was, therefore, without any co-operation between them, that Isabel and young Charlton were both of them putting forth their best endeavor to defeat the plans of Smith Westcott, and avert the sad eclipse which threatened the life of little Katy. And their efforts in that direction were about equally fruitful in producing the result they sought to avoid. For whenever Isa talked to little Katy about Westcott, Katy in the goodness of her heart and the vehemence of her love was set upon finding out, putting in order, and enumerating all of his good qualities. And when Albert attacked him vehemently and called him a coxcomb, and a rake, and a heartless villain, she cried, and cried, out of sheer pity for "poor Mr. Westcott;" she thought him the most persecuted man in the world, and she determined that she would love him more fervently and devotedly than ever, that she would! Her love should atone for all the poor fellow suffered. And "poor Mr. Westcott" was not slow in finding out that "feelin' sorry for a feller was Katy's soft side, by George! he! he!" and having made this discovery he affected to be greatly afflicted at the treatment he received from Albert and from Miss Marlay; nor did he hesitate to impress Katy with the fact that he endured all these things out of pure devotion to her, and he told her that he could die for her, "by George! he! he!" any day, and that she mustn't ever desert him if she didn't want him to kill himself; he didn't care two cents for life except for her, and he'd just as soon go to sleep in the lake as not, "by George! he! he!" any day. And then he rattled his keys, and sang in a quite affecting way, to the simple-minded Kate, how for "bonnie Annie Laurie," with a look at Katy, he could "lay him down and dee," and added touchingly and recitatively the words "by George! he! he!" which made his emotion seem very real and true to Katy; she even saw a vision of "poor Mr. Westcott" dragged out of the lake dead on her account, and with that pathetic vision in her mind she vowed she'd rather die than desert him. And as for all the ills which her brother foreboded for her in case she should marry Smith Westcott, they did not startle

43

her at all. Such simple, loving natures as Katy Charlton's can not feel for self. It is such a pleasure to them to throw themselves away in loving.

Besides, Mrs. Plausaby put all her weight into the scale, and with the loving Katy the mother's word weighed more even than Albert's. Mrs. Plausaby didn't see why in the world Katy couldn't marry as she pleased without being tormented to death. Marrying was a thing everybody must attend to personally for themselves. Besides, Mr. Westcott was a nice-spoken man, and dressed very well, his shirt-bosom was the finest in Metropolisville, and he had a nice hat and wore lavender gloves on Sundays. And he was a store-keeper, and he would give Katy all the nice things she wanted. It was a nice thing to be a store-keeper's wife. She wished Plausaby would keep a store. And she went to the glass and fixed her ribbons, and reflected that if Plausaby kept a store she could get plenty of them.

And so all that Cousin Isa and Brother Albert said came to naught, except that it drove the pitiful Katy into a greater devotion to her lover, and made the tender-hearted Katy cry. And when she cried, the sentimental Westcott comforted her by rattling his keys in an affectionate way, and reminding her that the course of true love never did run smooth, "by George! he! he! he!"

44

CHAPTER X

PLAUSABY, ESQ., TAKES A FATHERLY INTEREST

Plausaby, Esq., felt a fatherly interest. He said so. He wanted Albert to make his way in the world. "You have great gifts, Albert," he said. But the smoother Mr. Plausaby talked, the rougher Mr. Albert felt. Mr. Plausaby felt the weight of all that Albert had said against the learned professions. He did, indeed. He would not care to say it so strongly. Not too strongly. Old men never spoke quite so strongly as young ones. But the time had been, he said, when Thomas Plausaby's pulse beat as quick and strong as any other young man's. Virtuous indignation was a beautiful emotion in a young man. For his part he never cared much for a young man who did not know how to show just such feeling on such questions. But one must not carry it too far. Not too far. Never too far. For his part ho did not like to see anything carried too far. It was always bad to carry a thing too far. A man had to make his bread somehow. It was a necessity. Every young man must consider that he had his way to make in the world. It was a fact to be considered. To be considered carefully. He would recommend that Albert consider it. And consider it carefully. Albert must make his way. For his part, he had a plan in view that he thought could not be objectionable to Albert's feelings. Not at all objectionable. Not in the least.

All this Plausaby, Esq., oozed out at proper intervals and in gentlest tones. Charlton for his mother's sake kept still, and reflected that Mr. Plausaby had not said a word as yet that ought to anger him. He therefore nodded his head and waited to hear the plan which Plausaby had concocted for him.

Mr. Plausaby proceeded to state that he thought Albert ought to pre-empt.

Albert said that he would like to pre-empt as soon as he should be of age, but that was some weeks off yet, and he supposed that when he got ready there would be few good claims left.

The matter of age was easily got over, replied Plausaby. Quite easily got over. Nothing easier, indeed. All the young men in the Territory who were over nineteen had pre-empted. It was customary. Quite customary, indeed. And custom was law. In some sense it was law. Of course there were some customs in regard to pre-emption that Plausaby thought no good man could approve. Not at all. Not in the least.

There was the building of a house on wheels and hauling it from claim to claim, and swearing it in on each claim as a house on that claim. Plausaby, Esq., did not approve of that. Not at all. Not in the least. He thought it a dangerous precedent. Quite dangerous. Quite so. But good men did it. Very good men, indeed. And then he had known men to swear that there was glass in the window of a house when there was only a whisky-bottle sitting in the window. It was amusing. Quite amusing, these devices. Four men just over in Town 21 had built a house on the corners of four quarter sections. The house partly on each of the four claims. Swore that house in on each claim. But such expedients were not to be approved. Not at all. They were not commendable. However, nearly all the claims in the Territory had been made irregularly. Nearly all of them. And the matter of age could be gotten over easily. Custom made law. And Albert was twenty-three in looks. Quite twenty-three. More than that, indeed. Twenty-five, perhaps. Some people were men at sixteen. And some were always men. They were, indeed. Always men. Always. Albert was a man in intellect. Quite a man. The spirit of the law was the thing to be looked at. The spirit, not the letter. Not the letter at all. The spirit of the law warranted Albert in pre-empting.

Here Plausaby, Esq., stopped a minute. But Albert said nothing. He detested Plausaby's ethics, but was not insensible to his flattery.

"And as for a claim, Albert, I will attend to that. I will see to it. I know a good chance for you to make two thousand dollars fairly hi a month. A very good chance. Very good, indeed. There is a claim adjoining this town-site which was filed on by a stage-driver. Reckless sort of a fellow. Disreputable. We don't want him to hold land here. Not at all. You would be a great addition to us. You would indeed. A great addition. A valuable addition to the town. And it would be a great comfort to your mother and to me to have you near us. It would indeed. A great comfort. We could secure this Whisky Jim's claim very easily for you, and you could lay it off into town lots. I have used my pre-emption right, or I would take that myself. I advise you to secure it. I do, indeed. You couldn't use your pre-emption right to a better advantage. I am sure you couldn't."

"Well," said Albert, "if Whisky Jim will sell out, why not get him to hold it for me for three weeks until I am of age?"

"He wouldn't sell, but he has forfeited it. He neglected to stay on it. Has been away from it more than thirty days. You have a perfect right to jump it and pre-empt it. I am well acquainted with Mr. Shamberson, the brother-in-law of the receiver. Very well acquainted. He is a land-office lawyer, and they do say that a fee of

46

fifty dollars to him will put the case through, right or wrong. But in this case we should have right on our side, and should make a nice thing. A very nice thing, indeed. And the town would be relieved of a dissipated man, and you could then carry out your plan of establishing a village library here."

"But," said Albert between his teeth, "I hear that the reason Jim didn't come back to take possession of his claim at the end of his thirty days is his sickness. He's sick at the Sod Tavern."

"Well, you see, he oughtn't to have neglected his claim so long before he was taken sick. Not at all. Besides, he doesn't add anything to the moral character of a town. I value the moral character of a settler above all I do, indeed. The moral character. If he gets that claim, he'll get rich off my labors, and be one of our leading citizens. Quite a leading citizen. It is better that you should have it. A great deal better. Better all round. The depot will be on one corner of the east forty of that claim, probably. Now, you shouldn't neglect your chance to get on. You shouldn't, really. This is the road to wealth and influence. The road to wealth. And influence. You can found your school there. You'll have money and land. Money to build with. Land on which to build. You will have both."

"You want me to swear that I am twenty-one when I am not, to bribe the receiver, and to take a claim and all the improvements on it from a sick man?" said Albert with heat.

"You put things wrong. Quite so. I want to help you to start. The claim is now open. It belongs to Government, with all improvements. Improvements go with the claim. If you don't take it, somebody will. It is a pity for you to throw away your chances."

"My chances of being a perjured villain and a thief! No, thank you, sir," said the choleric Charlton, getting very red in the face, and stalking out of the room.

"Such notions!" cried his mother. "Just like his father over again. His father threw away all his chances just for notions. I tell you, Plausaby, he never got any of those notions from me. Not one."

"No, I don't think he did," said Plausaby. "I don't think he did. Not at all. Not in the least."

47

CHAPTER XI

ABOUT SEVERAL THINGS

Albert Charlton, like many other very conscientious men at his time of life, was quarrelsomely honest. He disliked Mr. Plausaby's way of doing business, and he therefore determined to satisfy his conscience by having a row with his step-father. And so he startled his sister and shocked his mother, and made the house generally uncomfortable, by making, in season and out of season, severe remarks on the subject of land speculation, and particularly of land-sharks. It was only Albert's very disagreeable way of being honest. Even Isabel Marlay looked with terror at what she regarded as signs of an approaching quarrel between the two men of the house.

But there was no such thing as a quarrel with Plausaby. Moses may have been the meekest of men, but that was in the ages before Plausaby, Esq. No manner of abuse could stir him. He had suffered many things of many men in his life, many things of outraged creditors, and the victims of his somewhat remarkable way of dealing; his air of patient long-suffering and quiet forbearance under injury had grown chronic. It was, indeed, part of his stock in trade, an element of character that redounded to his credit, while it cost nothing and was in every way profitable. It was as though the whole catalogue of Christian virtues had been presented to Plausaby to select from, and he, with characteristic shrewdness, had taken the one trait that was cheapest and most remunerative.

In these contests Albert was generally sure to sacrifice by his extravagance whatever sympathy he might otherwise have had from the rest of the family. When he denounced dishonest trading, Isabel knew that he was right, and that Mr. Plausaby deserved the censure, and even Mrs. Plausaby and the sweet, unreasoning Katy felt something of the justice of what he said. But Charlton was never satisfied to stop here. He always went further, and made a clean sweep of the whole system of town-site speculation, which unreasonable invective forced those who would have been his friends into opposition. And the beautiful meekness with which Plausaby, Esq., bore his step-son's denunciations never failed to excite the sympathy and admiration of all beholders. By never speaking an unkind word, by treating Albert with gentle courtesy, by never seeming to feel his innuendoes, Plausaby heaped coals of fire on his enemies' head, and had faith to believe that the coals were very hot. Mrs. Ferret, who once witnessed one of the contests between the two, or rather one of these attacks of Albert, for there could be no contest with embodied meekness, gave her verdict for Plausaby. He showed such a "Chrischen" spirit. She really thought he must have felt the power of grace. He seemed to hold schripcherral views, and show such a spirit of Chrischen forbearance, that she for her part thought he deserved the sympathy of good people. Mr. Charlton was severe, he was unchar-it-able—really unchar-it-able in his spirit. He pretended to a great deal of honesty, but people of unsound views generally whitened the outside of the sep-ul-cher. And Mrs. Ferret closed the sentence by jerking her face into an astringed smile, which, with the rising inflection of her voice, demanded the assent of her hearers.

The evidences of disapproval which Albert detected in the countenances of those about him did not at all decrease his irritation. His irritation did not tend to modify the severity of his moral judgments. And the fact that Smith Westcott had jumped the claim of Whisky Jim, of course at Plausaby's suggestion, led Albert into a strain of furious talk that must have produced a violent rupture in the family, had it not been for the admirable composure of Plausaby, Esq., under the extremest provocation. For Charlton openly embraced the cause of Jim; and much as he disliked all manner of rascality, he was secretly delighted to hear that Jim had employed Shamberson, the lawyer, who was brother-in-law to the receiver of the land-office, and whose retention in those days of mercenary lawlessness was a guarantee of his client's success. Westcott had offered the lawyer a fee of fifty dollars, but Jim's letter, tendering him a contingent fee of half the claim, reached him in the same mail, and the prudent lawyer, after talking the matter over with the receiver who was to decide the case, concluded to take half of the claim. Jim would have given him all rather than stand a defeat.

Katy, with more love than logic, took sides of course with her lover in this contest. Westcott showed her where he meant to build the most perfect little dove-house for her, by George, he! he! and she listened to his side of the story, and became eloquent in her denunciation of the drunken driver who wanted to cheat poor, dear Smith—she had got to the stage in which she called him by his Christian name now—to cheat poor, dear Smith out of his beautiful claim.

If I were writing a History instead of a Mystery of Metropolisville, I should have felt under obligation to begin with the founding of the town, in the year preceding the events of this story. Not that there were any mysterious rites or solemn ceremonies.

49

Neither Plausaby nor the silent partners interested with him cared for such classic customs. They sought first to guess out the line of a railroad; they examined corner-stakes; they planned for a future county-seat; they selected a high-sounding name, regardless of etymologies and tautologies; they built shanties, "filed" according to law, laid off a town-site, put up a hotel, published a beautiful colored map, and began to give away lots to men who would build on them. Such, in brief, is the unromantic history of the founding of the village of Metropolisville.

And if this were a history, I should feel bound to tell of all the maneuvers resorted to by Metropolisville, party of the second part, to get the county-seat removed from Perritaut, party of the first part, party in possession. But about the time that Smith Westcott's contest about the claim was ripening to a trial, the war between the two villages was becoming more and more interesting. A special election was approaching, and Albert of course took sides against Metropolisville, partly because of his disgust at the means Plausaby was using, partly because he thought the possession of the county-seat would only enable Plausaby to swindle more people and to swindle them more effectually, partly because he knew that Perritaut was more nearly central in the county, and partly because he made it a rule to oppose Plausaby on general principles. Albert was an enthusiastic and effective talker, and it was for this reason that Plausaby had wished to interest him by getting him to "jump" Whisky Jim's claim, which lay alongside the town. And it was because he was an enthusiastic talker, and because his entire disinterestedness and his relations to Plausaby gave his utterances peculiar weight, that the Squire planned to get him out of the county until after the election.

Mrs. Plausaby suggested to Albert that he should go and visit a cousin thirty miles away. Who suggested it to Mrs. Plausaby we may not guess, since we may not pry into the secrets of a family, or know anything of the conferences which a husband may hold with his wife in regard to the management of the younger members of the household. As an authentic historian, I am bound to limit myself to the simple fact, and the fact is that Mrs. Plausaby stated to Albert her opinion that it would be a nice thing for him to go and see Cousin John's folks at Glenfleld. She made the suggestion with characteristic maladroitness, at a moment when Albert had been holding forth on his favorite hobby of the sinfulness of land-speculation in general, and the peculiar wickedness of misrepresentation and all the other arts pertaining to town-site swindling. Perhaps Albert was too suspicious. He always saw the hand of Plausaby in everything proposed by his mother. He bluntly

50

refused to go. He wanted to stay and vote. He would be of age in time. He wanted to stay and vote against this carting of a county-seat around the country for purposes of speculation. He became so much excited at what he regarded as a scheme to get him out of the way, that he got up from the table and went out into the air to cool off. He sat down on the unpainted piazza, and took up Gerald Massey's poems, of which he never tired, and read until the light failed.

And then came Isa Marlay out in the twilight and said she wanted to speak to him, and he got her a chair and listened while she spoke in a voice as full of harmony as her figure was full of gracefulness. I have said that Isabel was not a beauty, and yet such was the influence of her form, her rhythmical movement, and her sweet, rich voice, that Charlton thought she was handsome, and when she sat down and talked to him, he found himself vibrating, as a sensitive nature will, under the influence of grace or beauty.

"Don't you think, Mr. Charlton, that you would better take your mother's suggestion, and go to your cousin's? You'll excuse me for speaking about what does not concern me?"

Charlton would have excused her for almost anything she might have said in the way of advice or censure, for in spite of all his determination that it should not be, her presence was very pleasant to him.

"Certainly I have no objection to receive advice, Miss Marlay; but have you joined the other side?"

"I don't know what you mean by the other side, Mr. Charlton. I don't belong to any side. I think all quarreling is unpleasant, and I hate it. I don't think anything you say makes any change in Uncle Plausaby, while it does make your mother unhappy."

"So you think, Miss Isabel, that I ought to go away from Wheat County and not throw my influence on the side of right in this contest, because my mother is unhappy?" Albert spoke with some warmth.

"I did not say so. I think that a useless struggle, which makes your mother unhappy, ought to be given over. But I didn't want to advise you about your duty to your mother. I was led into saying so much on that point. I came to say something else. It does seem to me that if you could take Katy with you, something might turn up that would offer you a chance to influence her. And that would be better than keeping the county-seat at Perritaut." And she got up to go in.

Charlton was profoundly touched by Isabel's interest in Katy. He rose to his feet and said: "You are right, I believe. And I am very, very much obliged."

And as the straightforward Isa said, "Oh! no, that is nothing," and walked away, Charlton looked after her and said, "What a charming woman!" He felt more than he said, and he immediately set himself loyally to work to enumerate all the points in which Miss Helen Minorkey was superior to Isa, and said that, after all, gracefulness of form and elasticity of motion and melodiousness of voice were only lower gifts, possessed in a degree by birds and animals, and he blamed himself for feeling them at all, and felt thankful that Helen Minorkey had those higher qualities which would up-lift—he had read some German, and compounded his words—up-lift a man to a higher level. Perhaps every loyal-hearted lover plays these little tricks of self-deception on himself. Every lover except the one whose "object" is indeed perfect. You know who that is. So do I. Indeed, life would be a very poor affair if it were not for these—what shall I call them? If Brown knew how much Jones's wife was superior to his own, Brown would be neither happier nor better for the knowledge. When he sees the superiority of Mrs. Jones's temper to Mrs. Brown's somewhat energetic disposition, he always falls back on Mrs. Brown's diploma, and plumes himself that at any rate Mrs. Brown graduated at the Hobson Female College. Poor Mrs. Jones had only a common-school education. How mortified Jones must feel when he thinks of it!

CHAPTER XII

AN ADVENTURE

That Katy should go with Albert to see the cousins at Glenfield was a matter easily brought about. Plausaby, Esq., was so desirous of Albert's absence that he threw all of Mrs. Plausaby's influence on the side of the arrangement which Charlton made a sine qua non. Albert felt a little mean at making such a compromise of principle, and Plausaby felt much as a man does who pays the maker of crank-music to begone. He did not like Katy's going; he wanted to further her marriage with so influential a person as Smith Westcott, the agent in charge of the interests of Jackson, Jones & Co., who not only owned the Emporium, but were silent partners in the town-site. But Katy must go. Plausaby affectionately proffered the loan of his horse and buggy, which Charlton could not well refuse, and so the two set out for Glenfleld with many kind adieus. Westcott came down, and smoked, and rattled his keys, and hoped they'd have a pleasant journey and get back soon, you know, Katy, by George! he! he! he! Couldn't live long without the light of her countenance. 'S a fact! By George! He! he! And when the carpet-bags and lunch-basket and all the rest were stowed away under the seat of the buggy, Mrs. Plausaby, with a magnificent number of streamers, kissed them, and she and Cousin Isa stood by the gate and nodded their heads to the departing buggy, as an expression of their feelings, and Mr. Plausaby lifted his hat in such a way as to conceal his feelings, which, written out, would be, "Good riddance!" And Smith Westcott blandly waved his good-by and bowed to the ladies at the gate, and started back to the store. He was not feeling very happy, apparently, for he walked to the store moodily, rattling the coppers and keys in his right pantaloons-pocket. But he seemed to see a little daylight, for just as he arrived in front of the Emporium, he looked up and said, as if he had just thought of something, "By George! he! he! he!"

Owing to some delay in fixing the buggy, Charlton had not got off till about noon, but as the moon would rise soon after dark, he felt sure of reaching Glenfleld by nine in the evening. One doesn't mind a late arrival when one is certain of a warm welcome. And so they jogged on quietly over the smooth road, the slow old horse walking half the time. Albert was not in a hurry. For the first time since his return, he felt that for a moment he possessed little Katy again. The shadow had gone; it might come back; he would rejoice in the light while he could. Katy was glad to be relieved of the perpetual conflict at home, and, with a feeling entirely childish, she rejoiced that Albert was not now reproving her. And so Albert talked in his old pedagogic fashion, telling Katy of all the strange things he could think of, and delighting himself in watching the wonder and admiration in her face. The country was now smooth and now broken, and Albert thought he had never seen the grass so green or the flowers so bright as they were this morning. The streams they crossed were clear and cold, the sun shone hot upon them, but the sky was so blue and the earth so green that they both abandoned themselves to the pleasure of living with such a sky above and such a world beneath. There were here and there a few settlers' houses, but not yet a great many. The country was not a lonely one for all that. Every now and then the frightened prairie-chickens ran across the road or rose with their quick, whirring flight; ten thousand katydids and grasshoppers were jumping, fluttering, flying, and fiddling their rattling notes, and the air seemed full of life. They were considerably delayed by Albert's excursions after new insects, for he had brought his collecting-box and net along. So that when, about the middle of the afternoon, as they stopped, in fording a brook, to water old Prince, and were suddenly startled by the sound of thunder, Albert felt a little conscience-smitten that he had not traveled more diligently toward his destination. And when he drove on a quarter of a mile, he found himself in a most unpleasant dilemma, the two horns being two roads, concerning which those who directed him had neglected to give him any advice. Katy had been here before, and she was very sure that to the right hand was the road. There was now no time to turn back, for the storm was already upon them—one of those fearful thunderstorms to which the high Minnesota table-land is peculiarly liable. In sheer desperation, Charlton took the right-hand road, not doubting that he could at least find shelter for the night in some settler's shanty. The storm was one not to be imagined by those who have not seen its like, not to be described by any one. The quick succession of flashes of lightning, the sudden, sharp, unendurable explosions, before, behind, and on either side, shook the nerves of Charlton and drove little Katy frantic. For an hour they traveled through the drenching rain, their eyes blinded every minute by lightning; for an hour they expected continually that the next thunder-bolt would smite them. All round them, on that treeless prairie, the lightning seemed to fall, and with every new blaze they held their breath for fear of sudden death. Charlton wrapped Katy in every way he could, but still the storm penetrated all the wrapping, and the cold rain chilled them both to the core. Katy, on her part, was frightened, lest

54

the lightning should strike Brother Albert. Muffled in shawls, she felt tolerably safe from a thunderbolt, but it was awful to think that Brother Albert sat out there, exposed to the lightning. And in this time of trouble and danger, Charlton held fast to his sister. He felt a brave determination never to suffer Smith Westcott to have her. And if he had only lived in the middle ages, he would doubtless have challenged the fellow to mortal combat. Now, alas! civilization was in his way.

At last the storm spent itself a little, and the clouds broke away in the west, lighting up the rain and making it glorious. Then the wind veered, and the clouds seemed to close over them again, and the lightning, not quite so vivid or so frequent but still terrible, and the rain, with an incessant plashing, set in as for the whole night. Darkness was upon them, not a house was in sight, the chill cold of the ceaseless rain seemed beyond endurance, the horse was well-nigh exhausted and walked at a dull pace, while Albert feared that Katy would die from the exposure. As they came to the top of each little rise he strained his eyes, and Katy rose up and strained her eyes, in the vain hope of seeing a light, but they did not know that they were in the midst of—that they were indeed driving diagonally across—a great tract of land which had come into the hands of some corporation by means of the location of half-breed scrip. They had long since given up all hope of the hospitable welcome at the house of Cousin John, and now wished for nothing but shelter of any sort. Albert knew that he was lost, but this entire absence of settlers' houses, and even of deserted claim-shanties built for pre-emption purposes, puzzled him. Sometimes he thought he saw a house ahead, and endeavored to quicken the pace of the old horse, but the house always transformed itself to a clump of hazel-brush as he drew nearer. About nine o'clock the rain grew colder and the lightning less frequent. Katy became entirely silent— Albert could feel her shiver now and then. Thus, in numb misery, constantly hoping to see a house on ascending the next rise of ground and constantly suffering disappointment, they traveled on through the wretched monotony of that night. The ceaseless plash of the rain, the slow tread of the horse's hoofs in the water, the roar of a distant thunderbolt—these were the only sounds they heard during the next hour—during the longer hour following—during the hours after that. And then little Katy, thinking she must die, began to send messages to the folks at home, and to poor, dear Smith, who would cry so when she was gone.

But just in the moment of extremity, when Charlton felt that his very heart was chilled by this exposure in an open buggy to more than seven hours of terrific storm, he caught sight of something which cheered him. He had descended into what seemed to be a valley, there was water in the road, he could mark the road by the absence of grass, and the glistening of the water in the faint light. The water was growing deeper; just ahead of him was a small but steep hill; on top of the hill, which showed its darker form against the dark clouds, he had been able to distinguish by the lightning-light a hay-stack, and here on one side of the road the grass of the natural meadow gave unmistakable evidence of having been mowed. Albert essayed to cheer Katy by calling her attention to these signs of human habitation, but Katy was too cold and weary and numb to say much or feel much; an out-door wet-sheet pack for seven hours does not leave much of heart or hope in a human soul.

Albert noticed with alarm that the water under the horse's feet increased in depth continually. A minute ago it was just above the fetlocks; now it was nearly to the knees, and the horse was obliged to lift his feet still more slowly. The rain had filled the lowland with water. Still the grass grew on either side of the road, and Charlton did not feel much alarm until, coming almost under the very shadow of the bluff, the grass suddenly ceased abruptly, and all was water, with what appeared to be an inaccessible cliff beyond. The road which lost itself in this pool or pond, must come out somewhere on the other side. But where? To the right or left? And how bottomless might not the morass be if he should miss the road!

But in such a strait one must do something. So he selected a certain point to the left, where the hill on the other side looked less broken, and, turning the horse's head in that direction, struck him smartly with the whip. The horse advanced a step or two, the water rose quickly to his body, and he refused to go any farther. Neither coaxing nor whipping could move him. There was nothing to do now but to wait for the next flash of lightning. It was long to wait, for with the continuance of the storm the lightning had grown less and less frequent. Charlton thought it the longest five minutes that he ever knew. At last there came a blaze, very bright and blinding, leaving a very fearful darkness after it. But short and sudden as it was, it served to show Charlton that the sheet of water before him was not a pool or a pond, but a brook or a creek over all its banks, swollen to a river, and sweeping on, a wild torrent. At the side on which Charlton was, the water was comparatively still; the stream curved in such a way as to make the current dash itself against the rocky bluff.

CHAPTER XIII

A SHELTER

Albert drove up the stream, and in a fit of desperation again essayed to ford it. The staying in the rain all night with Katy was so terrible to him that he determined to cross at all hazards. It were better to drown together than to perish here. But again the prudent stubbornness of the old horse saved them. He stood in the water as immovable as the ass of Balaam. Then, for the sheer sake of doing something, Charlton drove down the stream to a point opposite where the bluff seemed of easy ascent. Here he again attempted to cross, and was again balked by the horse's regard for his own safety. Charlton did not appreciate the depth and swiftness of the stream, nor the consequent certainty of drowning in any attempt to ford it. Not until he got out of the buggy and tried to cross afoot did he understand how impossible it was.

When Albert returned to the vehicle he sat still. The current rippled against the body of the horse and the wheels of the buggy. The incessant rain roared in the water before him. There was nothing to be done. In the sheer exhaustion of his resources, in his numb despondency, he neglected even to drive the horse out of the water. How long he sat there it would be hard to say. Several times he roused himself to utter a "Halloo!" But the roar of the rain swallowed up his voice, which was husky with emotion.

After a while he heard a plashing in the water, which was not that of the rain. He thought it must be the sound of a canoe-paddle. Could anybody row against such a torrent? But he distinctly heard the plashing, and it was below him. Even Katy roused herself to listen, and strained her eyes against the blackness of the night to discover what it might be. It did not grow any nearer. It did not retreat. At the end of ten minutes this irregular but distinct dipping sound, which seemed to be in some way due to human agency, was neither farther nor nearer, neither slower nor more rapid than at first. Albert hallooed again and again at it, but the mysterious cause of this dipping and dashing was deaf to all cries for help. Or if not deaf, this oarsman seemed as incapable of giving reply as the "dumb old man" that rowed the "lily maid of Astolat" to the palace of Arthur.

But it was no oarsman, not even a dumb one. The lightning for which Albert prayed came at last, and illumined the water and the shores, dispelling all dreams of canoe or oarsman. Charlton saw

57

in an instant that there was a fence a few rods away, and that where the fence crossed the stream, or crossed from bank to bank of what was the stream at its average stage, long poles had been used, and one of these long and supple poles was now partly submerged. The swift current bent it in the middle until it would spring out of the water and drop back higher up. It was thus kept in a rotary motion, making the sound which he had mistaken for the paddling of a canoeman. With this discovery departed all thought of human help from that quarter.

But with the dissipating of the illusion came a new hope. Charlton turned the head of the horse back and drove him out of the water, or at least to a part of the meadow where the overflowed water did not reach to his knees. Here he tied him to a tree, and told Katy she must stay alone until he should cross the stream and find help, if help there should be, and return. It might take him half an hour. But poor Katy said that she could not live half an hour longer in this rain. And, besides, she knew that Albert would be drowned in crossing. So that it was with much ado that he managed to get away from her, and, indeed, I think she cried after he had gone. He called back to her when he got to the brook's bank, "All right, Katy!" but Katy heard him through the roar of the rain, and it seemed to her that he was being swallowed up in a Noachian deluge.

Charlton climbed along on the precarious footing afforded by the submerged pole, holding to the poles above while the water rushed about his feet. These poles were each of them held by a single large nail at each end, and the support was doubly doubtful. He might fall off, or the nails might come out. Even had he not been paralyzed by long exposure to the cold, he could have no hope of being able to swim in such a torrent.

In the middle of the stream he found a new difficulty. The posts to which these limber poles were nailed at either end sloped in opposite directions, so that while he started across on the upper side he found that when he got to the middle the pole fence began to slant so much up the stream that he must needs climb to the other side, a most difficult and dangerous performance on a fence of wabbling popple poles in the middle of a stream on a very dark night. When at last he got across the stream, he found himself in the midst of a hazel thicket higher than his head. He hallooed to Katy, and she was sure this time that it was his last drowning cry. Working his way out of the hazel-brush, he came to a halt against a fence and waited for lightning. That there was a house in the neighborhood he could not doubt, but whether it were inhabited or not was a question. And where was it?

For full five minutes—an eternal five minutes—the pitiless

rain poured down upon Charlton as he stood there by the fence, his eyes going forward to find a house, his heart running back to the perishing Katy. At last the lightning showed him a house, and from the roof of the house he saw a stovepipe. The best proof that it was not a deserted claim-shanty!

Stumbling round the fence in the darkness, Charlton came upon the house, a mere cabin, and tried three sides of it before he found the entrance. When he knocked, the door was opened by a tall man, who said:

"Right smart sprinkle, stranger! Where did you come from? Must 'a' rained down like a frog."

But Albert had no time for compliments. He told his story very briefly, and asked permission to bring his sister over.

"Fetch her right along, stranger. No lady never staid in this 'ere shed afore, but she's mighty welcome."

Albert now hurried back, seized with a fear that he would find Katy dead. He crossed on the poles again, shouting to Katy as he went. He found her almost senseless. He quickly loosed old Prince from the buggy, and tethered him with the lines where he would not suffer for either water or grass, and then lifted Kate from the buggy, and literally carried her to the place where they must needs climb along the poles. It was with much difficulty that he partly carried her, partly persuaded her to climb along that slender fence. How he ever got the almost helpless girl over into that hazel-brush thicket he never exactly knew, but as they approached the house, guided by a candle set in the window, she grew more and more feeble, until Albert was obliged to carry her in and lay her down in a swoon of utter exhaustion.

The inhabitant of the cabin ran to a little cupboard, made of a packing-box, and brought out a whisky-flask, and essayed to put it to her lips, but as he saw her lying there, white and beautiful in her helplessness, he started back and said, with a rude reverence, "Stranger, gin her some of this 'ere—I never could tech sech a creetur!"

And Albert gave her some of the spirits and watched her revive. He warmed her hands and chafed her feet before the fire which the backwoodsman had made. As she came back to consciousness, Charlton happened to think that he had no dry clothes for her. He would have gone immediately back to the buggy, where there was a portmanteau carefully stowed under the seat, but that the Inhabitant had gone out and he was left alone with Katy, and he feared that she would faint again if he should leave her. Presently the tall, lank, longhaired man came in.

"Mister," he said, "I made kinder sorter free with your things.

59

I thought as how as the young woman might want to shed some of them air wet feathers of her'n, and so I jist venter'd to go and git this yer bag 'thout axin' no leave nor license, while you was a-bringin' on her to. Looks pooty peart, by hokey! Now, mister, we ha'n't got no spar rooms here. But you and me'll jes' take to the loff thar fer a while, seein' our room is better nor our comp'ny. You kin change up stars."

They went to the loft by an outside ladder, the Inhabitant speaking very reverently in a whisper, evidently feeling sure that there was an angel down-stairs. They went down again after a while, and the Inhabitant piled on wood so prodigally that the room became too warm; he boiled a pot of coffee, fried some salt-pork, baked some biscuit, a little yellow and a little too short, but to the hungry travelers very palatable. Even Charlton found it easy to forego his Grahamism and eat salt-pork, especially as he had a glass of milk. Katy, for her part, drank a cup of coffee but ate little, though the Inhabitant offered her the best he had with a voice stammering with emotion. He could not speak to her without blushing to his temples. He tried to apologize for the biscuit and the coffee, but could hardly ever get through his sentence intelligibly, he was so full of a sentiment of adoration for the first lady into whose presence he had come in years. Albert felt a profound respect for the man on account of his reverence for Katy. And Katy of course loved him as she did everybody who was kind to her or to her friends, and she essayed once or twice to make him feel comfortable by speaking to him, but so great was his agitation when spoken to by the divine creature, that he came near dropping a plate of biscuit the first time she spoke, and almost upset the coffee the next time. I have often noticed that the anchorites of the frontier belong to two classes— those who have left humanity and civilization from sheer antagonism to men, a selfish, crabbed love of solitude, and those who have fled from their fellows from a morbid sensitiveness. The Inhabitant was of the latter sort.

60

CHAPTER XIV

THE INHABITANT

When Albert awoke next morning from a sound sleep on the buffalo-robe in the loft of the cabin of the Inhabitant, the strange being who had slept at his side had gone. He found him leaning against the foot of the ladder outside.

"Waitin', you know," he said when he saw Albert, "tell she gits up. I was tryin' to think what I could do to make this house fit fer her to stay in; fer, you see, stranger, they's no movin' on tell to-morry, fer though the rain's stopped, I 'low you can't git that buggy over afore to-morry mornin'. But blam'd ef 'ta'n't too bad fer sech as her to stay in sech a cabin! I never wanted no better place tell las' night, but ever sence that creetur crossed the door-sill. I've wished it was a palace of di'monds. She hadn't orter live in nothin' poarer."

"Where did you come from?" asked Charlton.

"From the Wawbosh. You see I couldn't stay. They treated me bad. I had a idee. I wanted to write somethin' or nother in country talk. I need to try to write potry in good big dictionary words, but I hadn't but 'mazin little schoolin', and lived along of a set of folks that talked jes' like I do. But a Scotchman what I worked along of one winter, he read me some potry, writ out by a Mr. Burns, in the sort of bad grammar that a Scotchman talks, you know. And I says, Ef a Scotchman could write poetry in his sort of bad grammar, why couldn't a Hoosier jest as well write poetry in the sort of lingo we talk down on the Wawbosh? I don't see why. Do you, now?"

Albert was captivated to find a "child of nature" with such an idea, and he gave it his entire approval.

"Wal, you see, when I got to makin' varses I found the folks down in Posey Kyounty didn' take to varses wrote out in their own talk. They liked the real dictionary po'try, like 'The boy stood on the burnin' deck' and 'A life on the ocean wave,' but they made fun of me, and when the boys got a hold of my poortiest varses, and said 'em over and over as they was comin' from school, and larfed at me, and the gals kinder fooled me, gittin' me to do some varses fer ther birthdays, and then makin' fun of 'em, I couldn' bar it no ways, and so I jist cleaned out and left to git shed of their talk. But I stuck to my idee all the same. I made varses in the country talk all the same, and sent 'em to editors, but they couldn' see nothin' in 'em. Writ back that I'd better larn to spell. When I could a-spelt down any one of 'em the best day they ever seed!"

"I'd like to see some of your verses," said Albert.

"I thought maybe you mout," and with that he took out a soiled blue paper on which was written in blue ink some verses.

"Now, you see, I could spell right ef I wanted to, but I noticed that Mr. Burns had writ his Scotch like it was spoke, and so I thought I'd write my country talk by the same rule."

And the picturesque Inhabitant, standing there in the morning light in his trapper's wolf-skin cap, from the apex of which the tail of the wolf hung down his back, read aloud the verses which he had written in the Hoosier dialect, or, as he called it, the country talk of the Wawbosh. In transcribing them, I have inserted one or two apostrophes, for the poet always complained that though he could spell like sixty, he never could mind his stops.

WHAT DUMB CRITTERS SAYS

The cat-bird poorty nigh splits his throat,
Ef nobody's thar to see.
The cat-bird poorty nigh splits his throat,
But ef I say, "Sing out, green coat,"
Why, "I can't" and "I shan't," says he.

I 'low'd the crows mout be afeard
Of a man made outen straw.
I 'low'd the crows mout be afeard,
But laws! they warn't the least bit skeered,
They larfed out, "Haw! haw-haw!"

A long-tail squir'l up in th' top
Of that air ellum tree,
A long-tail squir'l up in th' top,
A lis'nin' to the acorns drop,
Says, "Sh! sh-sh!" at me.

The big-eyed owl a-settin' on a limb
With nary a wink nur nod,
The big-eyed owl a-settin' on a limb,
Is a-singin' a sort of a solemn hymn
Of "Hoo! hoo-ah!" at God.

Albert could not resist a temptation to smile at this last line.

"I know, stranger. You think a owl can't sing to God. But I'd like to know why! Ef a mockin'-bird kin sing God's praises a-singin' trible, and so on through all the parts—you see I larnt the squar notes oncet at a singin'—why, I don't see to save me why the bass of the owl a'n't jest as good praisin' ef 'ta'n't quite sech fine singin'. Do you, now? An' I kinder had a feller-feelin' fer the owl. I says to him,' Well, ole feller, you and me is jist alike in one thing. Our notes a'n't appreciated by the public.' But maybe God thinks about as much of the real ginowine hootin' of a owl as he does of the highfalugeon whistlin' of a mockin'-bird all stole from somebody else. An' ef my varses is kinder humbly to hear, anyway they a'n't made like other folkses; they're all of 'em outen my head—sech as it is."

"You certainly have struck an original vein," said Albert, who had a passion for nature in the rough. "I wish you would read some of your verses to my sister."

"Couldn' do it," said the poet; "at least, I don't believe I could. My voice wouldn' hold up. Laid awake all las' night tryin' to make some varses about her. But sakes, stranger, I couldn' git two lines strung together. You mout as well try to put sunshine inter a gallon-jug, you know, as to write about that lovely creetur. An' I can't make poetry in nothin' 'ceppin' in our country talk; but laws! it seems sech a rough thing to use to say anything about a heavenly angel in. Seemed like as ef I was makin' a nosegay fer her, and hadn't no poseys but jimson-weeds, hollyhocks, and big yaller sunflowers. I wished I could 'a' made real dictionary poetry like Casabianca and Hail Columby. But I didn' know enough about the words. I never got nary wink of sleep a-thinkin' about her, and a-wishin' my house was finer and my clo'es purtier and my hair shorter, and I was a eddicated gentleman. Never wished that air afore."

Katy woke up a little dull and quite hungry, but not sick, and she good-naturedly set herself to work to show her gratitude to the Inhabitant by helping, him to get breakfast, at which he declared that he was never so flustrated in all his born days. Never.

They waited all that day for the waters to subside, and Katy taught the Poet several new culinary arts, while he showed her his traps and hunting gear, and initiated the two strangers into all the mysteries of mink and muskrat catching, telling them more about the habits of fur-bearing animals than they could have learned from books. And Charlton recited many pieces of "real dictionary poetry" to the poor fellow, who was at last prevailed on to read some of his dialect pieces in the presence of Katy. He read her one on "What the Sunflower said to the Hollyhock," and a love-poem, called "Polly in the Spring-house." The first strophe of this inartistic idyl will doubtless be all the reader will care to see.

Purtier'n dressed-up gals in town
Is peart and larfin' Polly Brown,
With curly hair a-hangin' down,
An' sleeves rolled clean above her elbow.
Barfeooted stan'in on the rocks,
A-pourin' milk in airthen crocks,
An' kiverin' 'em with clean white blocks—
Jest lis'en how my fool heart knocks—
Shet up, my heart! what makes you tell so?

"You see," he said, blushing and stammering, "you see, miss, I had a sort of a preju_dice_ agin town gals in them air days, I thought they was all stuck up and proud like; I didn' think the—the—well—you know I don't mean no harm nur nothin'—but I didn' expect the very purtiest on 'em all was ever agoin' to come into my shanty and make herself at home like as ef I was a eddicated gentleman. All I said agin town gals I take back. I—I—you see—" but finding it impossible to get through, the Poet remembered something to be attended to out of doors.

The ever active Charlton could not pass a day in idleness. By ten o'clock he had selected a claim and staked it out. It was just the place for his great school. When the country should have settled up, he would found a farm-school here and make a great institution out of it. The Inhabitant was delighted with the prospect of having the brother of an angel for a neighbor, and readily made a bargain to erect for Charlton a cabin like his own for purposes of pre-emption. Albert's lively imagination had already planned the building and grounds of his institution.

During the whole of that sunshiny day that Charlton waited for the waters of Pleasant Brook to subside, George Gray, the Inhabitant of the lone cabin, exhausted his ingenuity in endeavoring to make his hospitality as complete as possible. When Albert saw him standing by the ladder in the morning, he had already shot some prairie-chickens, which he carefully broiled. And after they had supped on wild strawberries and another night had passed, they breakfasted on some squirrels killed in a neighboring grove, and made into a delicious stew by the use of such vegetables as the garden of the Inhabitant afforded. Charlton and the Poet got the horse and buggy through the stream. When everything was ready for a start, the Inhabitant insisted that he would go "a piece" with them to show the way, and, mounted on his Indian pony, he kept them company to their destination. Then the trapper bade Albert an affectionate adieu, and gave a blushing, stammering, adoring farewell to Katy, and turned his little sorrel pony back toward his home, where he spent the next few days in trying to make some worthy verses in commemoration of the coming to the cabin of a trapper lonely, a purty angel bright as day, and how the trapper only wep' and cried when she went away. But his feelings were too deep for his rhymes, and his rhymes were poorer than his average, because his feeling was deeper. He must have burned up hundreds of couplets, triplets, and sextuplets in the next fortnight. For, besides his chivalrous and poetic gallantry toward womankind, he found himself hopelessly in love with a girl whom he would no more have thought of marrying than he would of wedding a real angel. Sometimes he dreamed of going to school and getting an education, "puttin' some school-master's hair-ile onter his talk," as he called it, but then the hopelessness of any attempt to change himself deterred him. But thenceforth Katy became more to him than Laura was to Petrarch. Habits of intemperance had crept upon him in his isolation and pining for excitement, but now he set out to seek an ideal purity, he abolished even his pipe, he scrupulously pruned his conversation of profanity, so that he wouldn' be onfit to love her any way, ef he didn' never marry her.

65

CHAPTER XV

AN EPISODE

I fear the gentle reader, how much more the savage one, will accuse me of having beguiled him with false pretenses. Here I have written XIV chapters of this story, which claims to be a mystery, and there stand the letters XV at the head of this chapter and I have not got to the mystery yet, and my friend Miss Cormorant, who devours her dozen novels a week for steady diet, and perhaps makes it a baker's dozen at this season of the year, and who loves nothing so well as to be mystified by labyrinthine plots and counterplots—Miss Cormorant is about to part company with me at this point. She doesn't like this plain sailing. Now, I will be honest with you, Miss Cormorant, all the more that I don't care if you do quit. I will tell you plainly that to my mind the mystery lies yet several chapters in advance, and that I shouldn't be surprised if I have to pass out of my teens and begin to head with double X's before I get to that mystery. Why don't I hurry up then? Ah! there's the rub. Miss Cormorant and all the Cormorant family are wanting me to hurry up with this history, and just so surely as I should skip over any part of the tale, or slight my background, or show any eagerness, that other family, the Critics—the recording angels of literature—take down their pens, and with a sad face joyfully write: "This book is, so-so, but bears evident marks of hurry in its execution. If the author shall ever learn the self-possession of the true artist, and come to tell his stories with leisurely dignity of manner—and so on—and so on—and so forth—he will—well, he will—do middling well for a man who had the unhappiness to be born in longitude west from Washington." Ah! well, I shrug my shoulders, and bidding both Cormorant and Critic to get behind me, Satan, I write my story in my own fashion for my gentle readers who are neither Cormorants nor Critics, and of whom I am sincerely fond.

For instance, I find it convenient to turn aside at this point to mention Dave Sawney, for how could I relate the events which are to follow to readers who had not the happiness to know Katy's third lover—or thirteenth—the aforesaid Dave? You are surprised, doubtless, that Katy should have so many lovers as three; you have not then lived in a new country where there are generally half-a-dozen marriageable men to every marriageable woman, and where, since the law of demand and supply has no application, every girl finds herself beset with more beaux than a heartless flirt could wish for. Dave was large, lymphatic, and conceited; he "come frum Southern Eelinoy," as he expressed it, and he had a comfortable conviction that the fertile Illinois Egypt had produced nothing more creditable than his own slouching figure and self-complaisant soul. Dave Sawney had a certain vividness of imagination that served to exalt everything pertaining to himself; he never in his life made a bargain to do anything—he always cawntracked to do it. He cawntracked to set out three trees, and then he cawntracked to dig six post-holes, and-when he gave his occupation to the census-taker he set himself down as a "cawntractor."

He had laid siege to Katy in his fashion, slouching in of an evening, and boasting of his exploits until Smith Westcott would come and chirrup and joke, and walk Katy right away from him to take a walk or a boat-ride. Then he would finish the yarn which Westcott had broken in the middle, to Mrs. Plausaby or Miss Marlay, and get up and remark that he thought maybe he mout as well be a-gittin' on.

In the county-seat war, which had raged about the time Albert had left for Glenfleld, Dave Sawney had come to be a man of importance. His own claim lay equidistant from the two rival towns. He bad considerable influence with a knot of a dozen settlers in his neighborhood, who were, like himself, without any personal interest in the matter. It became evident that a dozen or a half-dozen votes might tip the scale after Plausaby, Esq., had turned the enemy's flank by getting some local politician to persuade the citizens of Westville, who would naturally have supported the claims of Perritaut, that their own village stood the ghost of a chance, or at least that their interests would be served by the notoriety which the contest would give, and perhaps also by defeating Perritaut, which, from proximity, was more of a rival than Metropolisville. After this diversion had weakened Perritaut, it became of great consequence to secure even so small an influence as that of Dave Sawney. Plausaby persuaded Dave to cawntrack for the delivery of his influence, and Dave was not a little delighted to be flattered and paid at the same time. He explained to the enlightened people in his neighborhood that Squire Plausaby was a-goin' to do big things fer the kyounty; that the village of Metropolisville would erect a brick court-house and donate it; that Plausaby had already cawntracked to donate it to the kyounty free gratis.

This ardent support of Dave, who saw not only the price which the squire had cawntracked to pay him, but a furtherance of his suit with little Katy, as rewards of his zeal, would have turned the balance at once in favor of Metropolisville, had it not been for a woman. Was there ever a war, since the days of the Greek hobby-horse, since the days of Rahab's basket indeed, in which a woman did not have some part? It is said that a woman should not vote, because she can not make war; but that is just what a woman can do; she can make war, and she can often decide it. There came into this contest between Metropolisville and its rival, not a Helen certainly, but a woman. Perritaut was named for an old French trader, who had made his fortune by selling goods to the Indians on its site, and who had taken him an Indian wife—it helped trade to wed an Indian—and reared a family of children who were dusky, and spoke both the Dakota and the French à la Canadien. M. Perritaut had become rich, and yet his riches could not remove a particle of the maternal complexion from those who were to inherit the name and wealth of the old trader. If they should marry other half-breeds, the line of dusky Perritauts might stretch out the memory of a savage maternity to the crack of doom. Que voulez-vous? They must not many half-breeds. Each generation must make advancement toward a Caucasian whiteness, in a geometric ratio, until the Indian element should be reduced by an infinite progression toward nothing. But how? It did not take long for Perritaut père to settle that question. Voilà tout. The young men should seek white wives. They had money. They might marry poor girls, but white ones. But the girls? Eh bien! Money should wash them also, or at least money should bleach their descendants. For money is the Great Stain-eraser, the Mighty Detergent, the Magic Cleanser. And the stain of race is not the only one that money makes white as snow. So the old gentleman one day remarked to some friends who drank wine with him, that he would geeve one ten tousant tollare, begare, to te man tat maree his oltest daughtare, Mathilde. Eh bien, te man must vary surelee pe w'ite and re-spect-ah-ble. Of course this confidential remark soon spread abroad, as it was meant to spread abroad. It came to many ears. The most utterly worthless white men, on hearing it, generally drew themselves up in pride and vowed they'd see the ole frog-eatin' Frenchman hung afore they'd many his Injin. They'd druther marry a Injin than a nigger, but they couldn' be bought with no money to trust their skelp with a Injin.

Not so our friend Dave. He wurn't afeared of no Injin, he said; sartainly not of one what had been weakened down to half the strength. Ef any man dared him to marry a Injin and backed the dare by ten thousand dollars, blamed ef he wouldn't take the dare. He wouldn' be dared by no Frenchman to marry his daughter. He wouldn't. He wa'n't afeard to marry a Injin. He'd cawntrack to do it fer ten thousand.

The first effect of this thought on Dave's mind was to change his view of the county-seat question. He shook his head now when Plausaby's brick court-house was spoken of. The squire was awful 'cute; too 'cute to live, he said ominously.

Dave concluded that ten thousand dollars could be made much more easily by foregoing his preferences for a white wife in favor of a red one, than by cawntracting to set out shade-trees, dig post-holes, or drive oxen. So he lost no time in visiting the old trader.

He walked in, in his slouching fashion, shook hands with M. Perritaut, gave his name as David Sawney, cawntracter, and after talking a little about the county-seat question, he broached the question of marriage with Mathilde Perritaut.

"I hearn tell that you are willin' to do somethin' han'some fer a son-in-law."

"Varee good, Mistare Sonee. You air a man of bisnees, perhaps, maybe. You undairstand tese tings. Eh? Très bien—I mean vary well, you see. I want that my daughtare zhould maree one respect-ah-ble man. Vare good. You air one, maybe. I weel find out. Très bien, you see, my daughtare weel marree the man that I zay. You weel come ovare here next week. Eef I find you air respect-ah-ble, I weel then get my lawyare to make a marriage contract."

"A cawntrack?" said Dave, starting at the sound of his favorite word.

"Very well, musheer, I sign a cawntrack and live up to it."

"Vare good. Weel you have one leetle peench of snuff?" said the old man, politely opening his box.

"Yes, I'm obleeged, musheer," said Dave. "Don't keer ef I do." And by way of showing his good-will and ingratiating himself with the Frenchman, Dave helped himself to an amazingly large pinch. Indeed, not being accustomed to take snuff, he helped himself, as he did to chewing tobacco when it was offered free, with the utmost liberality. The result did not add to the dignity of his bearing, for he was seized with a succession of convulsions of sneezing. Dave habitually did everything in the noisiest way possible, and he wound up each successive fit of sneezing with a whoop that gave him the semblance of practicing an Indian war-song, by way of fitting himself to wed a half-breed wife.

"I declare," he said, when the sneezing had subsided, "I never did see no sech snuff."

"Vare good," resumed M. Perritaut. "I weel promees in the contract to geeve you one ten tousant tollars—deux mille—two tousant avery yare for fife yare. Très bien. My daughtare is edu_cate_; she stoody fife, seex yare in te convent at Montreal. Zhe

69

play on piano evare so many tune. Bien. You come Monday. We weel zee. Adieu. I mean good-by, Mistare Sonee."

"Adoo, musheer," said Dave, taking his hat and leaving. He boasted afterwards that he had spoke to the ole man in French when he was comin' away. Thought it mout kinder tickle him, you know. And he said he didn' mind a brown complexion a bit. Fer his part, seemed to him 'twas kinder purty fer variety. Wouldn' want all women reddish, but fer variety 'twas sorter nice, you know. He always did like sompin' odd.

And he now threw all his energy into the advocacy of Perritaut. It was the natural location ᴉ of a county-seat. Metropolisville never would be nawthin'.

Monday morning found him at Perritaut's house, ready to sell himself in marriage. As for the girl, she, poor brown lamb—or wolf, as the case may be—was ready, with true Indian stolidity, to be disposed of as her father chose. The parties who were interested in the town of Perritaut had got wind of Dave's proposition; and as they saw how important his influence might be in the coming election, they took pains to satisfy Monsieur Perritaut that Mr. Sawney was a very proper person to marry his tawny daughter and pocket his yellow gold-pieces. The lawyer was just finishing the necessary documents when Dave entered.

"Eh bien! How you do, Mistare Sonee? Is eet dat you weel have a peench of snuff?" For the Frenchman had quite forgotten Dave's mishap in snuff-taking, and offered the snuff out of habitual complaisance.

"No, musheer," said Dave, "I can't use no snuff of late yeers. 'Fection of the nose; makes me sneeze dreffle."

"Oh! Eh blen! C'est comme il faut. I mean dat is all right, vare good, mistare. Now, den, Monsieur l'Avocat, I mean ze lawyare, he is ready to read ze contract."

"Cawntrack? Oh! yes, that's right. We Americans marry without a cawntrack, you see. But I like cawntracks myself. It's my business, cawntracking is, you know. Fire away whenever you're ready, mister." This last to the lawyer, who was waiting to read.

Dave sat, with a knowing air, listening to the legal phraseology as though he had been used to marriage contracts from infancy. He was pleased with the notion of being betrothed in this awful diplomatic fashion. It accorded with his feelings to think that he was worth ten thousand dollars and the exhaustive verbiage of this formidable cawntrack.

But at last the lawyer read a part which made him open his eyes.

Something about its being further stipulated that the said

70

David Sawney, of the first part, in and for the consideration named, "hereby binds himself to have the children which shall issue from this marriage educated in the Roman Catholic faith," caught his ears.

"Hold on, mister, I can't sign that! I a'n't over-pertikeler about who I marry, but I can't go that."

"What part do you object to?"

"Well, ef I understand them words you've got kiled up there—an' I'm purty middlin' smart at big words, you see—I'm to eddicate the children in the Catholic faith, as you call it."

"Yes, that is it."

"Oui! vare good. Dat I must inseest on," said Perritaut.

"Well, I a'n't nothin' in a religious way, but I can't stan' that air. I'm too well raised. I kin marry a Injin, but to sell out my children afore they're born to Catholic priests, I couldn't do that air ef you planked down two ten thousands."

And upon this point Dave stuck. There is a sentiment down somewhere in almost any man, and there was this one point of conscience with Dave. And there was likewise this one scruple with Perritaut. And these opposing scruples in two men who had not many, certainly, turned the scale and gave the county-seat to Metropolisville, for Dave told all his Southern Illinois friends that if the county-seat should remain at Perritaut, the Catholics would build a nunnery an' a caythedral there, and then none of their daughters would be safe. These priests was a-lookin' arter the comin' generation. And besides, Catholics and Injins wouldn' have a good influence on the moral and religious kerecter of the kyounty. The influence of half-breeds was a bad thing fer civilization. Ef a man was half-Injin, he was half-Injin, and you couldn't make him white noways. And Dave distributed freely deeds to some valueless outlots, which Plausaby had given him for the purpose.

CHAPTER XVI
THE RETURN

As long as he could, Charlton kept Katy at Glenfield. He amused her by every means in his power; he devoted himself to her; he sought to win her away from Westcott, not by argument, to which she was invulnerable, but by feeling. He found that the only motive that moved her was an emotion of pity for him, so he contrived to make her estimate his misery on her account at its full value. But just when he thought he had produced some effect there would come one of Smith Westcott's letters, written not as he talked (it is only real simpleheartedness or genuine literary gift that can make the personality of the writer felt in a letter), but in a round business hand with plenty of flourishes, and in sentences very carefully composed. But he managed in his precise and prim way to convey to Katy the notion that he was pining away for her company. And she, missing the giggle and the playfulness from the letter, thought his distress extreme indeed. For it would have required a deeper sorrow than Smith Westcott ever felt to make him talk in the stiff conventional fashion in which his letters were composed.

And besides Westcott's letters there were letters from her mother, in which that careful mother never failed to tell how Mr. Westcott had come in, the evening before, to talk about Katy, and to tell her how lost and heart-broken he was. So that letters from home generally brought on a relapse of Katy's devotion to her lover. She was cruelly torn by alternate fits of loving pity for poor dear Brother Albert on the one hand, and poor, dear, dear Smith Westcott on the other. And the latter generally carried the day in her sympathies. He was such a poor dear fellow, you know, and hadn't anybody, not even a mother, to comfort him, and he had often said that if his charming and divine little Katy should ever prove false, he would go and drown himself in the lake. And that would be so awful, you know. And, besides, Brother Albert had plenty to love him. There was mother, and there was that quiet kind of a young lady at the City Hotel that Albert went to see so often, though how he could like anybody so cool she didn't know. And then Cousin Isa would love Brother Albert maybe, if he'd ask her. But he had plenty, and poor Smith had often said that he needed somebody to help him to be good. And she would cleave to him forever and help him. Mother and father thought she was right, and she couldn't anyway let Smith drown himself. How could she? That would be the same as murdering him, you know.

During the fortnight that Charlton and his sister visited in Glenfield, Albert divided his time between trying to impress Katy with the general unfitness of Smith Westcott to be her husband, and the more congenial employment of writing long letters to Miss Helen Minorkey, and receiving long letters from that lady. His were fervent and enthusiastic; they explained in a rather vehement style all the schemes that filled his brain for working out his vocation and helping the world to its goal: while hers discussed everything in the most dispassionate temper. Charlton had brought himself to admire this dispassionate temper. A man of Charlton's temper who is really in love, can bring himself to admire any traits in the object of his love. Had Helen Minorkey shown some little enthusiasm, Charlton would have exaggerated it, admired it, and rejoiced in it as a priceless quality. As she showed none, he admired the lack of it in her, rejoiced in her entire superiority to her sex in this regard, and loved her more and more passionately every day. And Miss Minorkey was not wanting in a certain tenderness toward her adorer. She loved him in her way, it made her happy to be loved in that ideal fashion.

Charlton found himself in a strait betwixt two. He longed to worship again at the shrine of his Minerva. But he disliked to return with Katy until he had done something to break the hold of Smith Westcott upon her mind. So upon one pretext or another he staid until Westcott wrote to Katy that business would call him to Glenfield the next week, and he hoped that she would conclude to return with him. Katy was so pleased with the prospect of a long ride with her lover, that she felt considerable disappointment when Albert determined to return at once. Brother Albert always did such curious things. Katy, who had given Albert a dozen reasons for an immediate return, now thought it very strange that he should be in such a hurry. Had he given up trying to find that new kind of grasshopper he spoke of the day before?

One effect of the unexpected arrival of Albert and Katy in Metropolisville, was to make Smith Westcott forget that he ever had any business that was likely to call him to Glenfield. Delighted to see Katy back. Would a died if she'd staid away another week. By George! he! he! he! Wanted to jump into the lake, you know. Always felt that way when Katy was out of sight two days. Curious. By George! Didn't think any woman could ever make such a fool of him. He! he! Felt like ole Dan Tucker when he came to supper and found the hot cakes all gone. He! he! he! By George! You know! Let's sing de forty-lebenth hymn! Ahem!

73

"If Diner was an apple,
And I was one beside her,
Oh! how happy we would be,
When we's skwushed into cider!
And a little more cider too, ah-hoo!
And a little more cider too!
And a little more cider too—ah—hoo!
And a little more cider too."

How much? Pailful! By George! He! he! he! That's so! You know. Them's my sentiments. 'Spresses the 'motions of my heart, bredren! Yah! yah! By hokey! And here comes Mr. Albert Charlton. Brother Albert! Just as well learn to say it now as after a while. Eh, Katy? How do, brother Albert? Glad to see you as if I'd stuck a nail in my foot. By George! he! he! You won't mind my carryin' on. Nobody minds me. I'm the privileged infant, you know. I am, by George! he! he! Come, Kate, let's take a boat-ride.

"Oh! come, love, come; my boat's by the shore;
If yer don't ride now, I won't ax you no more."

And so forth. Too hoarse to sing. But I am not too feeble to paddle my own canoe. Come, Katy Darling. You needn't mind your shawl when you've got a Westcott to keep you warm. He! he! By George!

And then he went out singing that her lips was red as roses or poppies or something, and "wait for the row-boat and we'll all take a ride."

Albert endeavored to forget his vexation by seeking the society of Miss Minorkey, who was sincerely glad to see him back, and who was more demonstrative on this evening than he had ever known her to be. And Charlton was correspondingly happy. He lay in his unplastered room that night, and counted the laths in the moonlight, and built golden ladders out of them by which to climb up to the heaven of his desires. But he was a little troubled to find that in proportion as he came nearer to the possession of Miss Minorkey, his ardor in the matter of his great Educational Institution—his American Philanthropinum, as he called it—abated.

I ought here to mention a fact which occurred about this time, because it is a fact that has some bearing on the course of the story, and because it may help us to a more charitable judgment in regard to the character of Mr. Charlton's step-father. Soon after Albert's return from Glenfield, he received an appointment to the postmastership of Metropolisville in such a way as to leave no doubt that it came through Squire Plausaby's influence. We are in the habit of thinking a mean man wholly mean. But we are wrong. Liberal Donor, Esq., for instance, has a great passion for keeping his left hand exceedingly well informed of the generous doings of his right. He gives money to found the Liberal Donor Female Collegiate and Academical Institute, and then he gives money to found the Liberal Donor Professorship of Systematic and Metaphysical Theology, and still other sums to establish the Liberal Donor Orthopedic Chirurgical Gratuitous Hospital for Cripples and Clubfooted. Shall I say that the man is not generous, but only ostentatious? Not at all. He might gratify his vanity in other ways. His vanity dominates over his benevolence, and makes it pay tribute to his own glory. But his benevolence is genuine, notwithstanding. Plausaby was mercenary, and he may have seen some advantages to himself in having the post-office in his own house, and in placing his step-son under obligation to himself. Doubtless these considerations weighed much, but besides, we must remember the injunction that includes even the Father of Evil in the number of those to whom a share of credit is due. Let us say for Plausaby that, land-shark as he was, he was not vindictive, he was not without generosity, and that it gave him sincere pleasure to do a kindness to his step-son, particularly when his generous impulse coincided so exactly with his own interest in the matter. I do not say that he would not have preferred to take the appointment himself, had it not been that he had once been a postmaster in Pennsylvania, and some old unpleasantness between him and the Post-Office Department about an unsettled account stood in his way. But in all the tangled maze of motive that, by a resolution of force, produced the whole which men called Plausaby the Land-shark, there was not wanting an element of generosity, and that element of generosity had much to do with Charlton's appointment. And Albert took it kindly. I am afraid that he was just a little less observant of the transactions in which Plausaby engaged after that. I am sure that he was much less vehement than before in his denunciations of land-sharks. The post-office was set up in one of the unfinished rooms of Mr. Plausaby's house, and, except at mail-times, Charlton was not obliged to confine himself to it. Katy or Cousin Isa or Mrs. Plausaby was always glad to look over the letters for any caller, to sell stamps to those who wanted them, and tell a Swede how much postage he must pay on a painfully-written letter to some relative in Christiana or Stockholm. And the three or four hundred dollars of income enabled Charlton to prosecute his studies. In his gratitude he lent the two hundred and twenty dollars—all that was left of his educational fund—to Mr. Plausaby, at two per cent a month, on demand, secured by a mortgage on lots in Metropolisville.

Poor infatuated George Gray—the Inhabitant of the Lone Cabin, the Trapper of Pleasant Brook, the Hoosier Poet from the Wawbosh country—poor infatuated George Gray found his cabin untenable after little Katy had come and gone. He came up to Metropolisville, improved his dress by buying some ready-made clothing, and haunted the streets where he could catch a glimpse now and then of Katy.

One night, Charlton, coming home from an evening with Miss Minorkey at the hotel, found a man standing in front of the fence.

"What do you want here?" he asked sharply.

"Didn' mean no harm, stranger, to nobody."

"Oh! it's you!" exclaimed Charlton, recognizing his friend the Poet.

"Come in, come in."

"Come in? Couldn' do it no way, stranger. Ef I was to go in thar amongst all them air ladies, my knees would gin out. I was jist a-lookin' at that purty creetur. But I 'druther die'n do her any harm. I mos' wish I was dead. But 'ta'n't no harm to look at her ef she don' know it. I shan't disturb her; and ef she marries a gentleman, I shan't disturb him nuther. On'y, ef he don' mind it, you know, I'll write po'try about her now and then. I got some varses now that I wish you'd show to her, ef you think they won't do her no harm, you know, and I don't 'low they will. Good-by, Mr. Charlton. Comin' down to sleep on your claim? Land's a-comin' into market down thar."

After the Poet left him, Albert took the verses into the house and read them, and gave them to Katy. The first stanza was, if I remember it rightly, something of this sort:

"A angel come inter the poar trapper's door,
    The purty feet tromped on the rough puncheon floor,
Her lovely head slep' on his prairie-grass piller—
    The cabin is lonesome and the trapper is poar,
    He hears little shoes a-pattin' the floor;
    He can't sleep at night on that piller no more;
His Hoosier harp hangs on the wild water-willer!"

CHAPTER XVII

SAWNEY AND HIS OLD LOVE

Self-conceit is a great source of happiness, a buffer that softens all the jolts of life. After David Sawney's failure to capture Perritaut's half-breed Atlantis and her golden apples at one dash, one would have expected him to be a little modest in approaching his old love again; but forty-eight hours after her return from Glenfield, he was paying his "devours," as he called them, to little Katy Charlton. He felt confident of winning—he was one of that class of men who believe themselves able to carry off anybody they choose. He inventoried his own attractions with great complacency; he had good health, a good claim, and, as he often boasted, had been "raised rich," or, as he otherwise stated it, "cradled in the lap of luxury." His father was one of those rich Illinois farmers who are none the less coarse for all their money and farms. Owing to reverses of fortune, Dave had inherited none of the wealth, but all of the coarseness of grain. So he walked into Squire Plausaby's with his usual assurance, on the second evening after Katy's return.

"Howdy, Miss Charlton," he said, "howdy! I'm glad to see you lookin' so smart. Howdy, Mrs. Ferret!" to the widow, who was present. "Howdy do, Mr. Charlton—back again?" And then he took his seat alongside Katy, not without a little trepidation, for he felt a very slight anxiety lest his flirtation With Perritaut's ten thousand dollars "mout've made his chances juberous," as he stated it to his friends. But then, he reflected, "she'll think I'm worth more'n ever when she knows I de-clined ten thousand dollars, in five annooal payments."

"Mr. Sawney," said the widow Ferret, beaming on him with one of her sudden, precise, pickled smiles, "Mr. Sawney, I'm delighted to hear that you made a brave stand against Romanism. It is the bane of this country. I respect you for the stand you made. It shows the influence of schripcheral training by a praying mother, I've no doubt, Mr. Sawney."

Dave was flattered and annoyed at this mention, and he looked at little Katy, but she didn't seem to feel any interest in the matter, and so he took heart.

"I felt it my dooty, Mrs. Ferret, indeed I did."

"I respect you for it, Mr. Sawney."

"For what?" said Albert irascibly. "For selling himself into a

77

mercenary marriage, and then higgling on a point of religious prejudice?"

Mrs. Ferret now focused her round eyes at Mr. Charlton, smiled her deprecating smile, and replied: "I do think, Mr. Charlton, that in this day of lax views on one side and priestcraft on the other, I respect a man who thinks enough of ee-vangelical truth to make a stand against any enemy of the holy religion of—"

"Well," said Charlton rudely, "I must say that I respect Perritaut's prejudices just as much as I do Dave's. Both of them were engaged in a contemptible transaction, and both of them showed an utter lack of conscience, except in matters of opinion. Religion is—"

But the company did not get the benefit of Mr. Albert's views on the subject of religion, for at that moment entered Mr. Smith Westcott.

"How do, Katy? Lookin' solemn, eh? How do, Brother Albert? Mrs. Ferret, how do? Ho! ho! Dave, is this you? I congratulate you on your escape from the savages. Scalp all sound, eh? Didn' lose your back-hair? By George! he! he! he!" And he began to show symptoms of dancing, as he sang:

"John Brown, he had a little Injun;
John Brown, he had a little Injun;
Dave Sawney had a little Injun;
One little Injun gal!

"Yah! yah! Well, well, Mr. Shawnee, glad to see you back."

"Looky hyer. Mister Wes'cott," said Dave, growing red, "you're a-makin' a little too free."

"Oh! the Shawnee chief shouldn' git mad. He! he! by George! wouldn' git mad fer ten thousand dollars. I wouldn', by George! you know! he! he! Ef I was worth ten thousand dollars live weight, bide and tallow throw'd in, I would—"

"See here, mister," said Dave, rising, "maybe, you'd like to walk out to some retired place, and hev your hide thrashed tell 'twouldn' hold shucks? Eh?"

"I beg pardon," said Westcott, a little frightened, "didn' mean no harm, you know, Mr. Sawney. All's fair in war, especially when it's a war for the fair. Sort of warfare, you know. By George! he! he! Shake hands, let's be friends, Dave. Don' mind my joking—nobody minds me. I'm the privileged infant, you know, he! he! A'n't I, Mr. Charlton?"

"You're infant enough, I'm sure," said Albert, "and whether

78

you are privileged or not, you certainly take liberties that almost any other man would get knocked down for."

"Oh! well, don't let's be cross. Spoils our faces and voices, Mr. Charlton, to be cross. For my part, I'm the laughin' philosopher—the giggling philosopher, by George! he! he! Come Katy, let's walk."

Katy was glad enough to get her lover away fro her brother. She hated quarreling, and didn't see why people couldn't be peaceable. And so she took Mr. Westcott's arm, and they walked out, that gentleman stopping to strike a match and light his cigar at the door, and calling back, "Dood by, all, dood by! Adieu, Monsieur Sawney, au revoir!" Before he had passed out of the gate he was singing lustily:

> "Ten little, nine little, eight little Injun;
> Seven little, six little, five little Injun;
> Four, little, three little, two little Injun;
> One little Injun girl!

"He! he! By George! Best joke, for the time of the year, I ever heard."

"I think," said Mrs. Ferret, after Katy and her lover had gone— she spoke rapidly by jerks, with dashes between—"I think, Mr. Sawney—that you are worthy of commendation—I do, indeed—for your praiseworthy stand—against Romanism. I don't know what will become of our liberties—if the priests ever get control—of this country."

Sawney tried to talk, but was so annoyed by the quick effrontery with which Westcott had carried the day that he could not say anything quite to his own satisfaction. At last Dave rose to go, and said he had thought maybe he mout git a chance to explain things to Miss Charlton ef Mr. Westcott hadn't gone off with her. But he'd come agin. He wanted to know ef Albert thought her feelin's was hurt by what he'd done in offerin to make a cawntrack with Perritaut. And Albert assured him he didn't think they were in the least. He had never heard Katy mention the matter, except to laugh about it.

At the gate Mr. Sawney met the bland, gentlemanly Plausaby, Esq., who took him by the hand soothingly, and spoke of his services in the late election matter with the highest appreciation.

Dave asked the squire what he thought of the chance of his succeeding with Miss Charlton. He recited to Plausaby his early advantages. "You know, Squire, I was raised rich, cradled in the lap of luxury. Ef I ha'n't got much book-stuffin' in my head, 'ta'n't fer want of schoolin'. I never larnt much, but then I had plenty of edication; I went to school every winter hand-runnin' tell I was twenty-two, and went to singin' every Sunday arternoon. 'Ta'n't like as ef I'd been brought up poar, weth no chance to larn. I've had the schoolin' anyway, and it's all the same. An' I've got a good claim, half timber, and runnin' water onter it, and twenty acre of medder. I s'pose mebbe she don't like my going' arter that air Frenchman's gal. But I didn't mean no 'fense, you know—ten thousand in yaller gold's a nice thing to a feller like me what's been raised rich, and's kinder used to havin' and not much used to gittin'. I wouldn't want her to take no 'fense, you know. 'Ta'n't like's ef I'd a-loved the red-skin Catholic. I hadn' never seed 'er. It wasn't the gal, it was the money I hankered arter. So Miss Charlton needn' be jealous, nor juberous, like's ef I was agoin' to wish I'd a married the Injun. I'd feel satisfied with Kate Charlton ef you think she'd be with David Sawney!"

"That's a delicate subject—quite a delicate subject for me to speak about, Mr. Sawney. To say anything about. But I may assure you that I appreciate your services in our late battle. Appreciate them highly. Quite highly. Very, indeed. I have no friend that I think more highly of. None. I think I could indicate to you a way by which you might remove any unfavorable impression from Miss Charlton's mind. Any unfavorable impression."

"Anythin' you tell me to do, squire, I'll do. I'd mos' skelp the ole man Perritaut, and his darter too, ef you said it would help me to cut out that insultin' Smith Westcott, and carry off Miss Charlton. I don't know as I ever seed a gal that quite come up to her, in my way of thinkin'. Now, squire, what is it?"

"Well, Mr. Sawney, we carried the election the other day and got the county-seat. Got it fairly, by six majority. After a hard battle. A very hard battle. Very. Expensive contest, too. I pay men that work for me. Always pay 'em. Always. Now, then, we are going to have trouble to get possession, unless we do something bold. Something bold. They mean to contest the election. They've got the court on their side. On their side, I'm afraid. They will get an injunction if we try to move the records. Sure to. Now, if I was a young man I'd move them suddenly before they had time. Possession is nine points. Nine points of law. They may watch the records at night. But they could be moved in the daytime by some man that they did not suspect. Easily. Quite so. County buildings are in the edge of town. Nearly everybody away at noon. Nearly everybody."

"Wal, squire, I'd cawntrack to do it"

"I couldn't make a contract, you see. I'm a magistrate. Conspiracy and all that. But I always help a man that helps me.

Always. In more ways than one. There are two reasons why a man might do that job. Two of them. One is love, and the other's money. Love and money. But I mustn't appear in the matter. Not at all. I'll do what I can for you. What I can. Katy will listen to me. She certainly will. Do what you think best."

"I a'n't dull 'bout takin' a hint, squire." And Dave winked his left eye at the squire in a way that said, "Trust me! I'm no fool!"

CHAPTER XVIII

A COLLISION

If this were a History of Metropolisville—but it isn't, and that is enough. You do not want to hear, and I do not want to tell you, how Dave Sawney, like another Samson, overthrew the Philistines; how he sauntered into the room where all the county officers did business together, he and his associates, at noon, when most of the officers were gone to dinner; how he seized the records—there were not many at that early day—loaded them into his wagon, and made off. You don't want to hear all that. If you do, call on Dave himself. He has told it over and over to everybody who would listen, from that time to this, and he would cheerfully get out of bed at three in the morning to tell it again, with the utmost circumstantiality, and with such little accretions of fictitious ornament as always gather about a story often and fondly told. Neither do you, gentle reader, who read for your own amusement, care to be informed of all the schemes devised by Plausaby for removing the county officers to their offices, nor of the town lots and other perquisites which accrued to said officers. It is sufficient for the purposes of this story that the county-seat was carted off to Metropolisville, and abode there in basswood tabernacles for a while, and that it proved a great advertisement to the town; money was more freely invested in Metropolisville, an "Academy" was actually staked out, and the town grew rapidly. Not alone on account of its temporary political importance did it advance, for about this time Plausaby got himself elected a director of the St. Paul and Big Gun River Valley Land Grant Railroad, and the speculators, who scent a railroad station at once, began to buy lots—on long time, to be 'sure, and yet to buy them. So much did the fortunes of Plausaby, Esq., prosper that he began to invest also—on time and at high rates of interest—in a variety of speculations. It was the fashion of '56 to invest everything you had in first payments, and then to sell out at an advance before the second became due.

But it is not about Plausaby or Metropolisville that I meant to tell you in this chapter. Nor yet about the wooing of Charlton. For in his case, true love ran smoothly. Too smoothly for the interest of this history. If Miss Minorkey had repelled his suit, if she had steadfastly remained cold, disdainful, exacting, it would have been better, maybe, for me who have to tell the story, and for you who have to read it. But disdainful she never was, and she did not remain cold. The enthusiasm of her lover was contagious, and she came to write and talk to him with much earnestness. Next to her own comfort and peace of mind and her own culture, she prized her lover. He was original, piquant, and talented. She was proud of him, and loved him with all her heart. Not as a more earnest person might have loved; but as heartily as she could. And she came to take on the color of her lover's habits of thought and feeling; she expressed herself even more warmly than she felt, so that Albert was happy, and this story was doomed to suffer because of his happiness. I might give zest to this dull love-affair by telling you that Mr. Minorkey opposed the match. Next to a disdainful lady-love, the best thing for a writer and a reader is a furious father. But I must be truthful at all hazards, and I am obliged to say that while Mr. Minorkey would have been delighted to have had for son-in-law some man whose investments might have multiplied Helen's inheritance, he was yet so completely under the influence of his admired daughter that he gave a consent, tacitly at least, to anything she chose to do. So that Helen became recognized presently as the prospective Mrs. Charlton. Mrs. Plausaby liked her because she wore nice dresses, and Katy loved her because she loved Brother Albert. For that matter, Katy did not need any reason for loving anybody. Even Isa stifled a feeling she was unable to understand, and declared that Miss Minorkey was smart, and just suited to Albert; and she supposed that Albert, with all his crotchets and theories, might make a person like Miss Minorkey happy. It wasn't every woman that could put up with them, you know.

But it was not about the prosperous but uninteresting courtship of two people with "idees" that I set out to tell in this chapter. If Charlton got on smoothly with Helen Minorkey, and if he had no more serious and one-sided outbreaks with his step-father, he did not get on with his sister's lover.

Westcott had been drinking all of one night with some old cronies of the Elysian Club, and his merry time of the night was subsiding into a quarrelsome time in the morning. He was able, when he was sober, to smother his resentment towards Albert, for there is no better ambush than an entirely idiotic giggle. But drink had destroyed his prudence. And so when Albert stepped on the piazza of the hotel where Westcott stood rattling his pocketful of silver change and his keys for the amusement of the bystanders, as was his wont, the latter put himself in Charlton's way, and said, in a dreary, half-drunk style:

"Mornin', Mr. Hedgehog! By George! he! he! he! How's the purty little girl? My little girl. Don't you wish she wasn't? Hard feller, I am. Any gal's a fool to marry me, I s'pose. Katy's a fool.

That's just what I want, by George I he! he! I want a purty fool. And she's purty, and she's—the other thing. What you goin' to do about it? He! he! he!"

"I'm going to knock you down," said Albert, "if you say another word about her."

"A'n't she mine? You can't help it, either. He! he! The purty little goose loves Smith Westcott like lots of other purty little—"

Before he could finish the sentence Charlton had struck him one savage blow full in the face, and sent him staggering back against the side of the house, but he saved himself from falling by seizing the window-frame, and immediately drew his Deringer. Charlton, who was not very strong, but who had a quick, lightning-like activity, knocked him down, seized his pistol, and threw it into the street. This time Charlton fell on him in a thoroughly murderous mood, and would perhaps have beaten and choked him to death in the frenzy of his long pent-up passion, for notwithstanding Westcott's struggles Albert had the advantage. He was sober, active, and angry enough to be ruthless. Westcott's friends interfered, but that lively gentleman's eyes and nose were sadly disfigured by the pummeling he had received, and Charlton was badly scratched and bruised.

Whatever hesitancy had kept Albert from talking to Katy about Smith Westcott was all gone now, and he went home to denounce him bitterly. One may be sure that the muddled remarks of Mr. Westcott about Katy—of which even he had grace to be a little ashamed when he was sober—were not softened in the repetition which Albert gave them at home. Even Mrs. Plausaby forgot her attire long enough to express her indignation, and as for Miss Marlay, she combined with Albert in a bayonet-charge on poor Katy.

Plausaby had always made it a rule not to fight a current. Wait till the tide turns, he used to say, and row with the stream when it flows your way. So now he, too, denounced Westcott, and Katy was fairly borne off her feet for a while by the influences about her. In truth, Katy was not without her own private and personal indignation against Westcott. Not because he had spoken of her as a fool. That hurt her feelings, but did not anger her much. She was not in the habit of getting angry on her own account. But when she saw three frightful scratches and a black bruise on the face of Brother Albert, she could not help thinking that Smith had acted badly. And then to draw a pistol, too! To threaten to kill her own dear, dear brother! She couldn't ever forgive him, she said. If she had seen the much more serious damage which poor, dear, dear Smith had suffered at the tender hands of her dear, dear brother, I doubt not she would have had an equally strong indignation against Albert.

For Westcott's face was in mourning, and the Privileged Infant had lost his cheerfulness. He did not giggle for ten days. He did not swear "by George" once. He did not he! he! The joyful keys and the cheerful ten-cent coins lay in his pocket with no loving hand to rattle them. He did not indulge in double-shuffles. He sang no high-toned negro-minstrel songs. He smoked steadily and solemnly, and he drank steadily and solemnly. His two clerks were made to tremble. They forgot Smith's bruised nose and swollen eye in fearing his awful temper. All the swearing he wanted to do and dared not do at Albert, he did at his inoffensive subordinates.

Smith Westcott had the dumps. No sentimental heart-break over Katy, though he did miss her company sadly in a town where there were no amusements, not even a concert-saloon in which a refined young man could pass an evening. If he had been in New York now, he wouldn't have minded it. But in a place like Metropolisville, a stupid little frontier village of pious and New Englandish tendencies—in such a place, as Smith pathetically explained to a friend, one can't get along without a sweetheart, you know.

A few days after Albert's row with Westcott he met George Gray, the Hoosier Poet, who had haunted Metropolisville, off and on, ever since he had first seen the "angel."

He looked more wild and savage than usual.

"Hello! my friend," said Charlton heartily. "I'm glad to see you. What's the matter?"

"Well, Mister Charlton, I'm playin' the gardeen angel."

"Guardian angel! How's that?"

"I'm a sorter gardeen of your sister. Do you see that air pistol? Hey? Jist as sure as shootin,' I'll kill that Wes'cott ef he tries to marry that angel. I don't want to marry her. I aint fit, mister, that's a fack. Ef I was, I'd put in fer her. But I aint. And ef she marries a gentleman, I haint got not a bit of right to object. But looky hyer! Devils haint got no right to angels. Ef I kin finish up a devil jest about the time he gits his claws onto a angel and let the angel go free, why, I say it's wuth the doin'. Hey?"

Charlton, I am ashamed to say, did not at first think the death of Smith Westcott by violence a very great crime or calamity, if it served to save Katy. However, as he walked and talked with Gray, the thought of murder made him shudder, and he made an earnest effort to persuade the Inhabitant to give up his criminal thoughts. But it is the misfortune of people like George Gray that the romance in their composition will get into their lives. They have not mental discipline enough to make the distinction between the world of sentiment and the world of action, in which inflexible conditions modify the purpose.

"Ef I hev to hang fer it I'll hang, but I'm goin' to be her gardeen angel."

"I didn't know that guardian angels carried pistols," said Albert, trying to laugh the half-crazed fellow out of a conceit from which he could not drive him by argument.

"Looky hyer, Mr. Charlton," said Gray, coloring, "I thought you was a gentleman, and wouldn' stoop to make no sech a remark. Ef you're goin' to talk that-a-way, you and me don't travel no furder on the same trail. The road forks right here, mister."

"Oh! I hope not, my dear friend. I didn't mean any offense. Give me your hand, and God bless you for your noble heart."

Gray was touched as easily one way as the other, and he took Charlton's hand with emotion, at the same time drawing his sleeve across his eyes and saying, "God bless you, Mr. Charlton. You can depend on me. I'm the gardeen, and I don't keer two cents fer life. It's a shadder, and a mush-room, as I writ some varses about it wonst. Let me say 'em over:

> "Life's a shadder,
>   Never mind it.
> A cloud kivers up the sun
> And whar is yer shadder gone?
>   Ye'll hey to be peart to find it!
>
> "Life's a ladder—
>   What about it?
> You've clim half-way t' the top,
> Down comes yer ladder ke-whop!
>   You can't scrabble up without it!
>
> "Nothin's no sadder,
>   Kordin to my tell,
> Than packin' yer life around.
> They's good rest under the ground
>   Ef a feller kin on'y die well."

Charlton, full of ambition, having not yet tasted the bitterness of disappointment, clinging to life as to all, was fairly puzzled to understand the morbid sadness of the Poet's spirit. "I'm sorry you feel that way, Gray," he said. "But at any rate promise me you won't do anything desperate without talking to me."

"I'll do that air, Mr. Charlton," and the two shook hands again.

CHAPTER XIX

STANDING GUARD IN VAIN

It was Isabel Marlay that sought Albert again. Her practical intellect, bothered with no visions, dazed with no theories, embarrassed by no broad philanthropies, was full of resource, and equally full, if not of general, at least of a specific benevolence that forgot mankind in its kindness to the individual.

Albert saw plainly enough that he could not keep Katy in her present state of feeling. He saw how she would inevitably slip through his fingers. But what to do he knew not. So, like most men of earnest and half-visionary spirit, he did nothing. Unbeliever in Providence that he was, he waited in the belief that something must happen to help him out of the difficulty. Isa, believer that she was, set herself to be her own Providence.

Albert had been spending an evening with Miss Minorkey. He spent nearly all his evenings with Miss Minorkey. He came home, and stood a minute, as was his wont, looking at the prairie landscape. A rolling prairie is like a mountain, in that it perpetually changes its appearance; it is delicately susceptible to all manner of atmospheric effects. It lay before him in the dim moonlight, indefinite; a succession of undulations running one into the other, not to be counted nor measured. All accurate notions of topography were lost; there was only landscape, dim, undeveloped, suggestive of infinitude. Standing thus in the happiness of loving and being loved, the soft indefiniteness of the landscape and the incessant hum of the field-crickets and katydids, sounds which came out of the everywhere, soothed Charlton like the song of a troubadour.

"Mr. Charlton!"

Like one awaking from a dream, Albert saw Isa Marlay, her hand resting against one of the posts which supported the piazza-roof, looking even more perfect and picturesque than ever in the haziness of the moonlight. Figure, dress, and voice were each full of grace and sweetness, and if the face was not exactly beautiful, it was at least charming and full of a subtle magnetism. (Magnetism! happy word, with which we cover the weakness of our thoughts, and make a show of comprehending and defining qualities which are neither comprehensible nor definable!)

"Mr. Charlton, I want to speak to you about Katy."

It took Albert a moment or two to collect his thoughts. When he first perceived Miss Marlay, she seemed part of the landscape.

There was about her form and motion an indefinable gracefulness that was like the charm of this hazy, undulant, moonlit prairie, and this blue sky seen through the lace of thin, milk-white clouds. It was not until she spoke Katy's name that he began to return to himself. Katy was the one jarring string in the harmony of his hopes.

"About Katy? Certainly, Miss Marlay. Won't you sit down?"

"No, I thank you."

"Mr. Charlton, couldn't you get Katy away while her relations with Westcott are broken? You don't know how soon she'll slip back into her old love for him."

"If—" and Albert hesitated. To go, he must leave Miss Minorkey. And the practical difficulty presented itself to him at the same moment. "If I could raise money enough to get away, I should go. But Mr. Plausaby has all of my money and all of Katy's."

Isabel was on the point of complaining that Albert should lend to Mr. Plausaby, but she disliked to take any liberty, even that of reproof. Ever since she knew that the family had thought of marrying her to Albert, she had been an iceberg to him. He should not dare to think that she had any care for him. For the same reason, another reply died unuttered on her lips. She was about to offer to lend Mr. Charlton fifty dollars of her own. But her quick pride kept her back, and, besides, fifty dollars was not half-enough. She said she thought there must be some way of raising the money. Then, as if afraid she had been too cordial and had laid her motives open to suspicion in speaking thus to Charlton, she drew herself up and bade him good-night with stiff politeness, leaving him half-fascinated by her presence, half-vexed with something in her manner, and wholly vexed with himself for having any feeling one way or the other. What did he care for Isabel Marlay? What if she were graceful and full of a subtle fascination of presence? Why should he value such things? What were they worth, after all? What if she were kind one minute and repellent the next? Isa Marlay was nothing to him!

Lying in his little unfinished chamber, he dismissed intellectual Miss Minorkey from his mind with regret; he dismissed graceful but practical Miss Marlay from his mind also, wondering that he had to dismiss her at all, and gave himself to devising ways and means of eloping with little Katy. She must be gotten away. It was evident that Plausaby would make no effort to raise money to help him and Katy to get away. Plausaby would prefer to detain Katy. Clearly, to proceed to pre-empt his claim, to persuade Plausaby to raise money enough for him to buy a land-warrant with, and then to raise two hundred dollars by mortgaging his land to

Minorkey or any other lover of mortgages with waiver clauses in them, was the only course open.

Plausaby, Esq., was ever prompt in dealing with those to whom he was indebted, so far as promises went. He would always give the most solemn assurance of his readiness to do anything one wished to have done; and so, when Albert explained to him that it was necessary for him to pre-empt because he wished to go East, Plausaby told him to go on and establish his residence on his claim, and when he got ready to prove up and pre-empt, to come to him. To come and let him know. To let him know at once. He made the promise so frankly and so repetitiously, and with such evident consciousness of his own ability and readiness to meet his debt to Albert on demand, that the latter went away to his claim in quietness and hopefulness, relying on Miss Marlay to stand guard over his sister's love affairs in his absence.

But standing guard was not of much avail. All of the currents that flowed about Katy's life were undermining her resolution not to see Smith Westcott. Katy, loving, sweet, tenderhearted, was far from being a martyr, in stubbornness at best; her resolutions were not worth much against her sympathies. And now that Albert's scratched face was out of sight, and there was no visible object to keep alive her indignation, she felt her heart full of ruth for poor, dear Mr. Westcott. How lonesome he must be without her! She could only measure his lonesomeness by her own. Her heart, ever eager to love, could not let go when once it had attached itself, and she longed for other evenings in which she could hear Smith's rattling talk, and in which he would tell her how happy she had made him. How lonesome he must be! What if he should drown himself in the lake?

Mr. Plausaby, at tea, would tell in the most incidental way of something that had happened during the day, and then, in his sliding, slipping, repetitious, back-stitching fashion, would move round from one indifferent topic to another until he managed at last to stumble over Smith Westcott's name.

"By the way," he would say, "poor Smith looks heartbroken. Absolutely heart-broken. I didn't know the fellow cared so much for Katy. Didn't think he had so much heart. So much faithfulness. But he looks down. Very much downcast. Never saw a fellow look so chopfallen. And, by the way, Albert did punish him awfully. He looks black and blue. Well, he deserved it. He did so. I suppose he didn't mean to say anything against Katy. But he had no business to let old friends coax him to drink. Still, Albert was pretty severe. Too severe, in fact. I'm sorry for Westcott. I am, indeed."

After some such talk as this, Cousin Isa would generally find Katy crying before bed-time.

"What is the matter, Katy, dear?" she would say in a voice so full of natural melody and genuine sympathy, that it never failed to move Katy to the depths of her heart. Then Katy would cry more than ever, and fling her arms about the neck of dear, dear, dear Cousin Isa, and lavish on her the tenderness of which her heart was full.

"O Cousin Isa! what must I do? I'm breaking poor Smith's heart. You don't know how much he loves me, and I'm afraid something dreadful will happen to him, you know. What shall I do?"

"I don't think he cares much, Katy. He's a bad man, I'm afraid, and doesn't love you really. Don't think any more of him." For Isabel couldn't find it in her heart to say to Katy just what she thought of Westcott.

"Oh! but you don't know him," Katy cries. "You don't know him. He says that he does naughty things sometimes, but then he's got such a tender heart. He made me promise I wouldn't throw him over, as he called it, for his faults. He said he'd come to be good if I'd only keep on loving him. And I said I would. And I haven't. Here's more than a week now that he hasn't been here, and I haven't been to the store. And he said he'd go to sleep in the lake some night if I ever, ever proved false to him. And I lie awake nearly all night thinking how hard and cruel I've been to him. And oh!"—here Katy cried awhile—"and oh! I think such awful things sometimes," she continued in a whisper broken by sobs. "You don't know, Cousin Isa. I think how cold, how dreadful cold the lake must be! Oo-oo!" And a shudder shook her frame. "If poor, dear Smith were to throw himself in! What if he is there now?" And she looked up at Isa with staring eyes. "Do you know what an awful thing I heard about that lake once?" She stopped and shivered. "There are leeches in it— nasty, black worms—and one of them bit my hand once. And they told me that if a person should be drowned in Diamond Lake the leeches would—oo!—take all their blood, and their faces would be white, and not black like other drowned people's faces. Oh! I can't bear to think about poor Smith. If I could only write him a note, and tell him I love him just a little! But I told Albert I wouldn't see him nor write to him. What shall I do? He mayn't live till morning. They say he looks broken-hearted. He'll throw himself into that cold lake to-night, maybe—and the leeches—the black worms—oo!—or else he'll kill himself with that ugly pistol."

It was in vain that Isabel talked to her, in vain that she tried to argue with a cataract of feeling. It was rowing against Niagara with a canoe-paddle. It was not wonderful, therefore, that before Albert

90

got back, Isa Marlay found Katy reading little notes from Westcott, notes that ho had intrusted to one of his clerks, who was sent to the post-office three or four times a day on various pretexts, until he should happen to find Katy in the office. Then he would hand her the notes. Katy did not reply. She had promised Albert she wouldn't. But there was no harm in her reading them, just to keep Smith from drowning himself among those black leeches in Diamond Lake.

Isabel Marlay, in her distressful sense of responsibility to Albert, could yet find no means of breaking up this renewed communication. In sheer desperation, she appealed to Mrs. Plausaby.

"Well, now," said that lady, sitting in state with the complacent consciousness of a new and more stunning head-dress than usual, "I'll tell you what it is, Isabel, I think Albert makes altogether too much fuss over Katy's affairs. He'll break the girl's heart. He's got notions. His father had. Deliver me from notions! Just let Katy take her own course. Marryin's a thing everybody must attend to personally for themselves. You don't like to be meddled with, and neither does Albert. You won't either of you marry to suit me. I have had my plans about you and Albert. Now, Isabel, Mr. Westcott's a nice-looking man. With all his faults he's a nice man. Cheerful and good-natured in his talk, and a good provider. He's a store-keeper, too. It's nice to have a storekeeper for a husband. I want Plausaby to keep store, so that I can get dresses and such things without having to pay for them. I felt mad at Mr. Westcott about his taking out his pistol so at Albert. But if Albert had let Mr. Westcott alone, I'm sure Smith wouldn't a-touched him. But your folks with notions are always troubling somebody else. For my part, I shan't meddle with Katy. Do you think this bow's nice? Too low down, isn't it?" and Mrs. Plausaby went to the glass to adjust it.

And so it happened that all Isa Marlay's watching could not keep Westcott away. For the land-office regulations at that time required that Albert should live on his claim thirty days. This gave him the right to buy it at a dollar and a quarter an acre, or to exchange a land-warrant for it. The land was already worth two or three times the government price. But that thirty days of absence, broken only by one or two visits to his home, was enough to overturn all that Charlton had done in breaking up his sister's engagement with Westcott. The latter knew how long Albert's absence must be, and arranged his approaches to correspond. He gave her fifteen days to get over her resentment, and to begin to pity him on account of the stories of his incurable melancholy she would hear. After he had thus suffered her to dream of his probable suicide for a fortnight, he contrived to send her one little lugubrious note, confessing that he had been intoxicated and begging her pardon. Then he waited three days, days of great anxiety to her. For Katy feared lest her neglect to return an answer should precipitate Westcott's suicide. But he did not need an answer. Her looks when she received the note had been reported to him. What could he need more? On the very evening after he had sent that contrite note to Katy, announcing that he would never drink again, he felt so delighted with what he had heard of its reception, that he treated a crony out of his private bottle as they played cards together in his room, and treated himself quite as liberally as he did his friend, got up in the middle of the floor, and assured his friend that he would be all right with his sweet little girl before the brother got back. By George! If folks thought he was going to commit suicide, they were fooled. Never broke his heart about a woman yet. Not much, by George! But when he set his heart on a thing, he generally got it. He! he! And he had set his heart on that little girl. As for jumping into the lake, any man was a fool to jump into the drink on account of a woman. When there were plenty of them. Large assortment constantly on hand. Pays yer money and takes yer ch'ice! Suicide? Not much, by George! he! he!

> Hung his coat on a hickory limb,
> Then like a wise man he jumped in,
> My ole dad! My ole dad!

Wondered what tune Charlton would sing when he found himself beat? Guess 'twould be:

> Can't stay in de wilderness.
> In a few days, in a few days,
> Can't stay in de wilderness,
> A few days ago.

Goin' to pre-empt my claim, too. I've got a month's leave, and I'll follow him and marry that girl before he gets far. Bruddern and sistern, sing de ole six hundredth toon. Ahem!

> I wish I was a married man,
> A married man I'd be!
> An' ketch the grub fer both of us
> A-fishin' in the sea.
> Big fish,
> Little fish,
> It's all the same to me!

92

I got a organ stop in my throat. Can't sing below my breath to save my life. He! he!

After three days had elapsed, Westcott sent a still more melancholy note to Katy. It made her weep from the first line to the last. It was full of heartbreak, and Katy was too unobserving to notice how round and steady and commercial the penmanship was, and how large and fine were the flourishes. Westcott himself considered it his masterpiece. He punched his crony with his elbow as he deposited it in the office, and assured him that it was the techin'est note ever written. It would come the sympathies over her. There was nothing like the sympathies to fetch a woman to terms. He knew. Had lots of experience. By George! You could turn a woman round yer finger if you could only keep on the tender side. Tears was what done it. Love wouldn' keep sweet without it was pickled in brine. He! he! he! By George!

CHAPTER XX

SAWNEY AND WESTCOTT

David Sawney was delighted with the news that Albert Charlton and Smith Westcott had quarreled. "Westcott's run of luck in that quarter's broke. When a feller has a run of luck right along, and they comes a break, 'ts all up with him. Broke luck can't be spliced. It's David Sawney's turn now. Poor wind that blows no whar. I'll bet a right smart pile I'll pack the little gal off yet."

But if an inscrutable Providence had omitted to make any Smith Westcotts, Dave Sawney wouldn't have stood the ghost of a chance with Katy. His supreme self-complacency gave her no occasion to pity him. Her love was close of kin to her tenderheartedness, and all pity was wasted on Dave. He couldn't have been more entirely happy than he was if he had owned the universe in fee simple.

However, Dave was resolved to try his luck, and so, soon after Albert's departure, he blacked up his vast boots and slicked his hair, and went to Plausaby's. He had the good luck to find Katy alone.

"Howdy! Howdy! Howdy git along? Lucky, ain't I, to find you in? Haw! haw! I'm one of the luckiest fellers ever was born. Always wuz lucky. Found a fip in a crack in the hearth 'fore I was three year old. 'Ts a fack. Found a two-and-a-half gole piece wunst. Golly, didn't I feel some! Haw! haw! haw! The way of't wuz this." But we must not repeat the story in all its meanderings, lest readers should grow as tired of it as Katy did; for Dave crossed one leg over the other, looked his hands round his knee, and told it with many a complacent haw! haw! haw! When he laughed, it was not from a sense of the ludicrous: his guffaw was a pure eruption of delighted self-conceit.

"I thought as how as I'd like to explain to you somethin' that might 'a' hurt yer feelin's, Miss Charlton. Didn't you feel a little teched at sompin'?"

"No, Mr. Sawney, you never hurt my feelings."

"Well, gals is slow to own up that they're hurt, you know. But I'm shore you couldn't help bein', and I'm ever so sorry. Them Injin goin'-ons of mine wuz enough to 'a' broke your heart."

"What do you mean?"

"Why, my sellin' out to Perritaut for ten thousand dollars, only I didn't. Haw! haw!" and Dave threw his head back to laugh. "You had a right to feel sorter bad to think I would consent to marry a

94

Injin. But 'tain't every feller as'll git ten thousand offered in five annooal payments; an' I wanted you to understand 'twan't the Injin, 'twas the cash as reached me. When it comes to gals, you're the posy fer me."

Katy grew red, but didn't know what to say or do.

"I heerd tell that that feller Westcott'd got his walkin' papers. Sarved him right, dancin' roun' like a rang-a-tang, and jos'lin' his keys and ten-cent pieces in his pocket, and sayin' imperdent things. But I could 'a' beat him at talk the bes' day he ever seed ef he'd on'y 'a' gi'n me time to think. I kin jaw back splendid of you gin me time. Haw! haw! haw! But he ain't far—don't never gin a feller time to git his thoughts gethered up, you know. He jumps around like the Frenchman's flea. Put yer finger on him an' he ain't thar, and never wuz. Haw! haw! haw! But jest let him stay still wunst tell I get a good rest on him like, and I'll be dog-on'd ef I don't knock the hine sights offen him the purtiest day he ever seed! Haw! haw! haw! Your brother Albert handled him rough, didn't he? Sarved him right. I say, if a man is onrespectful to a woman, her brother had orter thrash him; and your'n done it. His eye's blacker'n my boot. And his nose! Haw! haw! it's a-mournin' fer his brains! Haw I haw! haw! And he feels bad bekase you cut him, too. Jemently, ef he don' look like 's ef he'd kill hisself fer three bits."

Katy was so affected by this fearful picture of poor, dear Smith's condition, that she got up and hurried out of the room to cry.

"What on airth's the matter?" soliloquized Dave. "Bashful little creeter, I 'low. Thought I wuz a-comin to the p'int, maybe. Well, nex' time'll do. Haw! haw! Young things is cur'us now, to be shore. Mout's well be a gittin' on, I reckon. Gin her time to come round, I 'low."

With such wooing, renewed from time to time, the clumsy and complacent Dave whiled away his days, and comforted himself that he had the persimmon-tree all to himself, as he expressed it. Meanwhile, the notes of Westcott were fast undoing all that Albert had done to separate him from "the purty little girl."

Of course, when the right time came, he happened to meet Katy on the street, and to take off his hat and make a melancholy bow, the high-tragedy air of which confirmed Katy's suspicions that he meant to commit suicide at the first opportunity. Then he chanced to stop at the gate, and ask, in a tone sad enough to have been learned from the gatherers of cold victuals, if he might come in. In three days more, he was fully restored to favor and to his wonted cheerfulness. He danced, he sang, he chirruped, he rattled his keys, he was the Privileged Infant once more. He urged Katy to

95

marry him at once, but her heart was now rent by pity for Albert and by her eager anxiety lest he should do something desperate when he heard of her reconciliation. She trembled every day at thought of what might happen when he should return.

"Goin' to pre-empt in a few days, Katy. Whisky Jim come plaguey near to gittin' that claim. He got Shamberson on his side, and if Shamberson's brother-in-law hadn't been removed from the Land Office before it was tried, he'd a got it. I'm going to pre-empt and build the cutest little bird's nest for you.

> "If I was young and in my prime,
>   I'd lead a different life,
>   I'd save my money, and buy me a farm,
>   Take Dinah for my wife.
>   Oh! carry me back—

"Psha! Dat dah ain't de toon, bruddern. Ahem!

> "When you and I get married, love,
>   How jolly it will be!
>   We'll keep house in a store-box, then,
>   Just two feet wide by three!
>   Store-box!
>   Band-box!
>   All the same to me!

> "And when we want our breakfast, love,
>   We'll nibble bread and chee—
>   It's good enough for you, love,
>   And most too good for me!
>   White bread!
>   Brown bread!
>   All the same to me!

"Dog-on'd ef 'tain't. White bread's good as brown bread. One's jest as good as the other, and a good deal better. It's all the same to me, and more so besides, and something to carry. It's all the same, only 'tain't. Ahem:

> "Jane and Sukey and July Ann—
>   Too brown, too slim, too stout!
>   You needn't smile on this 'ere man,
>   Git out! git out! git out!
>   But the maiden fair

With bonny brown hair—
Let all the rest git out!"—

"Get out yourself!" thundered Albert Charlton, bursting in at that moment. "If you don't get your pack of tomfoolery out of here quick, I'll get it out for you," and he bore down on Westcott fiercely.

"I beg pardon, Mr. Charlton. I'm here to see your sister with her consent and your mother's, and—"

"And I tell you," shouted Albert, "that my sister is a little girl, and my mother doesn't understand such puppies as you, and I am my sister's protector, and if you don't get out of here, I'll kill you if I can."

"Albert, don't be so quarrelsome," said Mrs. Plausaby, coming in at the instant. "I'm sure Mr. Westcott's a genteel man, and good-natured to Katy, and—"

"Out! out! I say, confound you! or I'll break your empty head," thundered Charlton, whose temper was now past all softening. "Put your hand on that pistol, if you dare," and with that he strode at the Privileged Infant with clenched fist, and the Privileged Infant prudently backed out the door into the yard, and then, as Albert kept up his fierce advance, the Privileged Infant backed out of the gate into the street. He was not a little mortified to see the grinning face of Dave Sawney in the crowd about the gate, and to save appearances, he called back at Albert, who was returning toward the house, that he would settle this affair with him yet. But he did not know how thoroughly Charlton's blood was up.

"Settle it?" said Albert—yelled Albert, I should say—turning back on him with more fury than ever. "Settle it, will you? I'll settle it right here and now, you cowardly villain! Let's have it through, now," and he walked swiftly at Westcott, who walked away; but finding that the infuriated Albert was coming after him, the Privileged Infant hurried on until his retreat became a run, Westcott running down street, Charlton hotly pursuing him, the spectators running pell-mell behind, laughing, cheering, and jeering.

"Don't come back again if you don't want to get killed," the angry Charlton called, as he turned at last and went toward home.

"Now, Katy," he said, with more energy than tenderness, as he entered the house, "if you are determined to marry that confounded rascal, I shall leave at once. You must decide now. If you will go East with me next week, well and good. If you won't give up Smith Westcott, then I shall leave you now forever."

Katy couldn't bear to be the cause of any disaster to anybody; and just at this moment Smith was out of sight, and Albert, white and trembling with the reaction of his passion, stood before her. She felt, somehow, that she had brought all this trouble on Albert, and in her pity for him, and remorse for her own course, she wept and clung to her brother, and begged him not to leave her. And Albert said: "There, don't cry any more. It's all right now. I didn't mean to hurt your feelings. There, there!" There is nothing a man can not abide better than a woman in tears.

CHAPTER XXI

ROWING

To get away with Katy immediately. These were the terms of the problem now before Albert His plan was to take her to visit friends at the East, and to keep her there until Westcott should pass out of her mind, or until she should be forgotten by the Privileged Infant. This was not Westcott's plan of the campaign at all. He was as much bent on securing Katy as he could have been had he been the most constant, devoted, and disinterested lover. He would have gone through fire and flood. The vindictive love of opposition and lust for triumph is one of the most powerful of motives. Men will brave more from an empty desire to have their own way, than they could be persuaded to face by the most substantial motives.

Smith Westcott was not a man to die for a sentiment, but for the time he had the semblance of a most devoted lover. He bent everything to the re-conquest of Katy Charlton. His pride served him instead of any higher passion, and he plotted by night and managed by day to get his affairs into a position in which he could leave. He meant to follow Albert and Katy, and somewhere and somehow, by working on Katy's sympathies, to carry off the "stakes," as he expressed it. He almost ceased trifling, and even his cronies came to believe that he was really in love. They saw signs of intense and genuine feeling, and they mistook its nature. Mrs. Ferret expressed her sympathy for him—the poor man really loved Kate, and she believed that Kate had a right to marry anybody she pleased. She did not know what warrant there was in Scripcherr for a brother's exercising any authority. She thought Mrs. Plausaby ought to have brought up her son to have more respect for her authority, and to hold Scripcherral views. If he were her son, now! What she would have done with him in that case never fully appeared; for Mrs. Ferret could not bring herself to complete the sentence. She only said subjunctively: "If he were my son, now!" Then she would break off and give her head two or three awful and ominous shakes. What would have happened if such a young man as Albert had been her son, it would be hard to tell. Something unutterably dreadful, no doubt.

Even the charms of Miss Minorkey were not sufficient to detain Albert in his eager haste and passionate determination to rescue Katy. But to go, he must have money; to get money, he must collect it from Plausaby, or at least get a land-warrant with which he

99

could pre-empt his claim. Then he would mortgage his land for money to pay his traveling expenses. But it was so much easier to lend money to Plausaby, Esq., than it was to collect it. Plausaby, Esq., was always just going to have the money; Plausaby, Esq., had ever ready so many excuses for past failure, and so many assurances of payment in the immediate future, that Charlton was kept hoping and waiting in agony from week to week. He knew that he was losing ground in the matter of Westcott and Katy. She was again grieving over Smith's possible suicide, was again longing for the cheerful rattle of flattery and nonsense which rendered the Privileged Infant so diverting even to those who hated him, much more to her who loved him.

Albert's position was the more embarrassing that he was obliged to spend a part of his time on his claim to maintain a residence. One night, after having suffered a disappointment for the fifth time in the matter of Plausaby and money, he was walking down the road to cool his anger in the night air, when he met the Inhabitant of the Lone Cabin, again.

"Well, Gray," he said, "how are you? Have you written any fresh verses lately?"

"Varses? See here, Mr. Charlton, do you 'low this 'ere's a time fer varses?"

"Why not?"

"To be shore! Why not? I should kinder think yer own heart should orter tell you. You don' know what I'm made of. You think I a'n't good fer nothin' but varses. Now, Mr. Charlton, I'm not one of them air fellers as lets theirselves all off in varses that don' mean nothin'. What my pomes says, that my heart feels. And that my hands does. No, sir, my po'try 's like the corn crap in August. It's laid by. I ha'n't writ nary line sence I seed you afore. The fingers that holds a pen kin pull a trigger."

"What do you mean, Gray?"

"This 'ere," and he took out a pistol. "I wuz a poet; now I'm a gardeen angel. I tole you I wouldn' do nothin' desperate tell I talked weth you. That's the reason I didn' shoot him t'other night. When you run him off, I draw'd on him, and he'd a been a gone sucker ef't hadn' been fer yore makin' me promise t'other day to hold on tell I'd talked weth you. Now, I've talked weth you, and I don't make no furder promises. Soon as he gits to makin' headway agin, I'll drap him."

It was in vain that Charlton argued with him. Gray said life wurn't no 'count no how; he had sot out to be a Gardeen Angel, and he wuz agoin' through. These 'ere Yankees tuck blam'd good keer of their hides, but down on the Wawbosh, where he come from, they

100

didn't valley life a copper in a thing of this 'ere sort. Ef Smith Westcott kep' a shovin' ahead on his present trail, he'd fetch up kinder suddent all to wunst, weth a jolt.

After this, the dread of a tragedy of some sort did not decrease Albert's eagerness to be away. He began to talk violently to Plausaby, and that poor gentleman, harassed now by a suit brought by the town of Perritaut to set aside the county-seat election, and by a prosecution instituted against him for conspiracy, and by a suit on the part of the fat gentleman for damages on account of fraud in the matter of the two watery lots in block twenty-six, and by much trouble arising from his illicit speculation in claims—this poor Squire Plausaby, in the midst of this accumulation of vexations, kept his temper sweet, bore all of Albert's severe remarks with serenity, and made fair promises with an unruffled countenance. Smith Westcott had defeated Whisky Jim in his contest for the claim, because the removal of a dishonest receiver left the case to be decided according to the law and the regulations of the General Land Office, and the law gave the claim to Westcott. The Privileged Infant, having taken possession of Jim's shanty, made a feint of living in it, having moved his trunk, his bed, his whisky, and all other necessaries to the shanty. As his thirty days had expired, he was getting ready to pre-empt; the value of the claim would put him in funds, and he proposed, now that his blood was up, to give up his situation, if he should find it necessary, and "play out his purty little game" with Albert Charlton. It was shrewdly suspected, indeed, that if he should leave the Territory, he would not return. He knew nothing of the pistol which the Gardeen Angel kept under his wing for him, but Whisky Jim had threatened that he shouldn't enjoy his claim long. Jim had remarked to several people, in his lofty way, that Minnesoty wuz a healthy place fer folks weth consumption, but a dreffle sickly one fer folks what jumped other folks's claims when they wuz down of typus. And Jim grew more and more threatening as the time of Westcott's pre-emption drew near. While throwing the mail-bag off one day at the Metropolisville post-office he told Albert that he jest wished he knowed which mail Westcott's land-warrant would come in. He wouldn't steal it, but plague ef he wouldn't heave it off into the Big Gun River, accidentally a purpose, ef he had to go to penitensh'ry fer it.

But after all his weary and impatient waiting on and badgering of Plausaby, Albert got his land-warrant, and hurried off to the land-office, made his pre-emption, gave Mr. Minorkey a mortgage with a waiver in it, borrowed two hundred dollars at three per cent a month and five after maturity, interest to be settled every six months.

101

Then, though it was Friday evening, he would have packed everything and hurried away the next morning; but his mother interposed her authority. Katy couldn't be got ready. What was the use of going to Red Owl to stay over Sunday? There was no boat down Sunday, and they could just as well wait till Monday, and take the Tuesday boat, and so Albeit reluctantly consented to wait.

But he would not let Katy be out of his sight. He was determined that in these last hours of her stay in the Territory, Smith Westcott should not have a moment's opportunity for conversation with her. He played the tyrannical brother to perfection. He walked about the house in a fighting mood all the time, with brows drawn down and fist ready to clench.

He must have one more boat-ride with Helen Minorkey, and he took Katy with him, because he dared not leave her behind. He took them both in the unpainted pine row-boat which belonged to nobody in particular, and he rowed away across the little lake, looking at the grassy-green shores on the one side, and at the basswood trees that shadowed the other. Albert had never had a happier hour. Out in the lake he was safe from the incursions of the tempter. Rowing on the water, he relaxed the strain of his vigilance; out on the lake, with water on every side, he felt secure. He had Katy, sweet and almost happy; he felt sure now that she would be able to forget Westcott, and be at peace again as in the old days when he had built play-houses for the sunny little child. He had Helen, and she seemed doubly dear to him on the eve of parting. When he was alone with her, he felt always a sense of disappointment, for he was ever striving by passionate speeches to elicit some expression more cordial than it was possible for Helen's cool nature to utter. But now that Katy's presence was a restraint upon him, this discord between the pitch of his nature and of hers did not make itself felt, and he was satisfied with himself, with Helen, and with Katy. And so round the pebbly margin of the lake he rowed, while they talked and laughed. The reaction from his previous state of mental tension put Albert into a sort of glee; he was almost as boisterous as the Privileged Infant himself. He amused himself by throwing spray on Katy with his oars, and he even ventured to sprinkle the dignified Miss Minorkey a little, and she unbent enough to make a cup of her white palm and to dip it into the clear water and dash a good, solid handful of it into the face of her lover. She had never in her life acted in so undignified a manner, and Charlton was thoroughly delighted to have her throw cold water upon him in this fashion. After this, he rowed down to the outlet, and showed them where the beavers had built a dam, and prolonged his happy rowing and talking till the full moon came up out of the prairie and made a golden pathway on the ripples. Albert's mind dwelt on this boat-ride in the lonely year that followed. It seemed to him strange that he could have had so much happiness on the brink of so much misery. He felt as that pleasure party did, who, after hours of happy sport, found that they had been merry-making in the very current of the great cataract.

There are those who believe that every great catastrophe throws its shadow before it, but Charlton was never more hopeful than when he lifted his dripping oars from the water at half-past nine o'clock, and said: "What a grand ride we've had! Let's row together again to-morrow evening. It is the last chance for a long time."

CHAPTER XXII

SAILING

On the Saturday morning after this Friday evening boat-ride, Charlton was vigilant as ever, and yet Saturday was not a dangerous day. It was the busy day at the Emporium, and he had not much to fear from Westcott, whose good quality was expressed by one trite maxim to which he rigidly adhered. "Business before pleasure" uttered the utmost self-denial of his life. He was fond of repeating his motto, with no little exultation in the triumph he had achieved over his pleasure-loving disposition. To this fidelity to business he owed his situation as "Agent," or head-clerk, of the branch store of Jackson, Jones & Co. If he could have kept from spending money as fast as he made it, he might have been a partner in the firm. However, he rejoiced in the success he had attained, and, to admiring neophytes who gazed in admiration on his perilous achievement of rather reckless living and success in gaining the confidence of his employers, he explained the marvel by uttering his favorite adage in his own peculiar style: "Business before pleasure! By George! That's the doctrine! A merchant don't care how fast you go to the devil out of hours, if you keep his business straight. Business before pleasure! That's the ticket! He! he! By George!"

When evening came, and Charlton felt that he had but one more day of standing guard, his hopes rose, he talked to Isabel Marlay with something of exultation. And he thought it due to Miss Marlay to ask her to make one of the boating-party. They went to the hotel, where Miss Minorkey joined them. Albert found it much more convenient walking with three ladies than with two. Isa and Katy walked on arm-in-arm, and left Albert to his tête-à-tête with Helen. And as Sunday evening would be the very last on which he should see her before leaving for the East, he found it necessary to walk slowly and say much. For lovers who see each other a great deal, have more to say the more they are together.

At the lake a disappointment met them. The old pine boat was in use. It was the evening of the launching of the new sail-boat, "The Lady of the Lake," and there was a party of people on the shore. Two young men, in a spirit of burlesque and opposition, had seized on the old boat and had chalked upon her bow, "The Pirate's Bride." With this they were rowing up and down the lake, and exciting much merriment in the crowd on the shore.

Ben Towle, who was one of the principal stockholders in "The

Lady of the Lake," and who had been suspected of a tender regard for Isabel Marlay, promptly offered Albert and his party seats in the boat on her first trip. There were just four vacancies, he said. The three ladies had stepped aboard, and Albert was following, when the ex-sailor who held the rudder touched his arm and said, "I don't think it's safe, Mr. Charlton, fer nobody else to git in. She's got 'leven now, and ef the wind freshens, twelve would be dangerous."

"Oh! I'll stay out!" said Albert, retreating.

"Come, Albert, take my place," said Towle. "You're welcome to it."

"No, I won't, Ben; you sit still, and I'll stand on the shore and cheer."

Just as the boat was about to leave her moorings, Smith Westcott came up and insisted on getting in.

"'Twon't do, Mr. Wes'cott. 'Ta'n't safe," said the helmsman. "I jest begged Mr. Charlton not to go. She's got a full load now."

"Oh! I don't weigh anything. Lighter'n a feather. Only an infant. And besides, I'm going anyhow, by George!" and with that he started to get aboard. But Albert had anticipated him by getting in at the other end of the boat and taking the only vacant seat. The Privileged Infant scowled fiercely, but Charlton affected not to see him, and began talking in a loud tone to Ben Towle about the rigging. The line was thrown off and the boat pushed out, the wind caught the new white sail, and the "Lady of the Lake" started along in the shallows, gradually swinging round toward the open water. Soon after her keel had ceased to grind upon the gravel, Albert jumped out, and, standing over boot-top in water, waved his hat and wished them a pleasant voyage, and all the ladies in the boat waved their handkerchiefs at him, appreciating his efforts to keep the boat from being overloaded, but not thinking of the stronger motive Charlton had for keeping Smith Westcott ashore. They could not know how much exultation Albert felt as he sat down on the green grass and poured the water from his boots.

There was a fine breeze, the boat sailed admirably, the party aboard laughed and talked and sang; their voices made merry music that reached the shore. The merry music was irritating discord to the ears of Westcott, it made him sweur bitterly at Charlton. I am afraid that it made Charlton happy to think of Westcott swearing at him. There is great comfort in being the object of an enemy's curses sometimes—When the enemy is down, and you are above and master. I think the consciousness that Westcott was swearing at him made even the fine sunset seem more glorious to Charlton. The red clouds were waving banners of victory.

But in ten minutes the situation had changed. Albert saw

Westcott walking across the beaver-dam at the lower end of the lake, and heard him hallooing to the young men who were rowing the "Pirate's Bride" up and down and around the "Lady of the Lake," for the ugly old boat was swiftest. The Pirate's Bride landed and took Westcott aboard, and all of Albert's rejoicing was turned to cursing, for there, right before his eyes, the Pirate's Bride ran her brown hull up alongside the white and graceful Lady of the Lake, and Smith Westcott stepped from the one to the other. The beauty of the sunset was put out. The new boat sailed up and down the little lake more swiftly and gracefully than ever as the breeze increased, but Albert hated it.

By some change or other in seats Westcott at last got alongside Katy. Albert distinctly saw the change made, and his anger was mingled with despair. For Isabel and Helen were in the other end of the boat, and there were none to help. And so on, on, in the gray dusk of the evening, the boat kept sailing from one end of the lake to the other, and as it passed now and then near him, he could see that Smith was in conversation with little Katy.

"You needn't worry, Mr. Charlton, I'll fix him." It was the voice of the Guardian Angel. "I'll fix him, shore as shootin'." And there he stood looking at Albert. For the first time now it struck Albert that George Gray was a little insane. There was a strange look in his eyes. If he should kill Westcott, the law would not hold him accountable. Nobody would be accountable, and Katy would be saved.

But in a moment Albert's better feeling was uppermost. The horribleness of murder came distinctly before him. He shuddered that he should have entertained the thought of suffering it.

"You see, Mr. Charlton," said Gray, with eyes having that strange mysterious look that only belongs to the eyes of people who are at least on the borders of insanity, "you see this 'ere pistol's got five bar'ls, all loadened. I tuck out the ole loads las' night and filled her up weth powder what's shore to go off. Now you leave that air matter to me, will you?"

"Let me see your revolver," said Albert.

Gray handed it to him, and Charlton examined it a minute, and then, with a sudden resolution, he got to his feet, ran forward a few paces, and hurled the pistol with all his might into the lake.

"Don't let us commit murder," he said, turning round and meeting the excited eyes of the half-insane poet.

"Well, maybe you're right, but I'll be hanged ef I think it's hardly far and squar and gentlemanly to wet a feller's catridges that-a-way."

"I had to," said Albert, trembling. "If I hadn't, you or I would have been a murderer before morning."

"Maybe so, but they ain't nothin else to be done. Ef you don't let me kill the devil, why, then the devil will pack your sister off, and that's the end on't."

The moon shone out, and still the boat went sailing up and down the lake, and still the party in the boat laughed and talked and sang merry songs, and still Charlton walked up and down the shore, though almost all the rest of the spectators had gone, and the Poet sat down in helpless dejection. And still Smith Westcott sat and talked to Katy. What he said need not be told: how, while all the rest laughed and sang, the Privileged Infant was serious; and how he appealed to Katy's sympathies by threatening to jump off into the lake; and how he told her that they must be married, and have it all over at once. Then, when it was all over, Albert wouldn't feel bad about it any more. Brothers never did. When he and Albert should get to be brothers-in-law, they'd get on splendidly. By George! Some such talk as this he had as they sailed up and down the lake. Just what it was will never be known, whether he planned an elopement that very night, or on Sunday night, or on the night which they must pass in Red Owl Landing, nobody knows. Isabel Marlay, who saw all, was sure that Smith had carried all his points. He had convinced the sweet and trusting Katy that an immediate marriage would be best for Brother Albert as well as for themselves.

And as the boat sailed on, tacking to and fro, even the pilot got over his anxiety at the overloading which had taken place when Westcott got in. The old tar said to Towle that she carried herself beautifully.

Five minutes after he made the remark, while Westcott was talking to Katy, and playfully holding his fingers in the water as he leaned over the gunwale that almost dipped, there came a flaw in the wind, and the little boat, having too much canvas and too much loading, careened suddenly and capsized.

There was a long, broken, mingled, discordant shriek as of a dozen voices on different keys uttering cries of terror and despair. There was the confusion of one person falling over another; there was the wild grasping for support, the seizing of each other's garments and arms, the undefined and undefinable struggle of the first desperate minute after a boat has capsized, the scream that dies to a gurgle in the water and then breaks out afresh, louder and sharper than before, and then is suddenly smothered into a gurgle again. There were all these things, there was an alarm on the shore, a rush of people, and then there came stillness, and those minutes of desperate waiting, in which the drowning people cling to rigging and boat, and test the problem of human endurance. It is a race between the endurance of frightened, chilled, drowning people, and the stupid lack of presence of mind of those on shore. All the inmates of the boat got hold of something, and for a minute all their heads were out of water. Their eyes were so near to the water, that not even the most self-possessed of them could see what exertions were being made by people on shore to help them. Thus they clung a minute, no one saying anything, when Jane Downing, who held to the rigging at some distance from the boat, paralyzed by fear, let go, and slowly sank out of sight, saying never a word as she went down, but looking with beseeching eyes at the rest, who turned away as the water closed over her, and held on more tenaciously than ever, and wondered whether help ever would reach them. And this was only at the close of the first minute. There were twenty-nine other minutes before help came.

108

CHAPTER XXIII

SINKING

Isabel Marlay's first care had been to see that little Katy had a good hold. Helen Minorkey was quite as self-possessed, but her chief care was to get into a secure position herself. Nothing brings out character more distinctly than an emergency such as this. Miss Minorkey was resolute and bent on self-preservation from the first moment. Miss Marlay was resolute, but full of sympathy for the rest. With characteristic practical sense, she did what she could to make herself and those within her reach secure, and then with characteristic faith she composed her mind to death if it should come, and even ventured with timid courage to exhort Katy and Miss Minorkey to put their trust in Christ, who could forgive their sins, and care for them living or dying. Even the most skeptical of us respect a settled belief in a time of trial. There was much broken praying from others, simply the cry of terror-stricken spirits. In all ages men have cried in their extremity to the Unseen Power, and the drowning passengers in Diamond Lake uttered the same old cry. Westcott himself, in his first terror, prayed a little and swore a little by turns.

The result of self-possession in the case of Isa Marlay and Helen Minorkey was the same. They did not waste their strength. When people drown, it is nearly always from a lack of economy of force. Here was poor little Katy so terrified at thoughts of drowning, and of the cold slimy bed at the bottom of the lake, and more than all at thoughts of the ugly black leeches that abounded at the bottom, that she was drawing herself up head and shoulders out of the water all the time, and praying brokenly to God and Brother Albert to come and help them. Isa tried to soothe her, but she shuddered, and said that the lake was so cold, and she knew she should drown, and Cousin Isa, and Smith, and all of them. Two or three times, in sheer desperation, little Katy let go, but each time Isa Marlay saved her and gave her a better hold, and cheered her with assurances that all would be well yet.

While one party on the shore were building a raft with which to reach the drowning people, Albert Charlton and George Gray ran to find the old boat. But the young men who had rowed in it, wishing to keep it for their own use, had concealed it in a little estuary on the side of the lake opposite to the village, so that the two rescuers were obliged to run half the circumference of the lake before they found it. And even when they reached it, there were no oars to be found, the party rowing last having carefully hidden them in the deep grass of the slough by the outlet. George Gray's quick frontiersman's instinct supplied the deficiency with sticks broken from a fallen tree. But with the time consumed in finding the boat, and the time lost in searching for the oars, and the slowness of the progress made in rowing with these clumsy poles, and the distance of the boat's starting-point from the scene of the disaster, the raft had greatly the advantage of them, though Charlton and Gray used their awkward paddles with the energy of desperation. The wrecked people had clung to their frail supports nearly a quarter of an hour, listening to the cries and shouts of their friends ashore, unable to guess what measures were being taken for their relief, and filled with a distrustful sense of having been abandoned by God and man. It just then occurred to Westcott, who had recovered from his first fright, and who for some time had neither prayed to God nor cursed his luck, that he might save himself by swimming. In his boyish days, before he had weakened his texture by self-indulgence and shattered his nerves by debauchery, he had been famous for his skill and endurance in the water, and it now occurred to him that he might swim ashore and save Katy Charlton at the same time. It is easy enough for us to see the interested motives he had in proposing to save little Katy. He would wipe out the censure sure to fall on him for overloading the boat, he would put Katy and her friends under lasting obligations to him, he would win his game. It is always easy to see the selfish motive. But let us do him justice, and say that these were not the only considerations. Just as the motives of no man are good without some admixture of evil, so are the motives of no man entirely bad. I do not think that Westcott, in taking charge of Katy, was wholly generous, yet there was a generous, and after a fashion, maybe, a loving feeling for the girl in the proposal. That good motives were uppermost, I will not say. They were somewhere in the man, and that is enough to temper our feeling toward him.

Isa Marlay was very unwilling to have Katy go. But the poor little thing was disheartened where she was—the shore did not seem very far away, looking along the water horizontally—the cries of the people on the bank seemed near—she was sure she could not hold on much longer—she was so anxious to get out of this cold lake—she was so afraid to die—she dreaded the black leeches at the bottom— she loved and trusted Smith as such women as she always love and trust—and so she was glad to accept his offer. It was so good of Smith to love her so and to save her. And so she took hold of his coat-collar as he bade her, and Westcott started to swim toward the nearest shore. He had swam his two miles once, when he was a boy, testing his endurance in the waters of the North River, and Diamond Lake was not a mile wide. There seemed no reason to doubt that he could swim to the shore, which could not in any event be more than half a mile away, and which seemed indeed much nearer as he looked over the surface of the water. But Westcott had not taken all the elements into the account. He had on his clothing, and before he had gone far, his boots seemed to fetter him, his saturated sleeves dragged through the water like leaden weights. His limbs, too, had grown numb from remaining so long in the water, and his physical powers had been severely taxed of late years by his dissipations. Add to this that he was encumbered by Katy, that his fright now returned, and that he made the mistake so often made by the best of swimmers under excitement, of wasting power by swimming too high, and you have the causes of rapid exhaustion.

"The shore seems so far away," murmured Katy. "Why don't Albert come and save us?" and she held on to Smith with a grasp yet more violent, and he seemed more and more embarrassed by her hold.

"Let go my arm, or we'll both drown," he cried savagely, and the poor little thing took her left hand off his arm, but held all the more firmly to his collar; but her heart sank in hopelessness. She had never heard him speak in that savage tone before She only called out feebly, "Brother Albert!" and the cry, which revealed to Westcott that she put no more trust in him, but turned now to the strong heart of her brother, angered him, and helped him to take the resolution he was already meditating. For his strength was fast failing; he looked back and could see the raft nearing the capsized boat, but he felt that he had not strength enough left to return; he began to sink, and Katy, frightened out of all self-control as they went under the water, clutched him desperately with both hands. With one violent effort Smith Westcott tore her little hands from him, and threw her off. He could not save her, anyhow. He must do that, or drown. He was no hero or martyr to drown with her. That is all. It cost him a pang to do it, I doubt not.

Katy came up once, and looked at him. It was not terror at thought of death, so much as it was heart-break at being thus cast off, that looked at him out of her despairing eyes. Then she clasped her hands, and cried aloud, in broken voice: "Brother Albert!"

And then with a broken cry she sank.

Oh! Katy! Katy! It were better to sink. I can hardly shed a tear for thee, as I see thee sink to thy cold bed at the lake-bottom among the slimy water-weeds and leeches; but for women who live to trust professions, and who find themselves cast off and sinking— neglected and helpless in life—for them my heart is breaking.

Oh! little Katy. Sweet, and loving, and trustful! It were better to sink among the water-weeds and leeches than to live on. God is more merciful than man.

111

CHAPTER XXIV

DRAGGING

Yes, God is indeed more merciful than man. There are many things worse than death. There is a fold where no wolves enter; a country where a loving heart shall not find its own love turned into poison; a place where the wicked cease from troubling—yes, even in this heretical day, let us be orthodox enough to believe that there is a land where no Smith Westcotts ever come.

There are many cases in which it were better to die. It is easy enough to say it before it comes. Albert Charlton had said—how many times!—that he would rather see Katy dead than married to Westcott. But, now that Katy was indeed dead, how did he feel?

Charlton and Gray had paddled hard with crooked limbs, the boat was unmanageable, and they could with difficulty keep her in her coarse. As they neared the capsized boat, they saw that the raft had taken the people from it, and Albert heard the voice—there could be no mistake as to the voice, weak and shivering as it was—of Isa Marlay, calling to him from the raft:

"We are all safe. Go and save Katy and—him!"

"There they air!" said Gray, pointing to two heads just visible above the water. "Pull away, by thunder!" And the two half-exhausted young men swung the boat round, and rowed. How they longed for the good oars that had sent the "Pirate's Bride" driving through the water that afternoon! How they grudged the time spent in righting her when she veered to right or left! At last they heard Katy's voice cry out, "Brother Albert!"

"O God!" groaned Charlton, and bent himself to his oar again.

"Alb—" The last cry was half-drowned in the water, and when the boat, with half-a-dozen more strokes, reached the place where Westcott was, so that he was able to seize the side, there was no Kate to be seen. Without waiting to lift the exhausted swimmer into the boat, Charlton and Gray dived. But the water was twenty feet deep, the divers were utterly out of breath with rowing, and their diving was of no avail. They kept trying until long after all hope had died out of their hearts. At last Charlton climbed back into the boat, and sat down. Then Gray got in. Westcott was so numb and exhausted from staying in the water so long that he could not get in, but he held to the boat desperately, and begged them to help him.

"Help him in," said Charlton to Gray. "I can't."

"I'd like to help him out ef he wuz in, mighty well. I can't kill a

112

drownin' man, but blamed ef I gin him a leetle finger of help. I'd jest as soon help a painter outen the water when I know'd he'd swaller the fust man he come to."

But Charlton got up and reached a hand to the sinking Westcott. He shut his eyes while he pulled him in, and was almost sorry he had saved him. Let us not be too hard on Albert. He was in the first agony of having reached a hand to save little Katy and missed her. To come so near that you might have succeeded by straining a nerve a little more somewhere—that is bitterest of all. If Westcott had only held on a minute!

It was with difficulty that Albert and Gray rowed to the shore, where Plausaby met them, and persuaded them to change their clothes. They were both soon on the shore again, where large fires were blazing, and the old boat that had failed to save little Katy alive, was now in use to recover her body. There is no more hopeless and melancholy work than dragging for the body of a drowned person. The drag moves over the bottom; the man who holds the rope, watching for the faintest sensation of resistance in the muscles of his arm, at last feels something drawing against the drag, calls to the oarsmen to stop rowing, lets the line slip through his fingers till the boat's momentum is a little spent, lest he should lose his hold, then he draws on his line gently, and while the boat drifts back, he reverently, as becomes one handling the dead, brings the drag to the surface, and finds that its hooks have brought up nothing but water-weeds, or a waterlogged bough. And when at last, after hours of anxious work, the drag brings the lifeless body to the surface, the disappointment is bitterest of all. For all the time you have seemed to be seeking the drowned person, and now at last you have got—what?

It was about eleven o'clock when they first began to drag. Albert had a sort of vague looking for something, a superstitious feeling that by some sort of a miracle Katy would yet be found alive. It is the hardest work the imagination has to do—this realizing that one who has lived by us will never more be with us. It is hard to project a future for ourselves, into which one who has filled a large share of our thought and affection shall never come. And so there lingers a blind hope, a hopeless hope of something that shall make unreal that which our impotent imaginations refuse to accept as real. It is a means by which nature parries a sudden blow.

Charlton walked up and down the shore, and wished he might take the drag-line into his own hands; but the mistaken kindness of our friends refuses us permission to do for our own dead, when doing anything would be a relief, and when doing for the dead would be the best possible utterance to the hopeless love which we call grief.

Mrs. Plausaby, weak and vain though she was, was full of natural affection. Her love for Albert was checked a little by her feeling that there was no perfect sympathy between him and her. But upon Katy she had lavished all her mother's love. People are apt to think that a love which is not intelligent is not real; there could be no greater mistake. And the very smallness of the area covered by Mrs. Plausaby's mind made her grief for Kate all the more passionate. Katy occupied Albert's mind jointly with Miss Minorkey, with ambition, with benevolence, with science, with literature, and with the great Philanthropinum that was to be built and to revolutionize the world by helping it on toward its "goal." But the interests that shared Mrs. Plausaby's thoughts along with Katy were very few. Of Albert she thought, and of her husband. But she gave the chief place to Katy and her own appearance. And so when the blow had come it was a severe one. At midnight, Albert went back to try to comfort his mother, and received patiently all her weeping upbraidings of him for letting his sister go in the boat, he might have known it was not safe. And then he hastened back again to the water, and watched the men in the boat still dragging without result. Everybody on the shore knew just where the "Lady of the Lake" had capsized, and if accurate information, plentifully given, could have helped to find the bodies, it would soon have been accomplished. The only difficulty was that this accurate information was very conflicting, no two of the positive eye-witnesses being able to agree. So there was much shouting along shore, and many directions given, but all the searching for a long time proved vain. All the shouting people hushed their shouting, and spoke in whispers whenever Albert came near. To most men there is nothing more reverend than grief. At half-past two o'clock, the man who held the rope felt a strange thrill, a sense of having touched one of the bodies. He drew up his drag, and one of the hooks held a piece of a black silk cape. When three or four more essays had been made, the body itself was brought to the surface, and the boat turned toward the shore. There was no more shouting of directions now, not a single loud word was spoken, the oarsman rowed with a steady funereal rhythm, while Ben Towle, who had held the drag-rope, now held half out of water the recovered corpse. Albert leaned forward anxiously to see the face of Katy, but it was Jane Downing, the girl who was drowned first. Her father took the body in his arms, drew it out on shore, and wept over it in a quiet fashion for a while. Then strong and friendly neighbors lifted it, and bore it before him to his house, while the man followed in a dumb grief.

114

Then the dragging for Katy was resumed; but as there was much more doubt in regard to the place where she went down than there was about the place of the accident, the search was more difficult and protracted. George Gray never left Albert for a moment. George wanted to take the drag-rope himself, but a feeling that he was eccentric, if not insane, kept those in charge of the boat from giving it to him.

When Sunday morning came, Katy's body had not yet been found, and the whole village flocked to the lake shore. These were the first deaths in Metropolisville, and the catastrophe was so sudden and tragic that it stirred the entire village in an extraordinary manner. All through that cloudy Sunday forenoon, in a weary waiting, Charlton sat on the bank of Diamond Lake.

"Mr. Charlton," said Gray, "git me into that air boat and I'll git done with this. I've watched them fellers go round the place tell I can't stan' it no longer."

The next time the boat faced toward the place where Charlton stood he beckoned to them, and the boat came to the shore.

"Let Mr. Gray row a few times, won't you?" whispered Albert. "I think he knows the place."

With that deference always paid to a man in grief, the man who had the oars surrendered them to the Hoosier Poet, who rowed gently and carefully toward the place where he and Albert had dived for Katy the night before. The quick instinct of the trapper stood him in good stead now. The perception and memory of locality and direction are developed to a degree that seems all but supernatural in a man who lives a trapper's life.

"Now, watch out!" said Gray to the man with the rope, as they passed what he thought to be the place. But the drag did not touch anything. Gray then went round and pulled at right angles across his former course, saying again, "Now, watch out!" as they passed the same spot. The man who held the rope advised him to turn a little to the right, but Gray stuck to his own infallible instinct, and crossed and re-crossed the same point six times without success.

"You see," he remarked, "you kin come awful closte to a thing in the water and not tech it. We ha'n't missed six foot nary time we passed thar. It may take right smart rowin' to do it yet. But when you miss a mark a-tryin' at it, you don't gain nothin' by shootin' wild. Now, watch out!"

And just at that moment the drag caught but did not hold. Gray noticed it, but neither man said a word. The Inhabitant turned the boat round and pulled slowly back over the same place. The drag caught, and Gray lifted his oars. The man with the rope, who had suddenly got a great reverence for Gray's skill, willingly allowed him to draw in the line. The Poet did so cautiously and tremblingly. When the body came above the water, he had all he could do to keep from fainting. He gently took hold of the arms and said to his companion, "Pull away now." And with his own wild, longing, desolate heart full of grief, Gray held to the little form and drew her through the water. Despite his grief, the Poet was glad to be the one who should bring her ashore. He held her now, if only her dead body, and his unselfish love found a melancholy recompense. Albert would have chosen him of all men for the office.

Poor little Kate! In that dread moment when she found herself sinking to her cold bed among the water-weeds, she had, failing all other support, clasped her left hand with her right and gone down to darkness. And as she went, so now came her lifeless body. The right hand clasped tightly the four little white fingers of the left.

Poor little Kate! How white as pearl her face was, turned up toward that Sabbath sky! There was not a spot upon it. The dreaded leeches had done their work.

She, whom everybody had called sweet, looked sweeter now than ever. Death had been kind to the child at the last, and had stroked away every trace of terror, and of the short anguish she had suffered when she felt herself cast off by the craven soul she trusted. What might the long anguish have been had she lived!

116

CHAPTER XXV

AFTERWARDS

The funeral was over, and there were two fresh graves—the only ones in the bit of prairie set apart for a graveyard. I have written enough in this melancholy strain. Why should I pause to describe in detail the solemn services held in the grove by the lake? It is enough that the land-shark forgot his illegal traffic in claims; the money-lender ceased for one day to talk of mortgages and per cent and foreclosure; the fat gentleman left his corner-lots. Plausaby's bland face was wet with tears of sincere grief, and Mr. Minorkey pressed his hand to his chest and coughed more despairingly than ever. The grove in which the meeting was held commanded a view of the lake at the very place where the accident occurred. The nine survivors sat upon the front seat of all; the friends of the deceased were all there, and, most pathetic sight of all, the two mute white faces of the drowned were exposed to view. The people wept before the tremulous voice of the minister had begun the service, and there was so much weeping that the preacher could say but little. Poor Mrs. Plausaby was nearly heart-broken. Nothing could have been more pathetic than her absurd mingling for two days of the sincerest grief and an anxious questioning about her mourning-dress. She would ask Isa's opinion concerning her veil, and then sit down and cry piteously the next minute. And now she was hopeless and utterly disconsolate at the loss of her little Katy, but wondering all the time whether Isa could not have fixed her bonnet so that it would not have looked quite so plain.

The old minister preached on "Remember now thy Creator in the days of thy youth." I am afraid he said some things which the liberalism of to-day would think unfit—we all have heresies nowadays; it is quite the style. But at least the old man reminded them that there were better investments than corner-lots, and that even mortgages with waivers in them will be brought into judgment. His solemn words could not have failed entirely of doing good.

But the solemn funeral services were over; the speculator in claims dried his eyes, and that very afternoon assigned a claim, to which he had no right, to a simple-minded immigrant for a hundred dollars. Minorkey was devoutly thankful that his own daughter had escaped, and that he could go on getting mortgages with waivers in them, and Plausaby turned his attention to contrivances for extricating himself from the embarrassments of his situation.

The funeral was over. That is the hardest time of all. You can bear up somehow, so long as the arrangements and cares and melancholy tributes of the obsequies last. But if one has occupied a large share of your thoughts, solicitudes, and affections, and there comes a time when the very last you can ever do for them, living or dead, is done, then for the first time you begin to take the full measure of your loss. Albert felt now that he was picking up the broken threads of another man's life. Between the past, which had been full of anxieties and plans for little Kate, and the future, into which no little Kate could ever come, there was a great chasm. There is nothing that love parts from so regretfully as its burdens.

Mrs. Ferret came to see Charlton, and smiled her old sudden puckered smile, and talked in her jerky complacent voice about the uses of sanctified affliction, and her trust that the sudden death of his sister in all the thoughtless vanity of youth would prove a solemn and impressive warning to him to repent in health before it should be with him everlastingly too late. Albert was very far from having that childlike spirit which enters the kingdom of heaven easily. Some natures, are softened by affliction, but they are not such as his. Charlton in his aggressiveness demanded to know the reason for everything. And in his sorrow his nature sent a defiant why back to the Power that had made Katy's fate so sad, and Mrs. Ferret's rasping way of talking about Katy's death as a divine judgment on him filled him with curses bitterer than Job's.

Miss Isa Marlay was an old-school Calvinist. She had been trained on the Assembly's Catechism, interpreted in good sound West Windsor fashion. In theory she never deviated one iota from the solid ground of the creed of her childhood. But while she held inflexibly to her creed in all its generalizations, she made all those sweet illogical exceptions which women of her kind are given to making. In general, she firmly believed that everybody who failed to have a saving faith in the vicarious atonement of Christ would be lost. In particular, she excepted many individual cases among her own acquaintance. And the inconsistency between her creed and her applications of it never troubled her. She spoke with so much confidence of the salvation of little Kate, that she comforted Albert somewhat, notwithstanding his entire antagonism to Isa's system of theology. If Albert had died, Miss Marlay would have fixed up a short and easy road to bliss for him also. So much, more generous is faith than logic! But it was not so much Isa's belief in the salvation of Katy that did Albert good, as it was her tender and delicate sympathy, expressed as much when she was silent as when she spoke, and when she spoke expressed more by the tones of her voice than by her words.

118

There was indeed one part of Isabel's theology that Charlton would have much liked to possess. He had accepted the idea of an Absolute God. A personal, sympathizing, benevolent Providence was in his opinion one of the illusions of the theologic stage of human development. Things happened by inexorable law, he said. And in the drowning of Katy he saw only the overloading of a boat and the inevitable action of water upon the vital organs of the human system. It seemed to him now an awful thing that such great and terrible forces should act irresistibly and blindly. He wished he could find some ground upon which to base a different opinion. He would like to have had Isabel's faith in the Paternity of God and in the immortality of the soul. But he was too honest with himself to suffer feeling to exert any influence on his opinions. He was in the logical stage of his development, and built up his system after the manner of the One-Hoss Shay. Logically he could not see sufficient ground to change, and he scorned the weakness that would change an opinion because of feeling. His soul might cry out in its depths for a Father in the universe. But what does Logic care for a Soul or its cry? After a while a wider experience brings in something better than Logic. This is Philosophy. And Philosophy knows what Logic can not learn, that reason is not the only faculty by which truth is apprehended—that the hungers and intuitions of the Soul are worth more than syllogisms.

Do what he would, Charlton could not conceal from himself that in sympathy Miss Minorkey was greatly deficient. She essayed to show feeling, but she had little to show. It was not her fault. Do you blame the dahlia for not having the fragrance of a tuberose? It is the most dangerous quality of enthusiastic young men and women that they are able to deceive themselves. Nine tenths of all conjugal disappointments come from the ability of people in love to see more in those they love than ever existed there. That love is blind is a fable. He has an affection of the eyes, but it is not blindness. Nobody else ever sees so much as he does. For here was Albert Charlton, bound by his vows to Helen Minorkey, with whom he had nothing in common, except in intellect, and already his sorrow was disclosing to him the shallowness of her nature, and the depth of his own; even now he found that she had no voice with which to answer his hungry cry for sympathy. Already his betrothal was becoming a fetter, and his great mistake was disclosing itself to him. The rude suspicion had knocked at his door before, but he had been able to bar it out. Now it stared at him in the night, and he could not rid himself of it. But he was still far enough from accepting the fact that the intellectual Helen Minorkey was destitute of all unselfish feeling. For Charlton was still in love with her. When one has fixed heart and hope and thought on a single person, love does not die with the first consciousness of disappointment. Love can subsist a long time on old associations. Besides, Miss Minorkey was not aggressively or obtrusively selfish—she never interfered with anybody else. But there is a cool-blooded indifference that can be moved by no consideration outside the Universal Ego. That was Helen.

CHAPTER XXVI

THE MYSTERY

I have before me, as one of the original sources of information for this history, a file of The Wheat County Weakly Windmill for 1856. It is not a large sheet, but certainly it is a very curious one. In its day this Windmill ground many grists, though its editorial columns were chiefly occupied with impartial gushing and expansive articles on the charms of scenery, fertility of soil, superiority of railroad prospects, admirableness of location, healthfulness, and general future rosiness of the various paper towns that paid tribute to its advertising columns. And the advertising columns! They abounded in business announcements of men who had "Money to Loan on Good Real Estate" at three, four, five, and six per cent a month, and of persons who called themselves "Attorneys-at-Law and Real Estate Agents," who stated that "All business relating to pre-emption and contested claims would be promptly attended to" at their offices in Perritaut. Even now, through the thin disguise of honest-seeming phrases, one can see the bait of the land-shark who speculated in imaginary titles to claims, or sold corner-lots in bubble-towns. And, as for the towns, it appears from these advertisements that there was one on almost every square mile, and that every one of them was on the line of an inevitable railroad, had a first-class hotel, a water-power, an academy, and an indefinite number of etcaeteras of the most delightful and remunerative kind. Each one of these villages was in the heart of the greatest grain-growing section of the State. Each, was the "natural outlet" to a large agricultural region. Each commanded the finest view. Each point was the healthiest in the county, and each village was "unrivaled." (When one looks at these town-site advertisements, one is tempted to think that member serious and wise who, about this time, offered a joint resolution in the Territorial Legislature, which read: "Resolved by the Senate and House of Representatives, That not more than two thirds of the area of this Territory should be laid out in town-sites and territorial roads, the remaining one third to be sacredly reserved for agricultural use.")

But I prize this old file of papers because it contains a graphic account of the next event in this narrative. And the young man who edited the Windmill at this time has told the story with so much sprightliness and vigor that I can not serve my reader a better turn than by clipping his account and pasting it just here in my manuscript. (I shall also rest myself a little, and do a favor to the patient printer, who will rejoice to get a little "reprint copy" in place of my perplexing manuscript.) For where else shall I find such a dictionariful command of the hights and depths—to say nothing of the lengths and breadths—of the good old English tongue? This young man must indeed have been a marvel of eloquent verbosity at that period of his career. The article in question has the very flavor of the golden age of Indian contracts, corner-lots, six per cent a month, and mortgages with waiver clauses. There, is also visible, I fear, a little of the prejudice which existed at that time in Perritaut against Metropolisville.

I wish that an obstinate scruple on the part of the printers and the limits of a duodecimo page did not forbid my reproducing here, in all their glory, the unique head-lines which precede the article in question. Any pageant introduced by music is impressive, says Madame de Stael. At least she says something of that sort, only it is in French, and I can not remember it exactly. And so any newspaper article is startling when introduced by the braying of head-lines. Fonts of type for displayed lines were not abundant in the office of the Windmill, but they were very stunning, and were used also for giving prominence to the euphonious names of the several towns, whose charms were set forth in the advertisements. Of course the first of these head-lines ran "Startling Disclosures!!!!" and then followed "Tremendous Excitement in Metropolisville!" "Official Rascality!" "Bold Mail Robbery!" "Arrest of the Postmaster!" "No Doubt of his Guilt!" "An Unexplained Mystery!" "Sequel to the Awful Drowning Affair of Last Week!" Having thus whetted the appetite of his reader, and economized in type-setting by nearly a column of such broad and soul-stirring typography, the editor proceeds:

"Metropolisville is again the red-hot crater of a boiling and seething excitement. Scarcely had the rascally and unscrupulous county-seat swindle begun to lose something of its terrific and exciting interest to the people of this county, when there came the awful and sad drowning of the two young ladies, Miss Jennie Downing and Miss Katy Charlton, the belles of the village, a full account of which will be found in the Windmill of last week, some copies of which we have still on hand, having issued an extra edition. Scarcely had the people of Metropolisville laid these two charming and much-lamented young ladies in their last, long resting-place, the quiet grave, when there comes like an earthquake out of a clear sky, the frightful and somewhat surprising and stunning intelligence that the postmaster of the village, a young man of a hitherto unexceptionable and blameless reputation, has been arrested for robbing the mails. It is supposed that his depredations have been very extensive and long continued, and that many citizens of our own village may have suffered from them. Farther investigations will doubtless bring all his nefarious and unscrupulous transactions to light. At present, however, he is under arrest on the single charge of stealing a land-warrant.

"The name of the rascally, villainous, and dishonest postmaster is Albert Charlton, and here comes in the wonderful and startling romance of this strange story. The carnival of excitement in Metropolisville and about Metropolisville has all had to do with one family. Our readers will remember how fully we have exposed the unscrupulous tricks of the old fox Plausaby, the contemptible land-shark who runs Metropolisville, and who now has temporary possession of the county-seat by means of a series of gigantic frauds, and of wholesale bribery and corruption and nefarious ballot-box stuffing. The fair Katy Charlton, who was drowned by the heart-rending calamity of last week, was his step-daughter, and now her brother, Albert Charlton, is arrested as a vile and dishonest mail-robber, and the victim whose land-warrant he stole was Miss Kate Charlton's betrothed lover, Mr. Smith Westcott. There was always hatred and animosity, however, between the lover and the brother, and it is hinted that the developments on the trial will prove that young Charlton had put a hired and ruthless assassin on the track of Westcott at the time of his sister's death. Mr. Westcott is well known and highly esteemed in Metropolisville and also here in Perritaut. He is the gentlemanly Agent in charge of the branch store of Jackson, Jones & Co., and we rejoice that he has made so narrow an escape from death at the hands of his relentless and unscrupulous foe.

"As for Albert Charlton, it is well for the community that he has been thus early and suddenly overtaken in the first incipiency of a black career of crime. His poor mother is said to be almost insane at this second grief, which follows so suddenly on her heart-rending bereavement of last week. We wish there were some hope that this young man, thus arrested with the suddenness of a thunderbolt by the majestic and firm hand of public justice, would reform; but we are told that he is utterly hard, and refuses to confess or deny his guilt, sitting in moody and gloomy silence in the room in which he is confined. We again call the attention of the proper authorities to the fact that Plausaby has not kept his agreement, and that Wheat County has no secure jail. We trust that the youthful villain Charlton will not be allowed to escape, but that he will receive the long term provided by the law for thieving postmasters. He will be removed to

123

St. Paul immediately, but we seize the opportunity to demand in thunder-tones how long the citizens of this county are to be left without the accommodations of a secure jail, of which they stand in such immediate need? It is a matter in which we all feel a personal interest. We hope the courts will decide the county-seat question at once, and then we trust the commissioners will give us a jail of sufficient size and strength to accommodate a county of ten thousand people.

"We would not judge young Charlton before he has a fair trial. We hope he will have a fair trial, and it is not for us to express any opinions on the case in advance. If he shall be found guilty—and we do not for a moment doubt he will—we trust the court will give him the full penalty of the law without fear or favor, so that his case may prove a solemn and impressive warning that shall make a lasting impression on the minds of the thoughtless young men of this community in favor of honesty, and in regard to the sinfulness of stealing. We would not exult over the downfall of any man; but when the proud young Charlton gets his hair cropped, and finds himself clad in 'Stillwater gray,' and engaged in the intellectual employments of piling shingles and making vinegar-barrels, he will have plenty of time for meditation on that great moral truth, that honesty is generally the best policy."

CHAPTER XXVII

THE ARREST

The eloquent editor from whom I have just quoted told the truth when he said that Metropolisville was "the red-hot crater of a boiling and seething excitement." For everybody had believed in Charlton. He was not popular. People with vicarious consciences are not generally beloved unless they are tempered by much suavity. And Charlton was not. But everybody, except Mrs. Ferret, believed in his honesty and courage. Nobody had doubted his sincerity, though Smith Westcott had uttered many innuendoes. In truth, Westcott had had an uncomfortable time during the week that followed the drowning. There had been much shaking of the head about little Katy's death. People who are not at all heroic like to have other people do sublime things, and there were few who did not think that Westcott should have drowned with Katy, like the hero of a romance. People could not forgive him for spoiling a good story. So Smith got the cold shoulder, and might have left the Territory, but that his land-warrant had not come. He ceased to dance and to appear cheerful, and his he! he! took on a sneering inflection. He grew mysterious, and intimated to his friends that he'd give Metropolisville something else to talk about before long. By George! He! he! And when the deputy of the United States marshal swooped down upon the village and arrested the young post-master on a charge of abstracting Smith Westcott's land-warrant from the mail, the whole town was agog. "Told you so. By George!" said Westcott.

At first the villagers were divided in opinion about Albert. Plenty of people, like Mrs. Ferret, were ready to rejoice that he was not so good as he might be, you know. But many others said that he wouldn't steal. A fellow that had thrown away all his chances of making money wouldn't steal. To which it was rejoined that if Charlton did not care for money he was a good hater, and that what such a man would not do for money he might do for spite. And then, too, it was known that Albert had been very anxious to get away, and that he wanted to get away before Westcott did. And that everything depended on which should get a land-warrant first. What more natural than that Charlton should seize upon Smith Westcott's land-warrant, and thus help himself and retard his rival? This sort of reasoning staggered those who would have defended him on the ground of previous good character.

But that which shook the popular confidence in Albert most

125

was his own behavior when arrested. He was perfectly collected until he inquired what evidence there was against him. The deputy marshal said that it was very clear evidence, indeed. "The land-warrant with which you pre-empted your claim bore a certain designating number. The prosecution can prove that that warrant was mailed at Red Owl on the 24th of August, directed to Smith Westcott, Metropolisville, and that he failed to receive it. The stolen property appearing in your hands, you must account for it in some way."

At this Charlton's countenance fell, and he refused to make any explanations or answer any questions. He was purposely kept over one day in Metropolisville in hope that something passing between him and his friends, who were permitted to have free access to him, might bring further evidence to light. But Charlton sat, pale and dejected, ready enough to converse about anything else, but declining to say one word in regard to his guilt or innocence of the crime charged. It is not strange that some of his best friends accepted the charge as true, and only tried to extenuate the offense on the ground that the circumstances made the temptation a very great one, and that the motive was not mercenary. Others stood out that it would yet be discovered that Plausaby had stolen the warrant, until half-a-dozen people remembered that Plausaby himself had been in Red Owl at that very time—he had spent a week there laying out a marshy shore in town lots down to the low-water mark, and also laying out the summit of a bluff three hundred and fifty feet high and sixty degrees steep. These sky and water lots were afterward sold to confiding Eastern speculators, and a year or two later the owner of the water privileges rowed all over his lots in a skiff. Whether the other purchaser used a balloon to reach his is not known. But the operation of staking out these ineligible "additions" to the city of Red Owl had attracted much attention, and consequently Plausaby's alibi was readily established. So that the two or three who still believed Albert innocent did so by "naked faith," and when questioned about it, shook their heads, and said that it was a great mystery. They could not understand it, but they did not believe him guilty. Isabel Marlay believed in Albert's innocence as she believed the hard passages in the catechism. She knew it, she believed it, she could not prove it, but she would not hear to anything else. She was sure of his innocence, and that was enough. For when a woman of that sort believes anything, she believes in spite of all her senses and all reason. What are the laws of evidence to her! She believes with the heart.

Poor Mrs. Plausaby, too, sat down in a dumb despair, and wept and complained and declared that she knew her Albert had

126

notions and such things, but people with such notions wouldn't do anything naughty. Albert wouldn't, she knew. He hadn't done any harm, and they couldn't find out that he had. Katy was gone, and now Albert was in trouble, and she didn't know what to do. She thought Isa might do something, and not let all these troubles come on her in this way. For the poor woman had come to depend on Isa not only in weighty matters, such as dresses and bonnets, but also in all the other affairs of life. And it seemed to her a grievous wrong that Isabel, who had saved her from so many troubles, should not have kept Katy from drowning and Albert from prison.

The chief trouble in the mind of Albert was not the probability of imprisonment, nor the overthrow of his educational schemes—though all of these were cups of bitterness. But the first thought with him was to ask what would be the effect of his arrest on Miss Minorkey. He had felt some disappointment in not finding Helen the ideal woman he had pictured her, but, as I said a while ago, love does not die at the first disappointment. If it finds little to live on in the one who is loved, it will yet find enough in the memories, the hopes, and the ideals that dwell within the lover. Charlton, in the long night after his arrest, reviewed everything, but in thinking of Miss Minorkey, he did not once recur to her lack of deep sympathy with him in his sorrow for Katy. The Helen he thought of was the radiant Helen that sat by his beloved Katy in the boat on that glorious evening in which he rowed in the long northern twilight, the Helen that had relaxed her dignity enough to dip her palm in the water and dash spray into his face. He saw her like one looking back through clouds of blackness to catch a sight of a bit of sky and a single shining star. As the impossibility of his marrying Helen became more and more evident to him, she grew all the more glorious in her culture, her quietness, her thoughtfulness. That she would break her heart for him, he did not imagine, but he did hope—yes, hope—that she would suffer acutely on his account.

And when Isa Marlay bravely walked through the crowd that had gathered about the place of his confinement, and asked to see him, and he was told that a young lady wanted to be admitted, he hoped that it might be Helen Minorkey. When he saw that it was Isabel he was glad, partly because he would rather have seen her than anybody else, next to Helen, and partly because he could ask her to carry a message to Miss Minorkey. He asked her to take from his trunk, which had already been searched by the marshal's deputy, all the letters of Miss Minorkey, to tie them in a package, and to have the goodness to present them to that lady with his sincere regards.

127

"Shall I tell her that you are innocent?" asked Isabel, wishing to strengthen her own faith by a word of assurance from Albert.

"Tell her—" and Albert cast down his eyes a moment in painful reflection—"tell her that I will explain some day. Meantime, tell her to believe what you believe about me."

"I believe that you are innocent."

"Thank you, Miss Isabel," said Albert warmly, but then he stopped and grew red in the face. He did not give her one word of assurance. Even Isa's faith was staggered for a moment. But only for a moment. The faith of a woman like Isabel Marlay laughs at doubt.

I do not know how to describe the feelings with which Miss Marlay went out from Albert. Even in the message, full of love, which he had sent to his mother, he did not say one word about his guilt or innocence. And yet Isabel believed in her heart that he had not committed the crime. While he was strong and free from suspicion, Isa Marlay had admired him. He seemed to her, notwithstanding his eccentricities, a man of such truth, fervor, and earnestness of character, that she liked him better than she was willing to admit to herself. Now that he was an object of universal suspicion, her courageous and generous heart espoused his cause vehemently. She stood ready to do anything in the world for him. Anything but what he had asked her to do. Why she did not like to carry messages from him to Miss Minorkey she did not know. As soon as she became conscious of this jealous feeling in her heart, she took herself to task severely. Like the good girl she was, she set her sins out in the light of her own conscience. She did more than that. But if I should tell you truly what she did with this naughty feeling, how she dragged it out into the light and presence of the Holy One Himself, I should seem to be writing cant, and people would say that I was preaching. And yet I should only show you the source of Isa's high moral and religious culture. Can I write truly of a life in which the idea of God as Father, Monitor, and Friend is ever present and dominant, without showing you the springs of that life?

When Isabel Marlay, with subdued heart, sought Miss Minorkey, it was with her resolution fixed to keep the trust committed to her, and, as far as possible, to remove all suspicions from Miss Minorkey's mind. As for any feeling in her own heart—she had no right to have any feeling but a friendly one to Albert. She would despise a woman who could love a man that did not first declare his love for her. She said this to herself several times by way of learning the lesson well.

Isa found Miss Minorkey, with her baggage packed, ready for a move. Helen told Miss Marlay that her father found the air very bad for him, and meant to go to St. Anthony, where there was a

128

mineral spring and a good hotel. For her part, she was glad of it, for a little place like Metropolisville was not pleasant. So full of gossip. And no newspapers or books. And very little cultivated society.

Miss Marlay said she had a package of something or other, which Mr. Charlton had sent with his regards. She said "something or other" from an instinctive delicacy.

"Oh! yes; something of mine that he borrowed, I suppose," said Helen. "Have you seen him? I'm really sorry for him. I found him a very pleasant companion, so full of reading and oddities. He's the last man I should have believed could rob the post-office."

"Oh! but he didn't," said Isa.

"Indeed! Well, I'm glad to hear it. I hope he'll be able to prove it. Is there any new evidence?"

Isa was obliged to confess that she had heard of none, and Miss Minorkey proceeded like a judge to explain to Miss Marlay how strong the evidence against him was. And then she said she thought the warrant had been taken, not from cupidity, but from a desire to serve Katy. It was a pity the law could not see it in that way. But all the time Isa protested with vehemence that she did not believe a word of it. Not one word. All the judges and juries and witnesses in the world could not convince her of Albert's guilt. Because she knew him, and she just knew that he couldn't do it, you see.

Miss Minorkey said it had made her father sick. "I've gone with Mr. Charlton so much, you know, that it has made talk," she said. "And father feels bad about it. And"—seeing the expression of Isa's countenance, she concluded that it would not do to be quite so secretive—"and, to tell you the truth, I did like him. But of course that is all over. Of course there couldn't be anything between us after this, even if he were innocent."

Isa grew indignant, and she no longer needed the support of religious faith and high moral principle to enable her to plead the cause of Albert Charlton with Miss Minorkey.

"But I thought you loved him," she said, with just a spice of bitterness.

"The poor fellow believes that you love him."

Miss Minorkey winced a little. "Well, you know, some people are sentimental, and others are not. It is a good thing for me that I'm not one of those that pine away and die after anybody. I suppose I am not worthy of a high-toned man, such as he seemed to be. I have often told him so. I am sure I never could marry a man that had been in the penitentiary, if he were ever so innocent. Now, could you. Miss Marlay?"

Isabel blushed, and said she could if he were innocent. She

thought a woman ought to stand by the man she loved to the death, if he were worthy. But Helen only sighed humbly, and said that she never was made for a heroine. She didn't even like to read about high-strung people in novels. She supposed it was her fault—people had to be what they were, she supposed. Miss Marlay must excuse her, though. She hadn't quite got her books packed, and the stage would be along in an hour. She would be glad if Isabel would tell Mr. Charlton privately, if she had a chance, how sorry she felt for him. But please not say anything that would compromise her, though.

And Isa Marlay went out of the hotel full of indignation at the cool-blooded Helen, and full of a fathomless pity for Albert, a pity that made her almost love him herself. She would have loved to atone for all Miss Minorkey's perfidy. And just alongside of her pity for Charlton thus deserted, crept in a secret joy. For there was now none to stand nearer friend to Albert than herself.

And yet Charlton did not want for friends. Whisky Jim had a lively sense of gratitude to him for his advocacy of Jim's right to the claim as against Westcott; and having also a lively antagonism to Westcott, he could see no good reason why a man should serve a long term in State's-prison for taking from a thief a land-warrant with which the thief meant to pre-empt another man's claim. And the Guardian Angel had transferred to the brother the devotion and care he once lavished on the sister. It was this unity of sentiment between the Jehu from the Green Mountains and the minstrel from the Indiana "Pocket" that gave Albert a chance for liberty.

The prisoner was handcuffed and confined in an upper room, the windows of which were securely boarded up on the outside. About three o'clock of the last night he spent in Metropolisville, the deputy marshal, who in the evening preceding had helped to empty two or three times the ample flask of Mr. Westcott, was sleeping very soundly. Albert, who was awake, heard the nails drawn from the boards. Presently the window was opened, and a familiar voice said in a dramatic tone:

"Mr. Charlton, git up and foller."

Albert arose and went to the window.

"Come right along, I 'low the coast's clear," said the Poet.

"No, I can not do that, Gray," said Charlton, though the prospect of liberty was very enticing.

"See here, mister, I calkilate es this is yer last chance fer fifteen year ur more," put in the driver, thrusting his head in alongside his Hoosier friend's.

"Come," added Gray, "you an' me'll jest put out together fer the Ingin kedentry ef you say so, and fetch up in Kansas under some fancy names, and take a hand in the wras'le that's agoin' on thar. Nobody'll ever track you. I've got a Yankton friend as'll help us through."

"My friends, I'm ever so thankful to you—"

"Blame take yer thanks! Come along," broke in the Superior Being. "It's now ur never."

"I'll be dogged ef it haint," said the Poet.

Charlton looked out wistfully over the wide prairies. He might escape and lead a wild, free life with Gray, and then turn up in some new Territory under an assumed name and work out his destiny. But the thought of being a fugitive from justice was very shocking to him.

"No! no! I can't. God bless you both. Good-by!" And he went back to his pallet on the floor. When the rescuers reached the ground the Superior Being delivered himself of some very sulphurous oaths, intended to express his abhorrence of "idees."

"There's that air blamed etarnal infarnal nateral born eejiot'll die in Stillwater penitensh'ry jest fer idees. Orter go to a 'sylum."

But the Poet went off dejectedly to his lone cabin on the prairie.

And there was a great row in the morning about the breaking open of the window and the attempted rescue. The deputy marshal told a famous story of his awaking in the night and driving off a rescuing party of eight with his revolver. And everybody wondered who they were. Was Charlton, then, a member of a gang?

131

CHAPTER XXVIII

THE TEMPTER

Albert was conveyed to St. Paul, but not until he had had one heart-breaking interview with his mother. The poor woman had spent nearly an hour dressing herself to go to him, for she was so shaken with agitation and blinded with weeping, that she could hardly tie a ribbon or see that her breast-pin was in the right place. This interview with her son shook her weak understanding to its foundations, and for days afterward Isa devoted her whole time to diverting her from the accumulation of troubled thoughts and memories that filled her with anguish—an anguish against the weight of which her feeble nature could offer no supports.

When Albert was brought before the commissioner, he waived examination, and was committed to await the session of the district court. Mr. Plausaby came up and offered to become his bail, but this Charlton vehemently refused, and was locked up in jail, where for the next two or three months he amused himself by reading the daily papers and such books as he could borrow, and writing on various subjects manuscripts which he never published.

The confinement chafed him. His mother's sorrow and feeble health oppressed him. And despite all he could do, his own humiliation bowed his head a little. But most of all, the utter neglect of Helen Minorkey hurt him sorely. Except that she had sent, through Isabel Marlay, that little smuggled message that she was sorry for him—like one who makes a great ado about sending you something which turns out to be nothing—except this mockery of pity, he had no word or sign from Helen. His mind dwelt on her as he remembered her in the moments when she had been carried out of herself by the contagion of his own enthusiasm, when she had seemed to love him devotedly. Especially did he think of her as she sat in quiet and thoughtful enjoyment in the row-boat by the side of Katy, playfully splashing the water and seeming to rejoice in his society. And now she had so easily accepted his guilt!

These thoughts robbed him of sleep, and the confinement and lack of exercise made him nervous. The energetic spirit, arrested at the very instant of beginning cherished enterprises, and shut out from hope of ever undertaking them, preyed upon itself, and Albert had a morbid longing for the State's prison, where he might weary himself with toil.

His counsel was Mr. Conger. Mr. Conger was not a great

jurist. Of the philosophy of law he knew nothing. For the sublime principles of equity and the great historic developments that underlie the conventions which enter into the administration of public justice, Mr. Conger cared nothing. But there was one thing Mr. Conger did understand and care for, and that was success. He was a man of medium hight, burly, active, ever in motion. When he had ever been still long enough to read law, nobody knew. He said everything he had to say with a quick, vehement utterance, as though he grudged the time taken to speak fully about anything. He went along the street eagerly; he wrote with all his might. There were twenty men in the Territory, at that day, any one of whom knew five times as much law as he. Other members of the bar were accustomed to speak contemptuously of Conger's legal knowledge. But Conger won more cases and made more money than any of them. If he did not know law in the widest sense, he did know it in the narrowest. He always knew the law that served his turn. When he drew an assignment for a client, no man could break it. And when he undertook a case, he was sure to find his opponent's weak point. He would pick flaws in pleas; he would postpone; he would browbeat witnesses; he would take exceptions to the rulings of the court in order to excite the sympathy of the jury; he would object to testimony on the other side, and try to get in irrelevant testimony on his own; he would abuse the opposing counsel, crying out, "The counsel on the other side lies like thunder, and he knows it!" By shrewdness, by an unwearying perseverance, by throwing his whole weight into his work, Conger made himself the most successful lawyer of his time in the Territory. And preserved his social position at the same time, for though he was not at all scrupulous, he managed to keep on the respectable side of the line which divides the lawyer from the shyster.

Mr. Conger had been Mr. Plausaby's counsel in one or two cases, and Charlton, knowing no other lawyer, sent for him. Mr. Conger had, with his characteristic quickness of perception, picked up the leading features of the case from the newspapers. He sat down on the bed in Charlton's cell with his brisk professional air, and came at once to business in his jerky-polite tone.

"Bad business, this, Mr. Charlton, but let us hope we'll pull through. We generally do pull through. Been in a good many tight places in my time. But it is necessary, first of all, that you trust me. The boat is in a bad way—you hail a pilot—he comes aboard. Now— hands off the helm—you sit down and let the pilot steer her through. You understand?" And Mr. Conger looked as though he might have smiled at his own illustration if he could have spared the time. But he couldn't. As for Albert, he only looked more dejected.

133

"Now," he proceeded, "let's get to business. In the first place, you must trust me with everything. You must tell me whether you took the warrant or not." And Mr. Conger paused and scrutinized his client closely.

Charlton said nothing, but his face gave evidence of a struggle.

"Well, well, Mr. Charlton," said the brisk man with the air of one who has gotten through the first and most disagreeable part of his business, and who now proposes to proceed immediately to the next matter on the docket. "Well, well, Mr. Charlton, you needn't say anything if the question is an unpleasant one. An experienced lawyer knows what silence means, of course," and there was just a trifle of self-gratulation in his voice. As for Albert, he winced, and seemed to be trying to make up his mind to speak.

"Now," and with this now the lawyer brought his white fat hand down upon his knee in an emphatic way, as one who says "nextly." "Now—there are several courses open to us. I asked you whether you took the warrant or not, because the line of defense that presents itself first is to follow the track of your suspicions, and fix the guilt on some one else if we can. I understand, however, that that course is closed to us?"

Charlton nodded his head.

"We might try to throw suspicion—only suspicion, you know—on the stage-driver or somebody else. Eh? Just enough to confuse the jury?"

Albert shook his head a little impatiently.

"Well, well, that's so—not the best line. The warrant was in your hands. You used it for pre-emption. That is very ugly, very. I don't think much of that line, under the circumstances. It might excite feeling against us. It is a very bad case. But we will pull through, I hope. We generally do. Give the case wholly into my hands. We'll postpone, I think. I shall have to make an affidavit that there are important witnesses absent, or something of the sort. But we'll have the case postponed. There's some popular feeling against you, and juries go as the newspapers do. Now, I see but one way, and that is to postpone until the feeling dies down. Then we can manage the papers a little and get up some sympathy for you. And there's no knowing what may happen. There's nothing like delay in a bad case. Wait long enough, and something is sure to turn up."

"But I don't want the case postponed," said Charlton decidedly.

"Very natural that you shouldn't like to wait. This is not a pleasant room. But it is better to wait a year or even two years in this jail than to go to prison for fifteen or twenty. Fifteen or twenty

134

years out of the life of a young man is about all there is worth the having."

Here Charlton shuddered, and Mr. Conger was pleased to see that his words took effect.

"You'd better make up your mind that the case is a bad one, and trust to my experience. When you're sick, trust the doctor. I think I can pull you through if you'll leave the matter to me."

"Mr. Conger," said Charlton, lifting up his pale face, twitching with nervousness, "I don't want to get free by playing tricks on a court of law. I know that fifteen or twenty years in prison would not leave me much worth living for, but I will not degrade myself by evading justice with delays and false affidavits. If you can do anything for me fairly and squarely, I should like to have it done."

"Scruples, eh?" asked Mr. Conger in surprise.

"Yes, scruples," said Albert Charlton, leaning his head on his hands with the air of one who has made a great exertion and has a feeling of exhaustion.

"Scruples, Mr. Charlton, are well enough when one is about to break the law. After one has been arrested, scruples are in the way."

"You have no right to presume that I have broken the law," said Charlton with something of his old fire.

"Well, Mr. Charlton, it will do no good for you to quarrel with your counsel. You have as good as confessed the crime yourself. I must insist that you leave the case in my hands, or I must throw it up. Take time to think about it. I'll send my partner over to get any suggestions from you about witnesses. The most we can do is to prove previous good character. That isn't worth anything where the evidence against the prisoner is so conclusive—as in your case. But it makes a show of doing something." And Mr. Conger was about leaving the cell when, as if a new thought had occurred to him, he turned back and sat down again and said: "There is one other course open to you. Perhaps it is the best, since you will not follow my plan. You can plead guilty, and trust to the clemency of the President. I think strong political influences could be brought to bear at Washington in favor of your pardon?"

Charlton shook his head, and the lawyer left him "to think the matter over," as he said. Then ensued the season of temptation. Why should he stand on a scruple? Why not get free? Here was a conscienceless attorney, ready to make any number of affidavits in regard to the absence of important witnesses; ready to fight the law by every technicality of the law. His imprisonment had already taught him how dear liberty was, and, within half an hour after Conger left him, a great change came over him. Why should he go to prison? What justice was there in his going to prison? Here he was, taking a long sentence to the penitentiary, while such men as Westcott and Conger were out. There could be no equity in such an arrangement. Whenever a man begins to seek equality of dispensation, he is in a fair way to debauch his conscience. And another line of thought influenced Charlton. The world needed his services. What advantage would there be in throwing away the chances of a lifetime on a punctilio? Why might he not let the serviceable lawyer do as he pleased? Conger was the keeper of his own conscience, and would not be either more or less honest at heart for what he did or did not do. All the kingdoms of the earth could not have tempted Charlton to serve himself by another man's perjury. But liberty on one hand and State's-prison on the other, was a dreadful alternative. And so, when the meek and studious man whom Conger used for a partner called on him, he answered all his questions, and offered no objection to the assumption of the quiet man that Mr. Conger would carry on the case in his own fashion.

Many a man is willing to be a martyr till he sees the stake and fagots.

CHAPTER XXIX

THE TRIAL

From the time that Charlton began to pettifog with his conscience, he began to lose peace of mind. His self-respect was impaired, and he became impatient, and chafed under his restraint. As the trial drew on, he was more than ever filled with questionings in regard to the course he should pursue. For conscience is like a pertinacious attorney. When a false decision is rendered, he is forever badgering the court with a bill of exceptions, with proposals to set aside, with motions for new trials, with applications for writs of appeal, with threats of a Higher Court, and even with contemptuous mutterings about impeachment. If Isa had not written to him, Albert might have regained his moral aplomb in some other way than he did—he might not. For human sympathy is Christ's own means of regenerating the earth. If you can not counsel, if you can not preach, if you can not get your timid lips to speak one word that will rebuke a man's sin, you can at least show the fellowship of your heart with his. There is a great moral tonic in human brotherhood. Worried, desperate, feeling forsaken of God and man, it is not strange that Charlton should shut his teeth together and defy his scruples. He would use any key he could to get out into the sunlight again. He quoted all those old, half-true, half-false adages about the lawlessness of necessity and so on. Then, weary of fencing with himself, he wished for strength to stand at peace again, as when he turned his back on the temptations of his rescuers in Metropolisville. But he had grown weak and nervous from confinement—prisons do not strengthen the moral power—and he had moreover given way to dreaming about liberty until he was like a homesick child, who aggravates his impatience by dwelling much on the delightfulness of the meeting with old friends, and by counting the slow-moving days that intervene.

But there came, just the day before the trial, a letter with the post-mark "Metropolisville" on it. That post-mark always excited a curious feeling in him. He remembered with what boyish pride he had taken possession of his office, and how he delighted to stamp the post-mark on the letters. The address of this letter was not in his mother's undecided penmanship—it was Isa Marlay's straightforward and yet graceful writing, and the very sight of it gave him comfort. The letter was simply a news letter, a vicarious letter from Isabel because Mrs. Plausaby did not feel well enough to write; this is what Isa said it was, and what she believed it to be, but Charlton knew that Isa's own friendly heart had planned it. And though it ran on about this and that unimportant matter of village intelligence, yet were its commonplace sentences about commonplace affairs like a fountain in the desert to the thirsty soul of the prisoner. I have read with fascination in an absurdly curious book that people of a very sensitive fiber can take a letter, the contents and writer of which are unknown, and by pressing it for a time against the forehead can see the writer and his surroundings. It took no spirit of divination in Charlton's case. The trim and graceful figure of Isa Marlay, in perfectly fitting calico frock, with her whole dress in that harmonious relation of parts for which she was so remarkable, came before him. He knew that by this time she must have some dried grasses in the vases, and some well-preserved autumn leaves around the picture-frames. The letter said nothing about his trial, but its tone gave him assurance of friendly sympathy, and of a faith in him that could not be shaken. Somehow, by some recalling of old associations, and by some subtle influence of human sympathy, it swept the fogs away from the soul of Charlton, and he began to see his duty and to feel an inspiration toward the right. I said that the letter did not mention the trial, but it did. For when Charlton had read it twice, he happened to turn it over, and found a postscript on the fourth page of the sheet. I wonder if the habit which most women have of reserving their very best for the postscript comes from the housekeeper's desire to have a good dessert. Here on the back Charlton read:

"P.S.—Mr. Gray, your Hoosier friend, called on me yesterday, and sent his regards. He told me how you refused to escape. I know you well enough to feel sure that you would not do anything mean or unmanly. I pray that God will sustain you on your trial, and make your innocence appear. I am sure you are innocent, though I can not understand it. Providence will overrule it all for good, I believe."

Something in the simple-hearted faith of Isabel did him a world of good. He was in the open hall of the jail when he read it, and he walked about the prison, feeling strong enough now to cope with temptation. That very morning he had received a New Testament from a colporteur, and now, out of regard to Isa Marlay's faith, maybe—out of some deeper feeling, possibly—he read the story of the trial and condemnation of Jesus. In his combative days he had read it for the sake of noting the disagreements between the Evangelists in some of the details. But now he was in no mood for small criticism. Which is the shallower, indeed, the criticism that harps on disagreements in such narratives, or the pettifogging that strives to reconcile them, one can hardly tell. In Charlton's mood, in any deeply earnest mood, one sees the smallness of all disputes about sixth and ninth hours. Albert saw the profound essential unity of the narratives, he felt the stirring of the deep sublimity of the story, he felt the inspiration of the sublimest character in human history. Did he believe? Not in any orthodox sense. But do you think that the influence of the Christ is limited to them who hold right opinions about Him? If a man's heart be simple, he can not see Jesus in any light without getting good from Him. Charlton, unbeliever that he was, wet the pages with tears, tears of sympathy with the high self-sacrifice of Jesus, and tears of penitence for his own moral weakness, which stood rebuked before the Great Example.

And then came the devil, in the person of Mr. Conger. His face was full of hopefulness as he sat down in Charlton's cell and smote his fat white hand upon his knee and said "Now!" and looked expectantly at his client. He waited a moment in hope of rousing Charlton's curiosity.

"We've got them!" he said presently. "I told you we should pull through. Leave the whole matter to me."

"I am willing to leave anything to you but my conscience," said Albert.

"The devil take your conscience, Mr. Charlton. If you are guilty, and so awfully conscientious, plead guilty at once. If you propose to cheat the government out of some years of penal servitude, why, well and good. But you must have a devilish queer conscience, to be sure. If you talk in that way, I shall enter a plea of insanity and get you off whether you will or not. But you might at least hear me through before you talk about conscience. Perhaps even your conscience would not take offense at my plan, unless you consider yourself foreordained to go to penitentiary."

"Let's hear your plan, Mr. Conger," said Charlton, hoping there might be some way found by which he could escape.

Mr. Conger became bland again, resumed his cheerful and hopeful look, brought down his fat white hand upon his knee, looked up over his client's head, while he let his countenance blossom with the promise of his coming communication. He then proceeded to say with a cheerful chuckle that there was a flaw in the form of the indictment—the grand jury had blundered. He had told Charlton that something would certainly happen. And it had. Then Mr. Conger smote his knee again, and said "Now!" once more, and proceeded to say that his plan was to get the trial set late in the term, so that the grand jury should finish their work and be discharged before the case came on. Then he would have the indictment quashed.

He said this with so innocent and plausible a face that at first it did not seem very objectionable to Charlton.

"What would we gain by quashing the indictment, Mr. Conger?"

"Well, if the indictment were quashed on the ground of a defect in its substance, then the case falls. But this is only defective in form. Another grand jury can indict you again. Now if the District Attorney should be a little easy—and I think that, considering your age, and my influence with him, he would be—a new commitment might not issue perhaps before you could get out of reach of it. If you were committed again, then we gain time. Time is everything in a bad case. You could not be tried until the next term. When the next term comes, we could then see what could be done. Meantime you could get bail."

If Charlton had not been entirely clear-headed, or entirely in a mood to deal honestly with himself, he would have been persuaded to take this course.

"Let me ask you a question, Mr. Conger. If the case were delayed, and I still had nothing to present against the strong circumstantial evidence of the prosecution—if, in other words, delay should still leave us in our present position—would there be any chance for me to escape by a fair, stand-up trial?"

"Well, you see, Mr. Charlton, this is precisely a case in which we will not accept a pitched battle, if we can help it. After a while, when the prosecuting parties feel less bitter toward you, we might get some of the evidence mislaid, out of the way, or get some friend on the jury, or—well, we might manage somehow to dodge trial on the case as it stands. Experience is worth a great deal in these things."

"There are, then, two possibilities for me," said Charlton very quietly. "I can run away, or we may juggle the evidence or the jury. Am I right?"

"Or, we can go to prison?" said Conger, smiling.

"I will take the latter alternative," said Charlton.

"Then you owe it to me to plead guilty, and relieve me from responsibility. If you plead guilty, we can get a recommendation of mercy from the court."

"I owe it to myself not to plead guilty," said Charlton, speaking still gently, for his old imperious and self-confident manner had left him.

"Very well," said Mr. Conger, rising, "if you take your fate into your own hands in that way, I owe it to myself to withdraw from the case."

"Very well, Mr. Conger."

140

"Good-morning, Mr. Charlton!"

"Good-morning, Mr. Conger."

And with Mr. Conger's disappearance went Albert's last hope of escape. The battle had been fought, and lost—or won, as you look at it. Let us say won, for no man's case is desperate till he parts with manliness.

Charlton had the good fortune to secure a young lawyer of little experience but of much principle, who was utterly bewildered by the mystery of the case, and the apparently paradoxical scruples of his client, but who worked diligently and hopelessly for him. He saw the flaw in the indictment and pointed it out to Charlton, but told him that as it was merely a technical point he would gain nothing but time. Charlton preferred that there should be no delay, except what was necessary to give his counsel time to understand the case. In truth, there was little enough to understand. The defense had nothing left to do.

When Albert came into court he was pale from his confinement. He looked eagerly round the crowded room to see if he could find the support of friendly faces. There were just two. The Hoosier Poet sat on one of the benches, and by him sat Isa Marlay. True, Mr. Plausaby sat next to Miss Marlay, but Albert did not account him anything in his inventory of friends.

Isabel wondered how he would plead. She hoped that he did not mean to plead guilty, but the withdrawal of Conger from the case filled her with fear, and she had been informed by Mr. Plausaby that he could refuse to plead altogether, and it would be considered a plea of not guilty. She believed him innocent, but she had not had one word of assurance to that effect from him, and even her faith had been shaken a little by the innuendoes and suspicions of Mr. Plausaby.

Everybody looked at the prisoner. Presently the District Attorney moved that Albert Charlton be arraigned.

The Court instructed the clerk, who said, "Albert Charlton, come forward."

Albert here rose to his feet, and raised his right hand in token of his identity.

The District Attorney said, "This prisoner I have indicted by the grand jury."

"Shall we waive the reading of the indictment?" asked Charlton's counsel.

"No," said Albert, "let it be read," and he listened intently while the clerk read it.

"Albert Charlton, you have heard the charge. What say you: Guilty, or, Not guilty?" Even the rattling and unmeaning voice in

141

which the clerk was accustomed to go through with his perfunctory performances took on some solemnity.

There was dead silence for a moment. Isa Marlay's heart stopped beating, and the Poet from Posey County opened his mouth with eager anxiety. When Charlton spoke, it was in a full, solemn voice, with deliberation and emphasis.

"NOT GUILTY!"

"Thank God!" whispered Isa.

The Poet shut his mouth and heaved a sigh of relief.

The counsel for the defense was electrified. Up to that moment he had believed that his client was guilty. But there was so much of solemn truthfulness in the voice that he could not resist its influence.

As for the trial itself, which came off two days later, that was a dull enough affair. It was easy to prove that Albert had expressed all sorts of bitter feelings toward Mr. Westcott; that he was anxious to leave; that he had every motive for wishing to pre-empt before Westcott did; that the land-warrant numbered so-and-so—it is of no use being accurate here, they were accurate enough in court—had been posted in Red Owl on a certain day; that a gentleman who rode with the driver saw him receive the mail at Red Owl, and saw it delivered at Metropolisville; that Charlton pre-empted his claim—the S.E. qr. of the N.E. qr., and the N. 1/2 of the S.E. qr. of Section 32, T. so-and-so, R. such-and-such—with this identical land-warrant, as the records of the land-office showed beyond a doubt.

Against all this counsel for defense had nothing whatever to offer. Nothing but evidence of previous good character, nothing but to urge that there still remained perhaps the shadow of a doubt. No testimony to show from whom Charlton had received the warrant, not the first particle of rebutting evidence. The District Attorney only made a little perfunctory speech on the evils brought upon business by theft in the post-office. The exertions of Charlton's counsel amounted to nothing; the jury found him guilty without deliberation.

The judge sentenced him with much solemn admonition. It was a grievous thing for one so young to commit such a crime. He warned Albert that he must not regard any consideration as a justification for such an offense. He had betrayed his trust and been guilty of theft. The judge expressed his regret that the sentence was so severe. It was a sad thing to send a young man of education and refinement to be the companion of criminals for so many years. But the law recognized the difference between a theft by a sworn and trusted officer and an ordinary larceny. He hoped that Albert would profit by this terrible experience, and that he would so improve the time of his confinement with meditation, that what would remain to him of life when he should come out of the walls of his prison might be spent as an honorable and law-abiding citizen. He sentenced him to serve the shortest term permitted by the statute, namely, ten years.

The first deep snow of the winter was falling outside the court-house, and as Charlton stood in the prisoners' box, he could hear the jingling of sleigh-bells, the sounds that usher in the happy social life of winter in these northern latitudes. He heard the judge, and he listened to the sleigh-bells as a man who dreams—the world was so far off from him now—ten weary years, and the load of a great disgrace measured the gulf fixed between him and all human joy and sympathy. And when, a few minutes afterward, the jail-lock clicked behind him, it seemed to have shut out life. For burial alive is no fable. Many a man has heard the closing of the vault as Albert Charlton did.

CHAPTER XXX

THE PENITENTIARY

It was a cold morning. The snow had fallen heavily the day before, and the Stillwater stage was on runners. The four horses rushed round the street-corners with eagerness as the driver, at a little past five o'clock in the morning, moved about collecting passengers. From the up-town hotels he drove in the light of the gas-lamps to the jail where the deputy marshal, with his prisoner securely handcuffed, took his seat and wrapped the robes about them both. Then at the down-town hotels they took on other passengers. The Fuller House was the last call of all.

"Haven't you a back-seat?" The passenger partly spoke and partly coughed out his inquiry.

"The back-seat is occupied by ladies," said the agent, "you will have to take the front one."

"It will kill me to ride backwards," whined the desponding voice of Minorkey, but as there were only two vacant seats he had no choice. He put his daughter in the middle while he took the end of the seat and resigned himself to death by retrograde motion. Miss Helen Minorkey was thus placed exactly vis-à-vis with her old lover Albert Charlton, but in the darkness of six o'clock on a winter's morning in Minnesota, she could not know it. The gentleman who occupied the other end of the seat recognized Mr. Minorkey, and was by him introduced to his daughter. That lady could not wholly resist the exhilaration of such a stage-ride over snowy roads, only half-broken as yet, where there was imminent peril of upsetting at every turn. And so she and her new acquaintance talked of many things, while Charlton could not but recall his ride, a short half-year ago, on a front-seat, over the green prairies—had prairies ever been greener?—and under the blue sky, and in bright sunshine—had the sun ever shone so brightly?—with this same quiet-voiced, thoughtful Helen Minorkey. How soon had sunshine turned to darkness! How suddenly had the blossoming spring-time changed to dreariest winter!

It is really delightful, this riding through the snow and darkness in a covered coach on runners, this battling with difficulties. There is a spice of adventure in it quite pleasant if you don't happen to be the driver and have the battle to manage. To be a well-muffled passenger, responsible for nothing, not even for your own neck, is thoroughly delightful—provided always that you are

144

not the passenger in handcuffs going to prison for ten years. To the passenger in handcuffs, whose good name has been destroyed, whose liberty is gone, whose future is to be made of weary days of monotonous drudgery and dreary nights in a damp cell, whose friends have deserted him, who is an outlaw to society—to the passenger in handcuffs this dashing and whirling toward a living entombment has no exhilaration. Charlton was glad of the darkness, but dreaded the dawn when there must come a recognition. In a whisper he begged the deputy marshal to pull his cap down over his eyes and to adjust his woolen comforter over his nose, not so much to avoid the cold wind as to escape the cold eyes of Helen Minorkey. Then he hid his handcuffs under the buffalo robes so that, if possible, he might escape recognition.

The gentleman alongside Miss Minorkey asked if she had read the account of the trial of young Charlton, the post-office robber.

"Part of it," said Miss Minorkey. "I don't read trials much."

"For my part," said the gentleman, "I think the court was very merciful. I should have given him the longest term known to the law. He ought to go for twenty-one years. We all of us have to risk money in the mails, and if thieves in the post-office are not punished severely, there is no security."

There spoke Commerce! Money is worth so much more than humanity, you know!

Miss Minorkey said that she knew something of the case. It was very curious, indeed. Young Charlton was disposed to be honest, but he was high-tempered. The taking of the warrant was an act of resentment, she thought. He had had two or three quarrels or fights, she believed, with the man from whom he took the warrant. He was a very talented young man, but very ungovernable in his feelings.

The gentleman said that that was the very reason why he should have gone for a longer time. A talented and self-conceited man of that sort was dangerous out of prison. As it was, he would learn all the roguery of the penitentiary, you know, and then we should none of us be safe from him.

There spoke the Spirit of the Law! Keep us safe, O Lord! whoever may go to the devil!

In reply to questions from her companion, Miss Minorkey told the story of Albert's conflict with Westcott—she stated the case with all the coolness of a dispassionate observer.

There was no sign—Albert listened for it—of the slightest sympathy for or against him in the matter. Then the story of little Katy was told as one might tell something that had happened a hundred years ago, without any personal sympathy. It was simply a

145

curious story, an interesting adventure with which to beguile a weary hour of stage riding in the darkness. It would have gratified Albert to have been able to detect the vibration of a painful memory or a pitying emotion, but Helen did not suffer her placidity to be ruffled by disturbing emotion. The conversation drifted to other subjects presently through Mr. Minorkey's sudden recollection that the drowning excitement at Metropolisville had brought on a sudden attack of his complaint, he had been seized with a pain just under his ribs. It ran up to the point of the right shoulder, and he thought he should die, etc., etc., etc. Nothing saved him but putting his feet into hot water, etc., etc., etc.

The gray dawn came on, and Charlton was presently able to trace the lineaments of the well-known countenance. He was not able to recognize it again without a profound emotion, an emotion that he could not have analyzed. Her face was unchanged, there was not the varying of a line in the placid, healthy, thoughtful expression to indicate any deepening of her nature through suffering. Charlton's face had changed so that she would not have recognized him readily had it been less concealed. And by so much as his countenance had changed and hers remained fixed, had he drifted away from her. Albert felt this. However painful his emotion was, as he sat there casting furtive glances at Helen's face, there was no regret that all relation between them was broken forever. He was not sorry for the meeting. He needed such a meeting to measure the parallax of his progress and her stagnation. He needed this impression of Helen to obliterate the memory of the row-boat. She was no longer to remain in his mind associated with the blessed memory of little Kate. Hereafter he could think of Katy in the row-boat—the other figure was a dim unreality which might have come to mean something, but which never did mean anything to him.

I wonder who keeps the tavern at Cypher's Lake now? In those old days it was not a very reputable place; it was said that many a man had there been fleeced at poker. The stage did not reach it on this snowy morning until ten o'clock. The driver stopped to water, the hospitable landlord, whose familiar nickname was "Bun," having provided a pail and cut a hole through the ice of the lake for the accommodation of the drivers. Water for beasts—gentlemen could meantime find something less "beastly" than ice-water in the little low-ceiled bar-room on the other side of the road. The deputy-marshal wanted to stretch his legs a little, and so, trusting partly to his knowledge of Charlton's character, partly to handcuffs, and partly to his convenient revolver, he leaped out of the coach and stepped to the door of the bar-room just to straighten his legs, you know, and get a glass of whisky "straight" at the same

146

time. In getting into the coach again he chanced to throw back the buffalo-robe and thus exposed Charlton's handcuffs. Helen glanced at them, and then at Albert's face. She shivered a little, and grew red. There was no alternative but to ride thus face to face with Charlton for six miles. She tried to feel herself an injured person, but something in the self-possessed face of Albert—his comforter had dropped down now—awed her, and she affected to be sick, leaning her head on her father's shoulder and surprising that gentleman beyond measure. Helen had never shown so much emotion of any sort in her life before, certainly never so much confusion and shame. And that in spite of her reasoning that it was not she but Albert who should be embarrassed. But the two seemed to have changed places. Charlton was as cold and immovable as Helen Minorkey ever had been; she trembled and shuddered, even with her eyes shut, to think that his eyes were on her—looking her through and through—measuring all the petty meanness and shallowness of her soul. She complained of the cold and wrapped her blanket shawl about her face and pretended to be asleep, but the shameful nakedness of her spirit seemed not a whit less visible to the cool, indifferent eyes that she felt must be still looking at her from under the shadow of that cap-front. What a relief it was at last to get into the warm parlor of the hotel! But still she shivered when she thought of her ride.

It is one thing to go into a warm parlor of a hotel, to order your room, your fire, your dinner, your bed. It is quite another to drive up under the high, rough limestone outer wall of a prison—a wall on which moss and creeper refuse to grow—to be led handcuffed into a little office, to have your credentials for ten years of servitude presented to the warden, to have your name, age, nativity, hight, complexion, weight, and distinguishing marks carefully booked, to have your hair cropped to half the length of a prize-fighter's, to lay aside the dress which you have chosen and which seems half your individuality, and put on a suit of cheerless penitentiary uniform—to cease to be a man with a place among men, and to become simply a convict. This is not nearly so agreeable as living at the hotel. Did Helen Minorkey ever think of the difference?

There is little to be told of the life in the penitentiary. It is very uniform. To eat prison fare without even the decency of a knife or fork—you might kill a guard or a fellow-rogue with a fork—to sleep in a narrow, rough cell on a hard bed, to have your cell unlocked and to be marched out under guard in the morning, to go in a row of prisoners to wash your face, to go in a procession to a frugal breakfast served on tin plates in a dining-room mustier than a cellar, to be marched to your work, to be watched by a guard while you work, to know that the guard has a loaded revolver and is ready to draw it on slight provocation, to march to meals under awe of the revolver, to march to bed while the man with the revolver walks behind you, to be locked in and barred in and double-locked in again, to have a piece of candle that will burn two hours, to burn it out and lie down in the darkness—to go through one such day and know that you have to endure three thousand six hundred and fifty-two days like it—that is about all. The life of a blind horse in a treadmill is varied and cheerful in comparison.

Oh! yes, there is Sunday. I forgot the Sunday. On Sundays you don't have to work in the shops. You have the blessed privilege of sitting alone in your bare cell all the day, except the hour of service. You can think about the outside world and wish you were out. You can read, if you can get anything interesting to read. You can count your term over, think of a broken life, of the friends of other days who feel disgraced at mention of your name, get into the dumps, and cry a little if you feel like it. Only crying doesn't seem to do much good. Such is the blessedness of the holy Sabbath in prison!

But Charlton did not let himself pine for liberty. He was busy with plans for reconstructing his life. What he would have had it, it could not be. You try to build a house, and it is shaken down about your ears by an earthquake. Your material is, much of it, broken. You can never make it what you would. But the brave heart, failing to do what it would, does what it can. Charlton, who had hated the law as a profession, was now enamored of it. He thought rightly that there is no calling that offers nobler opportunities to a man who has a moral fiber able to bear the strain. When he should have finished his term, he would be thirty-one, and would be precluded from marriage by his disgrace. He could live on a crust, if necessary, and be the champion of the oppressed. What pleasure he would have in beating Conger some day! So he arranged to borrow law-books, and faithfully used his two hours of candle in studying. He calculated that in ten years—if he should survive ten years of life in a cell—he could lay a foundation for eminence in legal learning. Thus he made vinegar-barrels all day, and read Coke on Littleton on Blackstone at night. His money received from the contractor for over-work, he used to buy law-books.

Sometimes he hoped for a pardon, but there was only one contingency that was likely to bring it about. And he could not wish for that. Unless, indeed, the prison-officers should seek a pardon for him. From the beginning they had held him in great favor. When he had been six months in prison, his character was so well established with the guards that no one ever thought of watching him or of inspecting his work.

He felt a great desire to have something done in a philanthropic way for the prisoners, but when the acting chaplain, Mr. White, preached to them, he always rebelled. Mr. White had been a steamboat captain, a sheriff, and divers other things, and was now a zealous missionary among the Stillwater lumbermen. The State could not afford to give more than three hundred dollars a year for religious and moral instruction at this time, and so the several pastors in the city served alternately, three months apiece. Mr. White was a man who delivered his exhortations with the same sort of vehemence that Captain White had used in giving orders to his deck-hands in a storm; he arrested souls much as Sheriff White had arrested criminals. To Albert's infidelity he gave no quarter. Charlton despised the chaplain's lack of learning until he came to admire his sincerity and wonder at his success. For the gracefulest and eruditest orator that ever held forth to genteelest congregation, could not have touched the prisoners by his highest flight of rhetoric as did the earnest, fiery Captain-Sheriff-Chaplain White, who moved aggressively on the wickedness of his felonious audience.

When Mr. White's three months had expired, there came another pastor, as different from him as possible. Mr. Lurton was as gentle as his predecessor had been boisterous. There was a strong substratum of manly courage and will, but the whole was overlaid with a sweetness wholly feminine and seraphic. His religion was the Twenty-third Psalm. His face showed no trace of conflict. He had accepted the creed which he had inherited without a question, and, finding in it abundant sources of happiness, of moral development, and spiritual consolation, he thence concluded it true. He had never doubted. It is a question whether his devout soul would not have found peace and edification in any set of opinions to which he had happened to be born. You have seen one or two such men in your life. Their presence is a benison. Albert felt more peaceful while Mr. Lurton stood without the grating of his cell, and Lurton seemed to leave a benediction behind him. He did not talk in pious cant, he did not display his piety, and he never addressed a sinner down an inclined plane. He was too humble for that. But the settled, the unruffled, the unruffleable peacefulness and trustfulness of his soul seemed to Charlton, whose life had been stormier within than without, nothing less than sublime. The inmates of the prison could not appreciate this delicate quality in the young minister. Lurton had never lived near enough to their life for them to understand him or for him to understand them. He considered them all, on general principles, as lost sinners, bad, like himself, by nature, who had

149

superadded outward transgressions and the crime of rejecting Christ to their original guilt and corruption as members of the human family.

Charlton watched Lurton with intense interest, listened to all he had to say, responded to the influence of his fine quality, but found his own doubts yet unanswered and indeed untouched. The minister, on his part, took a lively interest in the remarkable young man, and often endeavored to remove his doubts by the well-knit logical arguments he had learned in the schools.

"Mr. Lurton," said Charlton impatiently one day, "were you ever troubled with doubt?"

"I do not remember that I ever seriously entertained a doubt in regard to religious truth in my life," said Lurton, after reflection.

"Then you know no more about my doubts than a blind man knows of your sense of sight." But after a pause, he added, laughing: "Nevertheless, I would give away my doubtativeness any day in exchange for your peacefulness." Charlton did not know, nor did Lurton, that the natures which have never been driven into the wilderness to be buffeted of the devil are not the deepest.

It was during Mr. Lurton's time as chaplain that Charlton began to receive presents of little ornamental articles, intended to make his cell more cheerful. These things were sent to him by the hands of the chaplain, and the latter was forbidden to tell the name of the giver. Books and pictures, and even little pots with flowers in them, came to him in the early spring. He fancied they might come from some unknown friend, who had only heard of him through the chaplain, and he was prone to resent the charity. He received the articles with thankful lips, but asked in his heart, "Is it not enough to be a convict, without being pitied as such?" Why anybody in Stillwater should send him such things, he did not know. The gifts were not expensive, but every one gave evidence of a refined taste.

At last there came one—a simple cross, cut in paper, intended to be hung up as a transparency before the window—that in some unaccountable way suggested old associations. Charlton had never seen anything of the kind, but he had the feeling of one who half-recognizes a handwriting. The pattern had a delicacy about it approaching to daintiness, an expression of taste and feeling which he seemed to have known, as when one sees a face that is familiar, but which one can not "place," as we say. Charlton could not place the memory excited by this transparency, but for a moment he felt sure that it must be from some one whom he knew. But who could there be near enough to him to send flower-pots and framed pictures without great expense? There was no one in Stillwater whom he had ever seen, unless indeed Helen Minorkey were there yet, and he had long since given up all expectation and all desire of receiving any attention at her hands. Besides, the associations excited by the transparency, the taste evinced in making it, the sentiment which it expressed, were not of Helen Minorkey. It was on Thursday that he hung it against the light of his window. It was not until Sunday evening, as he lay listlessly watching his scanty allowance of daylight grow dimmer, that he became sure of the hand that he had detected in the workmanship of the piece. He got up quickly and looked at it more closely and said: "It must be Isa Marlay!" And he lay down again, saying: "Well, it can never be quite dark in a man's life when he has one friend." And then, as the light grew more and more faint, he said: "Why did not I see it before? Good orthodox Isa wants to preach to me. She means to say that I should receive light through the cross."

And he lay awake far into the night, trying to divine how the flower-pots and pictures and all the rest could have been sent all the way from Metropolisville. It was not till long afterward that he discovered the alliance between Whisky Jim and Isabel, and how Jim had gotten a friend on the Stillwater route to help him get them through. But Charlton wrote Isa, and told her how he had detected her, and thanked her cordially, asking her why she concealed her hand. She replied kindly, but with little allusion to the gifts, and they came no more. When Isa had been discovered she could not bring herself to continue the presents. Save that now and then there came something from his mother, in which Isa's taste and skill were evident, he received nothing more from her, except an occasional friendly letter. He appreciated her delicacy too late, and regretted that he had written about the cross at all.

One Sunday, Mr. Lurton, going his round, found Charlton reading the New Testament.

"Mr. Lurton, what a sublime prayer the Pater-noster is!" exclaimed Charlton.

"Yes;" said Lurton, "it expresses so fully the only two feelings that can bring us to God—a sense of guilt and a sense of dependence."

"What I admired in the prayer was not that, but the unselfishness that puts God and the world first, and asks bread, forgiveness, and guidance last. It seems to me, Mr. Lurton, that all men are not brought to God by the same feelings. Don't you think that a man may be drawn toward God by self-sacrifice—that a brave, heroic act, in its very nature, brings us nearer to God? It seems to me that whatever the rule may be, there are exceptions; that God draws some men to Himself by a sense of sympathy; that He makes a sudden draft on their moral nature—not more than they can bear,

151

but all they can bear—and that in doing right under difficulties the soul finds itself directed toward God—opened on the side on which God sits."

Mr. Lurton shook his head, and protested, in his gentle and earnest way, against this doctrine of man's ability to do anything good before conversion.

"But, Mr. Lurton," urged Albert, "I have known a man to make a great sacrifice, and to find himself drawn by that very sacrifice into a great admiring of Christ's sacrifice, into a great desire to call God his father, and into a seeking for the forgiveness and favor that would make him in some sense a child of God. Did you never know such a case?"

"Never. I do not think that genuine conversions come in that way. A sense of righteousness can not prepare a man for salvation—only a sense of sin—a believing that all our righteousness is filthy rags. Still, I wouldn't discourage you from studying the Bible in any way. You will come round right after a while, and then you will find that to be saved, a man must abhor every so-called good thing that he ever did."

"Yes," said Charlton, who had grown more modest in his trials, "I am sure there is some truth in the old doctrine as you state it. But is not a man better and more open to divine grace, for resisting a temptation to vice?"

Mr. Lurton hesitated. He remembered that he had read, in very sound writers, arguments to prove that there could be no such thing as good works before conversion, and Mr. Lurton was too humble to set his judgment against the great doctors'. Besides, he was not sure that Albert's questions might not force him into that dangerous heresy attributed to Arminius, that good works may be the impulsive cause by which God is moved to give His grace to the unconverted.

"Do you think that a man can really do good without God's help?" asked Mr. Lurton.

"I don't think man ever tries to do right in humility and sincerity without some help from God," answered Albert, whose mode of thinking about God was fast changing for the better. "I think God goes out a long, long way to meet the first motions of a good purpose in a man's heart. The parable of the Prodigal Son only half-tells it. The parable breaks down with a truth too great for human analogies. I don't know but that He acts in the beginning of the purpose. I am getting to be a Calvinist—in fact, on some points, I out-Calvin Calvin. Is not God's help in the good purposes of every man?"

Mr. Lurton shook his head with a gentle gravity, and changed

152

the subject by saying, "I am going to Metropolisville next week to attend a meeting. Can I do anything for you?"

"Go and see my mother," said Charlton, with emotion. "She is sick, and will never get well, I fear. Tell her I am cheerful. And—Mr. Lurton—do you pray with her. I do not believe anything, except by fits and starts; but one of your prayers would do my mother good. If she could be half as peaceful as you are, I should be happy."

Lurton walked away down the gallery from Albert's cell, and descended the steps that led to the dining-room, and was let out of the locked and barred door into the vestibule, and out of that into the yard, and thence out through other locks into the free air of out-doors. Then he took a long breath, for the sight of prison doors and locks and bars and grates and gates and guards oppressed even his peaceful soul. And walking along the sandy road that led by the margin of Lake St. Croix toward the town, he recalled Charlton's last remark. And as he meditatively tossed out of the path with his boot the pieces of pine-bark which in this lumbering country lie about everywhere, he rejoiced that Charlton had learned to appreciate the value of Christian peace, and he offered a silent prayer that Albert might one day obtain the same serenity as himself. For nothing was further from the young minister's mind than the thought that any of his good qualities were natural. He considered himself a miracle of grace upon all sides. As if natural qualities were not also of God's grace!

CHAPTER XXXI

MR. LURTON

It was a warm Sunday in the early spring, one week after Mr. Lurton's conversation with Charlton, that the latter sat in his cell feeling the spring he could not see. His prison had never been so much a prison. To perceive this balminess creeping through the narrow, high window—a mere orifice through a thick wall—and making itself feebly felt as it fell athwart the damp chilliness of the cell, to perceive thus faintly the breath of spring, and not to be able to see the pregnant tree-buds bursting with the coming greenness of the summer, and not to be able to catch the sound of the first twittering of the returning sparrows and the hopeful chattering of the swallows, made Albert feel indeed that he and life had parted.

Mr. Lurton's three months as chaplain had expired, and there had come in his stead Mr. Canton, who wore a very stiff white necktie and a very straight-breasted long-tailed coat. Nothing is so great a bar to human sympathies as a clerical dress, and Mr. Canton had diligently fixed a great gulf between himself and his fellow-men. Charlton's old, bitter aggressiveness, which had well-nigh died out under the sweet influences of Lurton's peacefulness, came back now, and he mentally pronounced the new chaplain a clerical humbug and an ecclesiastical fop, and all such mild paradoxical epithets as he was capable of forming. The hour of service was ended, and Charlton was in his cell again, standing under the high window, trying to absorb some of the influences of the balmy air that reached him in such niggardly quantities. He was hungering for a sight of the woods, which he knew must be so vital at this season. He had only the geraniums and the moss-rose that Isa, had sent, and they were worse than nothing, for they pined in this twilight of the cell, and seemed to him smitten, like himself, with a living death. He almost stopped, his heart's beating in his effort to hear the voices of the birds, and at last he caught the harsh cawing of the crows for a moment, and then that died away, and he could hear no sound but the voice of the clergyman in long clothes talking perfunctorily to O'Neill, the wife-murderer, in the next cell. He knew that his turn would come next, and it did. He listened in silence and with much impatience to such a moral lecture as seemed to Mr. Canton befitting a criminal.

Mr. Canton then handed him a letter, and seeing that it was addressed in the friendly hand of Lurton, he took it to the window and opened it, and read:

154

"DEAR MR. CHARLTON:

"I should have come to see you and told you about my trip to Metropolisville, but I am obliged to go out of town again. I send this by Mr. Canton, and also a request to the warden to pass this and your answer without the customary inspection of contents. I saw your mother and your stepfather and your friend Miss Marlay. Your mother is failing very fast, and I do not think it would be a kindness for me to conceal from you my belief that she can not live many weeks. I talked with her and prayed with her as you requested, but she seems to have some intolerable mental burden. Miss Marlay is evidently a great comfort to her, and, indeed, I never saw a more faithful person than she in my life, or a more remarkable exemplification of the beauty of a Christian life. She takes every burden off your mother except that unseen load which seems to trouble her spirit, and she believes absolutely in your innocence. By the way, why did you never explain to her or to me or to any of your friends the real history of the case? There must at least have been extenuating circumstances, and we might be able to help you.

"But I am writing about everything except what I want to say, or rather to ask, for I tremble to ask it. Are you interested in any way other than as a friend in Miss Isabel Marlay? You will guess why I ask the question. Since I met her I have thought of her a great deal, and I may add to you that I have anxiously sought divine guidance in a matter likely to affect the usefulness of my whole life. I will not take a single step in the direction in which my heart has been so suddenly drawn, if you have any prior claim, or even the remotest hope of establishing one in some more favorable time. Far be it from me to add a straw to the heavy burden you have had to bear. I expect to be in Metropolisville again soon, and will see your mother once more. Please answer me with frankness, and believe me,
"Always your friend,
J.H. LURTON."

The intelligence regarding his mother's health was not new to Albert, for Isa had told him fully of her state. It would be difficult to describe the feeling of mingled pain and pleasure with which he read Lurton's confession of his sudden love for Isabel. Nothing since his imprisonment had so humbled Charlton as the recollection of the mistake he had made in his estimate of Helen Minorkey, and his preference for her over Isa. He had lain on his cot sometimes and dreamed of what might have been if he had escaped prison and had chosen Isabel instead of Helen. He had pictured to himself the

155

content he might have had with such a woman for a wife. But then the thought of his disgrace—a disgrace he could not share with a wife—always dissipated the beautiful vision and made the hard reality of what was, seem tenfold harder for the ravishing beauty of what might have been.

And now the vision of the might-have-been came back to him more clearly than ever, and he sat a long while with his head leaning on his hand. Then the struggle passed, and he lighted his little ration of candle, and wrote:

"SUNDAY EVENING.
"REV. J.H. LURTON:

"DEAR SIR: You have acted very honorably in writing me as you have, and I admire you now more than ever. You fulfill my ideal of a Christian. I never had the slightest claim or the slightest purpose to establish any claim on Isabel Marlay, for I was so blinded by self-conceit, that I did not appreciate her until it was too late. And now! What have I to offer to any woman? The love of a convicted felon! A name tarnished forever! No! I shall never share that with Isa Marlay. She is, indeed, the best and most sensible of women. She is the only woman worthy of such a man as you. You are the only man I ever saw good enough for Isabel. I love you both. God bless you!

"Very respectfully and gratefully, CHARLTON."

Mr. Lurton had staid during the meeting of the ecclesiastical body—Presbytery, Consociation, Convention, Conference, or what not, it does not matter—at Squire Plausaby's Albert had written about him, and Isa, as soon as she heard that he was to attend, had prompted Plausaby to enter a request with the committee on the entertainment of delegates for the assignment of Mr. Lurton to him as guest. His peacefulness had not, as Albert and Isabel hoped, soothed the troubled spirit of Mrs. Plausaby, who was in a great terror at thought of death. The skillful surgeon probes before he tries to heal, and Mr. Lurton set himself to find the cause of all this irritation in the mind of this weak woman. Sometimes she seemed inclined to tell him all, but it always happened that when she was just ready to speak, the placid face of Plausaby glided in at the door. On the appearance of her husband, Mrs. Plausaby would cease speaking. It took Lurton a long time to discover that Plausaby was the cause of this restraint. He did discover it, however, and endeavored to get an interview when there was no one present but

156

Isabel. In trying to do this, he made a fresh discovery—that Plausaby was standing guard over his wife, and that the restraint he exercised was intentional. The mystery of the thing fascinated him; and the impression that it had something to do with Charlton, and the yet stronger motive of a sense of duty to the afflicted woman, made him resolute in his determination to penetrate it. Not more so, however, than was Isabel, who endeavored in every way to secure an uninterrupted interview for Mr. Lurton, but endeavored in vain.

Lurton was thus placed in favorable circumstances to see Miss Marlay's qualities. Her graceful figure in her simple tasteful, and perfectly fitting frock, her rhythmical movement, her rare voice, all touched exquisitely so sensitive a nature as Lurton's. But more than that was he moved by her diligent management of the household, her unwearying patience with the querulous and feeble-minded sick woman, her tact and common-sense, and especially the entire truthfulness of her character.

Mr. Lurton made excuse to himself for another trip to Metropolisville that he had business in Perritaut. It was business that might have waited; it was business that would have waited, but for his desire to talk further with Mrs. Plausaby, and for his other desire to see and talk with Isabel Marlay again. For, if he should fail of her, where would he ever find one so well suited to help the usefulness of his life? Happy is he whose heart and duty go together! And now that Lurton had found that Charlton had no first right to Isabel, his worst fear had departed.

Even in his palpitating excitement about Isa, he was the true minister, and gave his first thought to the spiritual wants of the afflicted woman whom he regarded as providentially thrown upon his care. He was so fortunate as to find Plausaby absent at Perritaut. But how anxiously did he wait for the time when he could see the sick woman! Even Isa almost lost her patience with Mrs. Plausaby's characteristic desire to be fixed up to receive company. She must have her hair brushed and her bed "tidied," and, when Isabel thought she had concluded everything, Mrs. Plausaby would insist that all should be undone again and fixed m some other way. Part of this came from her old habitual vanity, aggravated by the querulous childishness produced by sickness, and part from a desire to postpone as long as she could an interview which she greatly dreaded. Isa knew that time was of the greatest value, and so, when she had complied with the twentieth unreasonable exaction of the sick woman, and was just about to hear the twenty-first, she suddenly opened the door of Mrs. Plausaby's sickroom and invited Mr. Lurton to enter.

157

And then began again the old battle—the hardest conflict of all—the battle with vacillation. To contend with a stubborn will is a simple problem of force against force. But to contend with a weak and vacillating will is fighting the air.

Mrs. Plausaby said she had something to say to Mr. Lurton. But—dear me—she was so annoyed! The room was not fit for a stranger to see. She must look like a ghost. There was something that worried her. She was afraid she was going to die, and she had—did Mr. Lurton think she would die? Didn't he think she might get well?

Mr. Lurton had to say that, in his opinion, she could never get well, and that if there was anything on her mind, she would better tell it.

Didn't Isa think she could get well? She didn't want to die. But then Katy was dead. Would she go to heaven if she died? Did Mr. Lurton think that if she had done wrong, she ought to confess it? Couldn't she be forgiven without that? Wouldn't he pray for her unless she confessed it? He ought not to be so hard on her. Would God be hard on her if she did not tell it all? Oh! she was so miserable!

Mr. Lurton told her that sometimes people committed sin by refusing to confess because their confession had something to do with other people. Was her confession necessary to remove blame from others?

"Oh!" cried the sick woman, "Albert has told you all about it! Oh, dear! now I shall have more trouble! Why didn't he wait till I'm dead? Isn't it enough to have Katy drowned and Albert gone to that awful place and this trouble? Oh! I wish I was dead! But then—maybe God would be hard on me! Do you think God would be hard on a woman that did wrong if she was told to do it? And if she was told to do it by her own husband? And if she had to do it to save her husband from some awful trouble? There, I nearly told it. Won't that do?"

And she turned her head over and affected to be asleep. Mr. Lurton was now more eager than ever that the whole truth should come out, since he began to see how important Mrs. Plausaby's communication might be. Beneath all his sweetness, as I have said, there was much manly firmness, and he now drew his chair near to the bedside, and began in a tone full of solemnity, with that sort of quiet resoluteness that a surgeon has when he decides to use the knife. He was the more resolute because he knew that if Plausaby returned before the confession should be made, there would be no possibility of getting it.

158

"Mrs. Plausaby," he said, but she affected to be asleep. "Mrs. Plausaby, suppose a woman, by doing wrong when her husband asks it, brings a great calamity on the only child she has, locking him in prison and destroying his good name—"

"Oh, dear, dear! stop! You'll kill me! I knew Albert had told you. Now I won't say a word about it. If he has told it, there is no use of my saying anything," and she covered up her face in a stubborn, childish petulance.

CHAPTER XXXII

A CONFESSION

Mr. Lurton wisely left the room. Mrs. Plausaby's fears of death soon awakened again, and she begged Isa to ask Mr. Lurton to come back. Like most feeble people, she had a superstitious veneration for ecclesiastical authority, and now in her weakened condition she had readily got a vague notion that Lurton held her salvation in his hands, and could modify the conditions if he would.

"You aren't a Catholic are you, Mr. Lurton?"

"No, I am not at all a Catholic."

"Well, then, what makes you want me to confess?"

"Because you are adding to your first sin a greater one in wronging your son by not confessing."

"Who told you that? Did Albert?"

"No, you told me as much as that, yourself."

"Did I? Why, then I might as well tell you all. But why won't that do?"

"Because, that much would not get Albert out of prison. You don't want to leave him in penitentiary when you're gone, do you?"

"Oh, dear! I can't tell. Plausaby won't let me. Maybe I might tell Isa."

"That will do just as well. Tell Miss Marlay." And Lurton walked out on the piazza.

For half an hour Mrs. Plausaby talked to Isa and told her nothing. She would come face to face with the confession, and then say that she could not tell it, that Plausaby would do something awful if he knew she had said so much.

At last Isabel was tired out with this method, and was desperate at the thought that Plausaby would return while yet the confession was incomplete. So she determined to force Mrs. Plausaby to speak.

"Now, Mrs. Plausaby," she said, "what did Uncle Plausaby say to you that made you take that letter of Smith Westcott's?"

"I didn't take it, did I? How do you know? I didn't say so?"

"You have told me part, and if you tell me the rest I will keep it secret for the present. If you don't tell me, I shall tell Uncle Plausaby what I know, and tell him that he must tell me the rest."

"You wouldn't do that, Isabel? You couldn't do that. Don't do that," begged the sick woman.

"Then tell me the truth," she said with sternness. "What made you take that land-warrant—for you know you did, and you must not tell me a lie when you're just going to die and go before God."

"There now, Isa, I knew you would hate me. That's the reason why I can't tell it. Everybody has been looking so hateful at me ever since I took the letter, I mean ever since—Oh! I didn't mean anything bad, but you know I have to do what Plausaby tells me I must do. He's such a man! And then he was in trouble. There was some old trouble from Pennsylvania. The men came on here, and made him pay money, all the money he could get, to keep them from having him put in prison. I don't know what it was all about, you know, I never could understand about business, but here was Albert bothering him about money to pay for a warrant, and these men taking all his money, and here was a trial about some lots that he sold to that fat man with curly hair, and he was afraid Albert would swear against him about that and about the county-seat, and so he wanted to get him away. And there was an awful bother about Katy and Westcott at the same time. And I wanted a changeable silk dress, and he couldn't get it for me because all his money was going to the men from Pennsylvania. But—I can't tell you any more. I'm afraid Plausaby might come. You won't tell, and you won't hate me, Isa, dear—now, will you? You used to be good to me, but you won't be good to me any more!"

"I'll always love you if you only tell me the rest."

"No, I can't. For you see Plausaby didn't mean any harm, and I didn't mean any harm. Plausaby wanted Albert to go away so they couldn't get Albert to swear against him. It was all Albert's fault, you know—he had such notions. But he was a good boy, and I can't sleep at night now for seeing him behind a kind of a grate, and he seems to be pointing his finger at me and saying, 'You put me in here.' But I didn't. That's one of his notions. It was Plausaby made me do it. And he didn't mean any harm. He said Westcott would soon be his son-in-law. He had helped Westcott to get the claim anyhow. It was only borrowing a little from his own son-in-law. He said that I must get the letter out of the office when Albert did not see me. He said it would be a big letter, with 'Red Owl' stamped on it, and that it would be in Mr. Westcott's box. And he said I must take the land-warrant out and burn up the letter and the envelope. And then he said I must give the land-warrant to Albert the next day, and tell him that a man that came up in the stage brought it from Plausaby. And he said he'd get another and bring it home with him and give it to Westcott, and make it all right. And that would keep him out of prison, and get Albert away so he couldn't swear against him in the suit with the fat man, and then he would be able to get me the changeable silk that I wanted so much. But things went all wrong

161

with him since, and I never got the changeable silk, and he said he would keep Albert out of penitentiary and he didn't, and Albert told me I musn't tell anybody about taking it myself, for he couldn't bear to have me go to prison. Now, won't that do? But don't you tell Plausaby. He looks at me sometimes so awfully. Oh, dear! if I could have told that before, maybe I wouldn't have died. It's been killing me all the time. Oh, dear! dear! I wish I was dead, if only I was sure I wouldn't go to the bad place."

Isa now acquainted Lurton briefly with the nature of Mrs. Plausaby's statement, and Lurton knelt by her bedside and turned it into a very solemn and penitent confession to God, and very trustfully prayed for forgiveness, and—call it the contagion of Lurton's own faith, if you will—at any rate, the dying woman felt a sense of relief that the story was told, and a sense of trust and more peace than she had ever known in her life. Lurton had led her feeble feet into a place of rest. And he found joy in thinking that, though his ministry to rude lumbermen and hardened convicts might be fruitless, he had at least some gifts that made him a source of strength and consolation to the weak, the remorseful, the bereaved, and the dying. He stepped out of the door of the sick-chamber, and there, right before him, was Plausaby, his smooth face making a vain endeavor to keep its hold upon itself. But Lurton saw at once that Plausaby had heard the prayer in which he had framed Mrs. Plausaby's confession to Isa into a solemn and specific confession to God. I know no sight more pitiful than that of a man who has worn his face as a mask, when at last the mask is broken and the agony behind reveals itself. Lurton had a great deal of presence of mind, and if he did not think much of the official and priestly authority of a minister, he had a prophet's sense of his moral authority. He looked calmly and steadily into the eyes of Plausaby, Esq., and the hollow sham, who had been unshaken till now, quailed; counterfeit serenity could not hold its head up and look the real in the face. Had Lurton been abashed or nervous or self-conscious, Plausaby might have assumed an air of indignation at the minister's meddling. But Lurton had nothing but a serene sense of having been divinely aided in the performance of a delicate and difficult duty. He reached out his hand and greeted Plausaby quietly and courteously and yet solemnly. Isabel, for her part, perceiving that Plausaby had overheard, did not care to conceal the indignation she felt. Poor Plausaby, Esq.! the disguise was torn, and he could no longer hide himself. He sat down and wiped the perspiration from his forehead, and essayed to speak, as before, to the minister, of his anxiety about his poor, dear wife, but he could not do it. Exert himself as he would, the color would not return to his pallid lips, and he had a shameful consciousness that the old serene and complacent look, when he tried it, was sadly crossed by rigid lines of hard anxiety and shame. The mask was indeed broken—the nakedness and villainy could no more be hidden! And even the voice, faithful and obedient hitherto, always holding the same rhythmical pace, had suddenly broken rein, galloping up and down the gamut in a husky jangling.

"Mr. Plausaby, let us walk," said Lurton, not affecting in the least to ignore Plausaby's agitation. They walked in silence through the village out to the prairie. Plausaby, habitually a sham, tried, to recover his ground. He said something about his wife's not being quite sane, and was going to caution Lurton about believing anything Mrs. Plausaby might say.

"Mr. Plausaby," said Lurton, "is it not better to repent of your sins and make restitution, than to hide them?"

Plausaby cleared his throat and wiped the perspiration from his brow, but he could not trust his voice to say anything.

It was vain to appeal to Plausaby to repent. He had saturated himself in falsehood from the beginning. Perhaps, after all, the saturation had began several generations back, and unhappy Plausaby, born to an inheritance of falsehood, was to be pitied as well as blamed. He was even now planning to extort from his vacillating wife a written statement that should contradict any confession of hers to Isa and Lurton.

Fly swiftly, pen! For Isa Marlay knew the stake in this game, and she did not mean that any chance of securing Charlton's release should be neglected. She knew nothing of legal forms, but she could write a straight-out statement after a woman's fashion. So she wrote a paper which read as follows:

"I do not expect to live long, and I solemnly confess that I took the land-warrant from Smith Westcott's letter, for which my son Albert Charlton is now unjustly imprisoned in the penitentiary, and I did it without the knowledge of Albert, and at the instigation of Thomas Plausaby, my husband."

This paper Isa read to Mrs. Plausaby, and that lady, after much vacillation, signed it with a feeble hand. Then Isabel wrote her own name as a witness. But she wanted another witness. At this moment Mrs. Ferret came in, having an instinctive feeling that a second visit from Lurton boded something worth finding out. Isa took her into Mrs. Plausaby's room and told her to witness this paper.

"Well," said pertinacious Mrs. Ferret, "I'll have to know what is in it, won't I?"

"No, you only want to know that this is Mrs. Plausaby's

signature," and Isa placed her fingers over the paper in such a way that Mrs. Ferret could not read it.

"Did you sign this, Mrs. Plausaby?"

The sick woman said she did.

"Do you know what is in it?"

"Yes, but—but it's a secret."

"Did you sign it of your own free will, or did Mr. Plausaby make you?"

"Mr. Plausaby! Oh! don't tell him about it. He'll make such an awful fuss! But it's true."

Thus satisfied that it was not a case of domestic despotism, Mrs. Ferret wrote her peculiar signature, and made a private mark besides.

And later in the evening Mrs. Plausaby asked Isa to send word to that nice-looking young woman that Albert loved so much. She said she supposed he must feel bad about her. She wanted Isa to tell her all about it. "But not till I'm dead," she added. "Do you think people know what people say about them after they're dead? And, Isa, when I'm laid out let me wear my blue merino dress, and do my hair up nice, and put a bunch of roses in my hand. I wish Plausaby had got that changeable silk. It would have been better than the blue merino. But you know best. Only don't forget to tell Albert's girl that he did not do it. But explain it all so she won't think I'm a—that I did it a-purpose, you know. I didn't mean to. What makes you look at me that way? Oh, dear! Isa, you won't ever love me any more!"

But Isa quieted her by putting her arms around her neck in a way that made the poor woman cry, and say, "That's just the way Katy used to do. When I die, Katy'll love me all the same. Won't she? Katy always did love a body so." Perhaps she felt that Isabel's love was not like Katy's. For pity is not love, and even Mrs. Plausaby could hardly avoid distinguishing the spontaneous affection of Katy from this demonstration of Isa's, which must have cost her some exertion.

CHAPTER XXXIII

DEATH

Mrs. Plausaby grew more feeble. Her remorse and her feeling of the dire necessity for confessing her sin had sustained her hitherto. But now her duty was done, she had no longer any mental stimulant. In spite of Isa's devoted and ingenious kindness, the sensitive vanity of Mrs. Plausaby detected in every motion evidence that Isa thought of her as a thief. She somehow got a notion that Mrs. Ferret knew all about it also, and from her and Mr. Lurton she half-hid her face in the cover. Lurton, perceiving that his mission to Mrs. Plausaby was ended, returned home, intending to see Isabel when circumstances should be more favorable. But the Ferret kept sniffing round after a secret which she knew lay not far away. Mrs. Plausaby having suddenly grown worse, Isa determined to sit by her during the night, but Plausaby strenuously objected that this was unnecessary. The poor woman secretly besought Isa not to leave her alone with Plausaby, and Isabel positively refused to go away from her bedside. For the first time Mr. Plausaby spoke harshly to Isa, and for the first time Isabel treated him with a savage neglect. A housekeeper's authority is generally supreme in the house, and Isa had gradually come to be the housekeeper. She sat stubbornly by the dying woman during the whole night.

Mr. Plausaby had his course distinctly marked out. In the morning he watched anxiously for the arrival of his trusted lawyer, Mr. Conger. The property which he had married with his wife, and which she had derived from Albert's father, had all been made over to her again to save it from Plausaby's rather eager creditors. He had spent the preceding day at Perritaut, whither Mr. Conger had gone to appear in a case as counsel for Plausaby, for the county-seat had recently returned to its old abode. Mr. Plausaby intended to have his wife make some kind of a will that would give him control of the property and yet keep it under shelter. By what legal fencing this was to be done nobody knows, but it has been often surmised that Mrs. Plausaby was to leave it to her husband in trust for the Metropolisville University. Mr. Plausaby had already acquired experience in the management of trust funds, in the matter of Isa's patrimony, and it would not be a feat beyond his ability for him to own his wife's bequest and not to own it at the same time. This was the easier that territorial codes are generally made for the benefit of absconding debtors. He had made many fair promises about a final

165

transfer of this property to Albert and Katy when they should both be of age, but all that was now forgotten, as it was intended to be.

Mr. Plausaby was nervous. His easy, self-possessed manner had departed, and that impenetrable coat of mail being now broken up, he shuddered whenever the honest, indignant eyes of Miss Marlay looked at him. He longed for the presence of the bustling, energetic man of law, to keep him in countenance.

When the lawyer came, he and Plausaby were closeted for half an hour. Then Plausaby, Esq., took a walk, and the attorney requested an interview with Isabel. She came in, stiff, cold, and self-possessed.

"Miss Marlay," said the lawyer, smiling a little as became a man asking a favor from a lady, and yet looking out at Isa in a penetrating way from beneath shadowing eyebrows, "will you have the goodness to tell me the nature of the paper that Mrs. Plausaby signed yesterday?"

"Did Mrs. Plausaby sign a paper yesterday?" asked Isabel diplomatically.

"I have information to that effect. Will you tell me whether that paper was of the nature of a will or deed or—in short, what was its character?"

"I will not tell you anything about it. It is Mrs. Plausaby's secret. I suppose you get your information from Mrs. Ferret. If she chooses to tell you the contents, she may."

"You are a little sharp, Miss Marlay. I understand that Mrs. Ferret does not know the contents of that paper. As the confidential legal adviser of Mr. Plausaby and of Mrs. Plausaby, I have a right to ask what the contents of that paper were."

"As the confidential legal adviser—" Isa stopped and stammered. She was about to retort that as confidential legal adviser to Mrs. Plausaby he might ask that lady herself, but she was afraid of his doing that very thing; so she stopped short and, because she was confused, grew a little angry, and told Mr. Conger that he had no right to ask any questions, and then got up and disdainfully walked out of the room. And the lawyer, left alone, meditated that women had a way, when they were likely to be defeated, of getting angry, or pretending to get angry. And you never could do anything with a woman when she was angry. Or, as Conger framed it in his mind, a mad dog was easier to handle than a mad woman.

As the paper signed the day before could not have been legally executed, Plausaby and his lawyer guessed very readily that it probably did not relate to property. The next step was an easy one to the client if not to the lawyer. It must relate to the crime—it was a

166

solution of the mystery. Plausaby knew well enough that a confession had been made to Lurton, but he had not suspected that Isabel would go so far as to put it into writing. The best that could be done was to have Conger frame a counter-declaration that her confession had been signed under a misapprehension—had been obtained by coercion, over-persuasion, and so forth. Plausaby knew that his wife would sign anything if he could present the matter to her alone. But, to get rid of Isabel Marlay?

A very coward now in the presence of Isa, he sent the lawyer ahead, while he followed close behind.

"Miss Marlay," said Mr. Conger, smiling blandly but speaking with decision, "it will be necessary for me to speak to Mrs. Plausaby for a few minutes alone."

It is curious what an effect a tone of authority has. Isa rose and would have gone out, but Mrs. Plausaby said, "Don't leave me, don't leave me, Isa; they want to arrest me, I believe."

Seeing her advantage, Miss Marlay said, "Mrs. Plausaby wishes me to stay."

It was in vain that the lawyer insisted. It was in vain that Mr. Plausaby stepped forward and told Mrs. Plausaby to ask Isabel to leave the room a minute. The sick woman only drew the cover over her eyes and held fast to Isabel's hand and said: "No, no, don't go— Isa, don't go."

"I will not go till you ask me," said Isa.

At last, however, Plausaby pushed himself close to his wife and said something in her ear. She turned pale, and when he asked if she wished Isabel to go she nodded her head.

"But I won't go at all now," said Isa stubbornly, "unless you will go out of the room first. Then, if Mrs. Plausaby tells me that she wishes to see you and this gentleman without my presence, I shall go."

Mr. Plausaby drew the attorney into one corner of the room for consultation. Nothing but the desperateness of his position and the energetic advice of Mr. Conger could have induced him to take the course which he now decided upon, for force was not a common resort with him, and with all his faults, he was a man of much kindness of heart.

"Isa," he said, "I have always been a father to you. Now you are conspiring against me. If you do not go out, I shall be under the painful necessity of putting you out, gently, but by main strength." The old smile was on his face. He seized her arms, and Isa, seeing how useless resistance would be, and how much harm excitement might do to the patient, rose to go. But at that moment, happening to look toward the bed, she cried out, "Mrs. Plausaby is dying!" and

167

she would not have been a woman if she could have helped adding, "See what you have done, now!"

There was nothing Mr. Plausaby wanted less than that his wife should die at this inconvenient moment. He ran off for the doctor, but poor, weak Mrs. Plausaby was past signing wills or recantations.

The next day she died.

And Isa wrote to Albert:

"METROPOLISVILLE, May 17th, 1857
"MR. CHARLTON:

"DEAR SIR: Your poor mother died yesterday. She suffered little in body, and her mind was much more peaceful after her last interview with Mr. Lurton, which resulted in her making a frank statement of the circumstances of the land-warrant affair. She afterward had it written down, and signed it, that it might be used to set you free. She also asked me to tell Miss Minorkey, and I shall send her a letter by this mail. I am so glad that your innocence is to be proved at last. I have said nothing about the statement your mother made to any one except Miss Minorkey, because I am unwilling to use it without your consent. You have great reason to be grateful to Mr. Lurton. Ho has shown himself your friend, indeed. I think him an excellent man. He comforted your mother a great deal. You had better let me put the writing your mother left, into his hands. I am sure he will secure your freedom for you.

"Your mother died without any will, and all the property is yours. Your father earned it, and I am glad it goes back to its rightful owner. You will not agree with me, but I believe in a Providence, now, more than ever.

"Truly your friend, ISABEL MARLAY."

The intelligence of his mother's death caused Albert a real sorrow. And yet he could hardly regret it. Charlton was not conscious of anything but a filial grief. But the feeling of relief modified his sorrow.

The letter filled him with a hope of pardon. Now that he could without danger to his mother seek release from an unjust incarceration, he became eager to get out. The possibility of release made every hour of confinement intolerable.

He experienced a certain dissatisfaction with Isa's letter. She had always since his imprisonment taken pains to write cordially. He had been "Dear Mr. Charlton," or "My Dear Mr. Charlton," and sometimes even "My Dear Friend." Isa was anxious that he should not feel any coldness in her letters. Now that he was about to be released and would naturally feel grateful to her, the case was very different. But Albert could not see why she should be so friendly with him when she had every reason to believe him guilty, and now that she knew him innocent should freeze him with a stranger-like coolness. He had resolved to care nothing for her, and yet here he was anxious for some sign that she cared for him.

Albert wrote in reply:

"HOUSE OF BONDAGE, May 20th, 1857

"MY DEAR, GOOD FRIEND: The death of my mother has given me a great deal of sorrow, though it did not surprise me. I remember now how many times of late years I have given her needless trouble. For whatever mistakes her personal peculiarities led her into, she was certainly a most affectionate mother. I can now see, and the reflection causes me much bitterness, that I might have been more thoughtful of her happiness without compromising my opinions. How much trouble my self-conceit must have given her! Your rebuke on this subject has been very fresh in mind since I heard of her death. And I am feeling lonely, too. Mother and Katy have gone, and more distant relatives will not care to know an outlaw.

"If I had not seen Mr. Lurton, I should not have known how much I owe to your faithful friendship. I doubt not God will reward you. For I, too, am coming to believe in a Providence!

"Sometimes I think this prison has done me good. There may be some truth, after all, in that acrid saying of Mrs. Ferret's about 'sanctified affliction,' though she does know how to make even truth hateful. I haven't learned to believe as you and Mr. Lurton would have me, and yet I have learned not to believe so much in my own infallibility. I have been a high-church skeptic—I thought as much of my own infallibility as poor O'Neill in the next cell does of the Pope's. And I suppose I shall always have a good deal of aggressiveness and uneasiness and all that about me—I am the same restless man yet, full of projects and of opinions. I can not be Lurton—I almost wish I could. But I have learned some things. I am yet very unsettled in my opinions about Christ—sometimes he seems to be a human manifestation of God, and at other times, when my skeptical habit comes back, he seems only the divinest of men. But I believe in him with all my heart, and may be I shall settle down on some definite opinion after a while. I had a mind to ask Lurton to baptize me the other day, but I feared he wouldn't do it.

169

All the faith I could profess would be that I believe enough in Christ to wish to be his disciple. I know Mr. Lurton wouldn't think that enough. But I don't believe Jesus himself would refuse me. His immediate followers couldn't have believed much more than that at first. And I don't think you would refuse me baptism if you were a minister.

"Mr. Lurton has kindly offered to endeavor to secure my release, and he will call on you for that paper. I hope you'll like Lurton as well as he does you. You are the only woman in the world good enough for him, and he is the only man fit for you. And if it should ever come to pass that you and he should be happy together, I shall be too glad to envy either of you.

"Do shield the memory of my mother. You know how little she was to blame. I can not bear that people should talk about her unkindly. She had such a dread of censure. I think that is what killed her. I am sorry you wrote to Helen Minorkey. I could not now share my disgrace with a wife; and if I could marry, she is one of the last I should ever think of seeking. I do not even care to have her think well of me.

"As to the property, I am greatly perplexed. Plausaby owned it once rightfully and legally, and there are innocent creditors who trusted him on the strength of his possession of it. I wish I did not have the responsibility of deciding what I ought to do.

"I have written a long letter. I would write a great deal more if I thought I could ever express the gratitude I feel to you. But I am going to be always,

"Your grateful and faithful friend,
"ALBERT CHARLTON"

This letter set Isabel's mind in a whirl of emotions. She sincerely admired Lurton, but she had never thought of him as a lover. Albert's gratitude and praises would have made her happy, but his confidence that she would marry Lurton vexed her. And yet the thought that Lurton might love her made it hard to keep from dreaming of a new future, brighter than any she had supposed possible to her.

170

CHAPTER XXXIV

MR. LURTON'S COURTSHIP

After the death of Mrs. Plausaby, Isa had broken at once with her uncle-in-law, treating him with a wholesome contempt whenever she found opportunity. She had made many apologies for Plausaby's previous offenses—this was too much even for her ingenious charity. For want of a better boarding-place, she had taken up her abode at Mrs. Ferret's, and had opened a little summer-school in the village schoolhouse. She began immediately to devise means for securing Charlton's release. Her first step was to write to Lurton, but she had hardly mailed the letter, when she received Albert's, announcing that Lurton was coming to see her; and almost immediately that gentleman himself appeared again in Metropolisville. He spent the evening in devising with Isa proper means of laying the evidences of Charlton's innocence before the President in a way calculated to secure his pardon. Lurton knew two Representatives and one Senator, and he had hope of being able to interest them in the case. He would go to Washington himself. Isa thought his offer very generous, and found in her heart a great admiration for him. Lurton, on his part, regarded Isabel with more and more wonder and affection. He told her at last, in a sweet and sincere humility, the burden of his heart. He confessed his love with a frankness that was very winning, and with a gentle deference that revealed him to her the man he was—affectionate, sincere, and unselfish.

If Isabel had been impulsive, she would have accepted at once, under the influence of his presence. But she had a wise, practical way of taking time to think. She endeavored to eliminate entirely the element of feeling, and see the offer in the light in which it would show itself after present circumstances had passed. For if Lurton had been a crafty man, he could not have offered himself at a moment more opportune. Isa was now homeless, and without a future. If you ask me why, then, she did not accept Lurton without hesitation, I answer that I can no more explain this than I can explain all the other paradoxes of love that I see every day. Was it that he was too perfect? Is it easier for a woman to love a man than a model? People are not apt to be enamored of monotony, even of a monotony of goodness. Was it, then, that Isa would have liked a man whose soul had been a battle-field, rather than one in whom goodness and faith had had an easy time? Did she feel more sympathy for one who had fought and overcome, like Charlton, than for one who had never known a great struggle? Perhaps I have not touched at all upon the real reason for Isa's hesitation. But she certainly did hesitate. She found it quite impossible to analyze her own feelings in the matter. The more she thought about it, the more hopeless her confusion became.

It is one of the unhappy results produced by some works of religious biography, that people who copy methods, are prone to copy those not adapted to their own peculiarities. Isabel, in her extremity of indecision, remembered that some saint of the latter part of the last century, whose biography she had read in a Sunday-school library-book, was wont, when undecided in weighty matters, to write down all the reasons, pro and con, and cipher out a conclusion by striking a logical balance. It naturally occurred to Isa that what so good and wise a person had found beneficial, might also prove an assistance to her. So she wrote down the following:

"REASONS IN FAVOR

"1. Mr. Lurton is one of the most excellent men in the world. I have a very great respect and a sincere regard for him. If he were my husband, I do not think I should ever find anything to prevent me loving him.

"2. The life of a minister's wife would open to me opportunities to do good. I could at least encourage and sustain him.

"3. It seems to be providential that the offer should come at this time, when I am free from all obligations that would interfere with it, and when I seem to have no other prospect.

"REASONS AGAINST

"1."—

But here she stopped. There was nothing to be said against Mr. Lurton, or against her accepting the offered happiness. She would then lead the quiet, peaceful life of a village-minister's wife who does her duty to her husband and her neighbors. Her generous nature found pleasure in the thought of all the employments that would fill her heart and hands. How much better it would be to have a home, and to have others to work for, than to lead the life of a stranger in other people's houses! And then she blushed, and was happy at the thought that there would be children's voices in the house—little stockings in the basket on a Saturday night—there would be the tender cares of the mother. How much better was such a life than a lonely one!

It was not until some hours of such thinking—of more castle-building than the sober-spirited girl had done in her whole life before—that she became painfully conscious that in all this dreaming of her future as the friend of the parishioners and the house-mother, Lurton himself was a figure in the background of her thoughts. He did not excite any enthusiasm in her heart. She took up her paper; she read over again the reasons why she ought to love Lurton. But though reason may chain Love and forbid his going wrong, all the logic in the world can not make him go where he will not. She had always acted as a most rational creature. Now, for the first time, she could not make her heart go where she would. Love in such cases seems held back by intuition, by a logic so high and fine that its terms can not be stated. Love has a balance-sheet in which all is invisible except the totals. I have noticed that practical and matter-of-fact women are most of all likely to be exacting and ideal in love affairs. Or, is it that this high and ideal way of looking at such affairs is only another manifestation of practical wisdom?

Certain it is, that though Isa found it impossible to set down a single reason for not loving so good a man with the utmost fervor, she found it equally impossible to love him with any fervor at all.

Then she fell to pitying Lurton. She could make him happy and help him to be useful, and she thought she ought to do it. But could she love Lurton better than she could have loved any other man? Now, I know that most marriages are not contracted on this basis. It is not given to every one to receive this saying. I am quite aware that preaching on this subject would be vain. Comparatively few people can live in this atmosphere. But noblesse oblige—noblesse does more than oblige—and Isa Marlay, against all her habits of acting on practical expediency, could not bring herself to marry the excellent Lurton without a consciousness of moral descending, while she could not give herself a single satisfactory reason for feeling so.

It went hard with Lurton. He had been so sure of divine approval and guidance that he had not counted failure possible. But at such times the man of trustful and serene habit has a great advantage. He took the great disappointment as a needed spiritual discipline; he shouldered this load as he had carried all smaller burdens, and went on his way without a murmur.

Having resigned his Stillwater pastorate from a conviction that his ministry among red-shirted lumbermen was not a great success, he armed himself with letters from the warden of the prison and the other ministers who had served as chaplains, and, above all, with Mrs. Plausaby's written confession, and set out for Washington. He easily secured money to defray the expense of the journey from Plausaby, who held some funds belonging to his wife's estate, and who yielded to a very gentle pressure from Lurton, knowing how entirely he was in Lurton's power.

It is proper to say here that Albert's scrupulous conscience was never troubled about the settlement of his mother's estate. Plausaby had an old will, which bequeathed all to him in fee simple. He presented it for probate, and would have succeeded, doubtless, in saving something by acute juggling with his creditors, but that he heard ominous whispers of the real solution of the mystery—where they came from he could not tell. Thinking that Isa was planning his arrest, he suddenly left the country. He turned up afterwards as president of a Nevada silver-mine company, which did a large business in stocks but a small one in dividends; and I have a vague impression that he had something to do with the building of the Union Pacific Railroad. His creditors made short work of the property left by Mrs. Plausaby.

CHAPTER XXXV

UNBARRED

Lurton was gone six weeks. His letters to Charlton were not very hopeful. People are slow to believe that a court has made a mistake.

I who write and you who read get over six weeks as smoothly as we do over six days. But six weeks in grim, gray, yellowish, unplastered, limestone walls, that are so thick and so high and so rough that they are always looking at you in suspicion and with stern threat of resistance! Six weeks in May and June and July inside such walls, where there is scarcely a blade of grass, hardly a cool breeze, not even the song of a bird! A great yard so cursed that the little brown wrens refuse to bless it with their feet! The sound of machinery and of the hammers of unwilling toilers, but no mellow voice of robin or chatter of gossiping chimney-swallows! To Albert they were six weeks of alternate hope and fear, and of heart-sickness.

The contractor gave a Fourth-of-July dinner to the convicts. Strawberries and cream instead of salt pork and potatoes. The guards went out and left the men alone, and Charlton was called on for a speech. But all eulogies of liberty died on his lips. He could only talk platitudes, and he could not say anything with satisfaction to himself. He tossed wakefully all that night, and was so worn when morning came that he debated whether he should not ask to be put on the sick-list.

He was marched to the water-tank as usual, then to breakfast, but he could not eat. When the men were ordered to work, one of the guards said:

"Charlton, the warden wants to see you in the office."

Out through the vestibule of the main building Charlton passed with a heart full of hope, alternating with fear of a great disappointment. He noticed, as he passed, how heavy the bolts and bars were, and wondered if these two doors would ever shut him in again. He walked across the yard, feeble and faint, and then ascended the long flight of steps which went up to the office-door. For the office was so arranged as to open out of the prison and in it also, and was so adapted to the uneven ground as to be on top of the prison-wail. Panting with excitement, the convict Charlton stopped at the top of this flight of steps while the guard gave an alarm, and the door was opened from the office side. Albert could not refrain from looking back over the prison-yard; he saw every familiar object again, he passed through the door, and stood face to face with the firm and kindly Warden Proctor. He saw Lurton standing by the warden, he was painfully alive to everything; the clerks had ceased to write, and were looking at him expectantly.

"Well, Charlton," said the warden kindly, "I am glad to tell you that you are pardoned. I never was so glad at any man's release."

"Pardoned?" Charlton had dreamed so much of liberty, that now that liberty had come he was incredulous. "I am very much obliged to you, Mr. Proctor," he gasped.

"That is the man to thank," said the warden, pointing to Lurton. But Charlton couldn't thank Lurton yet. He took his hand and looked in his face and then turned away. He wanted to thank everybody—the guard who conducted him out, and the clerk who was recording the precious pardon in one of the great books; but, in truth, he could say hardly anything.

"Come, Charlton, you'll find a change of clothes in the back-room. Can't let you carry those off!" said the warden.

Charlton put off the gray with eagerness. Clothes made all the difference. When once he was dressed like other men, his freedom became a reality. Then he told everybody good-by, the warden first, and then the guard, and then the clerks, and he got permission to go back into the prison, as a visitor, now, and tell the prisoners farewell.

Then Lurton locked arms with him, and Charlton could hardly keep back the tears. Human fellowship is so precious to a cleansed leper! And as they walked away down the sandy street by the shore of Lake St. Croix, Charlton was trying all the while to remember that walls and grates and bars and bolts and locks and iron gates and armed guards shut him in no longer. It seemed so strange that here was come a day in which he did not have to put up a regular stint of eight vinegar-barrels, with the privilege of doing one or two more, if he could, for pay. He ate some breakfast with Lurton. For freedom is a great tonic, and satisfied hopes help digestion. It is a little prosy to say so, but Lurton's buttered toast and coffee was more palatable than the prison fare. And Lurton's face was more cheerful than the dark visage of Ball, the burglar, which always confronted Charlton at the breakfast-table.

Charlton was impatient to go back to Metropolisville. For what, he could hardly say. There was no home there for him, but then he wanted to go somewhere. It seemed so fine to be able to go anywhere. Bidding Lurton a grateful adieu, he hurried to St. Paul. The next morning he was booked for Metropolisville, and climbed up to the driver's seat with the eager impatience of a boy.

"Wal, stranger, go tew thunder! I'm glad to see you're able to be aout. You've ben confined t' the haouse fer some time, I guess, p'r'aps?"

It was the voice of Whisky Jim that thus greeted Albert. If there was a half-sneer in the words, there was nothing but cordial friendliness in the tone and the grasp of the hand. The Superior Being was so delighted that he could only express his emotions by giving his leaders several extra slashes with his whip, and by putting on a speed that threatened to upset the coach.

"Well, Jim, what's the news?" said Charlton gayly.

"Nooze? Let me see. Nothin' much. Your father-in-law, or step-father, or whatever you call him, concluded to cut and run las' week. I s'pose he calkilated that your gittin' out might leave a vacancy fer him. Thought he might hev to turn in and do the rest of the ten years' job that's owin' to Uncle Sam on that land-warrant, eh? I guess you won't find no money left. 'Twixt him and the creditors and the lawyers and the jedges, they a'n't nary cent to carry."

"When did you hear from Gray?"

"Oh! he was up to Metropolisville las' week. He a'n't so much of a singster as he wus. Gone to spekilatin'. The St. Paul and Big Gun River Valley Railroad is a-goin' t' his taown."

Here the Superior Being stopped talking, and waited to be questioned.

"Laid off a town, then, has he?"

"Couldn' help hisself. The Wanosia and Dakota Crossing Road makes a junction there, and his claim and yourn has doubled in valoo two or three times."

"But I suppose mine has been sold under mortgage?"

"Under mortgage? Not much. Some of your friends jest sejested to Plausaby he'd better pay two debts of yourn. And he did. He paid Westcott fer the land-warrant, and he paid Minorkey's mortgage. Ole chap didn't want to be paid. Cutthroat mortgage, you know. He'd heerd of the railroad junction. Jemeny! they's five hundred people livin' on Gray's claim, and yourn's alongside."

"What does he call his town?" asked Albert.

Jim brought his whip down smartly on a lazy wheel-horse, crying out:

"Puck-a-chee! Seechy-do!" (Get out—bad.) For, like most of his class in Minnesota at that day, the Superior Being had enriched his vocabulary of slang with divers Indian words. Then, after a pause, he said: "What does he call it? I believe it's 'Charlton,' or suthin' of that sort. Git up!"

Albert was disposed at first to think the name a compliment to

177

himself, but the more he thought of it, the more clear it became to him that the worshipful heart of the Poet had meant to preserve the memory of Katy, over whom he had tried in vain to stand guard.

Of course part of Driver Jim's information was not new to Albert, but much of it was, for the Poet's letters had not been explicit in regard to the increased value of the property, and Charlton had concluded the claim would go out of his hands anyhow, and had ceased to take any further interest in it.

When at last he saw again the familiar balloon-frame houses of Metropolisville, he grew anxious. How would people receive him? Albert had always taken more pains to express his opinions dogmatically than to make friends; and now that the odium of crime attached itself to him, he felt pretty sure that Metropolisville, where there was neither mother nor Katy, would offer him no cordial welcome. His heart turned toward Isa with more warmth than he could have desired, but he feared that any friendship he might show to Isabel would compromise her. A young woman's standing is not helped by the friendship of a post-office thief, he reflected. He could not leave Metropolisville without seeing the best friend he had; he could not see her without doing her harm. He was thoroughly vexed that he had rashly put himself in so awkward a dilemma; he almost wished himself back in St. Paul.

At last the Superior Being roused his horses into a final dash, and came rushing up to the door of the "City Hotel" with his usual flourish.

"Hooray! Howdy! I know'd you'd be along to-night," cried the Poet. "You see a feller went through our town—I've laid off a town you know—called it Charlton, arter her you know—they wuz a feller come along yisterday as said as he'd come on from Washin'ton City weth Preacher Lurton, and he'd heern him tell as how as Ole Buck— the President I mean—had ordered you let out. An' I'm that glad! Howdy! You look a leetle slim, but you'll look peart enough when we git you down to Charlton, and you see some of your ground wuth fifteen dollar a front foot! You didn' think I'd ever a gin up po'try long enough to sell lots. But you see the town wuz named arter her you know—a sorter moniment to a angel, a kind of po'try that'll keep her name from bein' forgot arter my varses is gone to nothin'. An' I'm a-layin' myself out to make that town nice and fit to be named arter her, you know. I didn't think I could ever stan' it to have so many neighbors a drivin' away all the game. But I'm a-gittin' used to it."

Charlton could see that the Inhabitant was greatly improved by his contact with the practical affairs of life and by human society. The old half-crazed look had departed from his eyes, and the over-sensitive nature had found a satisfaction in the standing which the founding of a town and his improved circumstances had brought him.

"Don't go in thar!" said Gray as Charlton was about to enter the room used as office and bar-room for the purpose of registering his name. "Don't go in thar!" and Gray pulled him back. "Let's go out to supper. That devilish Smith Wes'cott's in thar, drunk's he kin be, and raisin' perdition. They turned him off this week fer drinkin' too steady, and he's tryin' to make a finish of his money and Smith Wes'cott too."

Charlton and Gray sat down to supper at the long table where the Superior Being was already drinking his third cup of coffee. The exquisite privilege of doing as he pleased was a great stimulant to Charlton's appetite, and knives and forks were the greatest of luxuries.

"Seems to me," said Jim, as he sat and watched Albert, "seems to me you a'n't so finicky 'bout vittles as you was. Sheddin' some of yer idees, maybe."

"Yes, I think I am."

"Wal, you see you hed too thick a coat of idees to thrive. I guess a good curryin' a'n't done you no pertickeler hurt, but blamed ef it didn't seem mean to me at first. I've cussed about it over and over agin on every mile 'twixt here and St. Paul. But curryin's healthy. I wish some other folks as I know could git put through weth a curry-comb as would peel the hull hide offen 'em."

This last remark was accompanied by a significant look at the rough board partition that separated the dining-room from the bar-room. For Westcott's drunken voice could be heard singing snatches of negro melodies in a most melancholy tone.

Somebody in the bar-room mentioned Charlton's name.

"Got out, did he?" said Westcott in a maudlin tone. "How'd 'e get out? How'd 'e like it fur's he went? Always liked simple diet, you know.

> "Oh! if I wuz a jail-bird,
>   With feathers like a crow,
>   I'd flop around and—

"Wat's the rest? Hey? How does that go? Wonder how it feels to be a thief? He! he! he!"

Somehow the voice and the words irritated Albert beyond endurance. He lost his relish for supper and went out on the piazza.

"Git's riled dreffle easy," said Jim as Charlton disappeared.

179

"Fellers weth idees does. I hope he'll gin Wes'cott another thrashin'."

"He's powerful techy," said the Poet. "Kinder curus, though. I wanted to salivate Wes'cott wunst, and he throwed my pistol into the lake."

CHAPTER XXXVI

ISABEL

What to do about going to see Isabel?

Albert knew perfectly well that he would be obliged to visit her. Isa had no doubt heard of his arrival before this time. The whole village must know it, for there was a succession of people who came on the hotel piazza to shake hands with him. Some came from friendliness, some from curiosity, but none remained long in conversation with him. For in truth conversation was quite embarrassing under the circumstances. You can not ask your acquaintance, "How have you been?" when his face is yet pale from confinement in a prison; you can not inquire how he liked Stillwater or Sing Sing, when he must have disliked what he saw of Stillwater or Sing Sing. One or two of the villagers asked Albert how he had "got along," and then blushed when they remembered that he couldn't have "got along" at all. Most of them asked him if Metropolisville had "grown any" since he left, and whether or not he meant to stay and set up here, and then floundered a little and left him. For most people talk by routine. Whatever may be thought of development from monkeys, it does seem that a strong case might be made out in favor of a descent from parrots.

Charlton knew that he must go to see Isa, and that the whole village would know where he had gone, and that it would give Isa trouble, maybe. He wanted to see Isa more than he wanted anything else in the world, but then he dreaded to see her. She had pitied him and helped him in his trouble, but her letters had something of constraint in them. He remembered how she had always mingled the friendliness of her treatment with something of reserve and coolness. He did not care much for this in other times. But now he found in himself such a hungering for something more from Isa, that he feared the effect of her cool dignity. He had braced himself against being betrayed into an affection for Isabel. He must not allow himself to become interested in her. As an honorable man he could not marry her, of course. But he would see her and thank her. Then if she should give him a few kind words he would cherish them as a comforting memory in all the loneliness of following years. He felt sorry for himself, and he granted to himself just so much indulgence.

Between his fear of compromising Isa and his feeling that on every account he must see her, his dread of meeting her and his desire to talk with her, he was in a state of compound excitement when he rose from his seat on the piazza of the City Hotel, and started down Plausaby street toward the house of Mrs. Ferret. He had noticed some women going to the weekly prayer-meeting, and half-hoped, but feared more than he hoped, that Isabel should have gone to meeting also. He knew how constant and regular she was in the performance of religious duties.

But Isa for once had staid at home. And had received from Mrs. Ferret a caustic lecture on the sin of neglecting her duty for the sake of anybody. Mrs. Ferret was afterward sorry she had said anything, for she herself wanted to stay to gratify her curiosity. But Isabel did not mind the rebuke. She put some petunias on the mantel-piece and some grasses over the looking-glass, and then tried to read, but the book was not interesting. She was alarmed at her own excitement; she planned how she would treat Albert with mingled cordiality and reserve, and thus preserve her own dignity; she went through a mental rehearsal of the meeting two or three times—in truth, she was just going over it the fourth time when Charlton stood between the morning-glory vines on the doorstep. And when she saw his face pale with suffering, she forgot all about the rehearsal, and shook his hand with sisterly heartiness—the word "sisterly" came to her mind most opportunely—and looked at him with the utmost gladness, and sat him down by the window, and sat down facing him. For the first time since Katy's death he was happy. He thought himself entitled to one hour of happiness after all that he had endured.

When Mrs. Ferret came home from prayer-meeting she entered by the back-gate, and judiciously stood for some time looking in at the window. Charlton was telling Isa something about his imprisonment, and Mrs. Ferret, listening to the tones of his voice and seeing the light in Isa's eyes, shook her head, and said to herself that it was scandalous for a Chrischen girl to act in such a way.

If the warmth of feeling shown in the interview between Albert and Isa had anything improper in it under the circumstances, Mrs. Ferret knew how to destroy it. She projected her iceberg presence into the room and froze them both.

Albert had many misgivings that night. He felt that he had not acted with proper self-control in his interview with Isabel. And just in proportion to his growing love for Isa did he chafe with the bitterness of the undeserved disgrace that must be an insurmountable barrier to his possessing her. How should he venture to hope that a woman who had refused Lurton, should be willing to marry him? And to marry his dishonor besides?

He lay thus debating what he should do, sometimes almost resolved to renounce his scruples and endeavor to win Isa, sometimes bravely determined to leave with Gray in the morning, never to come back to Metropolisville again. Sleep was not encouraged by the fact that Westcott occupied the bed on the other side of a thin board partition. He could hear him in that pitiful state of half-delirium that so often succeeds a spree, and that just touches upon the verge of mania-à-potu.

"So he's out, is he?" Charlton heard him say. "How the devil did he get out? Must a swum out, by George! That's the only way. Now her face is goin' to come. Always does come when I feel this way. There she is! Go 'way! What do you want? What do you look at me for? What makes you look that way? I can't help it. I didn't drown you. I had to get out some way. What do you call Albert for? Albert's gone to penitentiary. He can't save you. Don't look that way! If you're goin' to drown, why don't you do it and be done with it? Hey? You will keep bobbin' up and down there all night and staring at me like the devil all the time! I couldn't help it. I didn't want to shake you off. I would 'ave gone down myself if I hadn't. There now, let go! Pullin' me down again! Let go! If you don't let go, Katy, I'll have to shake you off. I couldn't help it. What made you love me so? You needn't have been a fool. Why didn't somebody tell you about Nelly? If you'd heard about Nelly, you wouldn't have—oh! the devil! I knew it! There's Nelly's face coming. That's the worst of all. What does she come for? She a'n't dead. Here, somebody! I want a match! Bring me a light!"

Whatever anger Albert may have had toward the poor fellow was all turned into pity after this night. Charlton felt as though he had been listening to the plaints of a damned soul, and moralized that it were better to go to prison for life than to carry about such memories as haunted the dreams of Westcott. And he felt that to allow his own attachment to Isa Marlay to lead to a marriage would involve him in guilt and entail a lifelong remorse. He must not bring his dishonor upon her. He determined to rise early and go over to Gray's new town, sell off his property, and then leave the Territory. But the Inhabitant was to leave at six o'clock, and Charlton, after his wakeful night, sank into a deep sleep at daybreak, and did not wake until half-past eight. When he came down to breakfast, Gray had been gone two hours and a half.

He sat around during the forenoon irresolute and of course unhappy. After a while decision came to him in the person of Mrs. Ferret, who called and asked for a private interview.

Albert led her into the parlor, for the parlor was always private enough on a pleasant day. Nobody cared to keep the

183

company of a rusty box stove, a tattered hair-cloth sofa, six wooden chairs, and a discordant tinny piano-forte, when the weather was pleasant enough to sit on the piazza or to walk on the prairie. To Albert the parlor was full of associations of the days in which he had studied botany with Helen Minorkey. And the bitter memory of the mistakes of the year before, was a perpetual check to his self-confidence now. So that he prepared himself to listen with meekness even to Mrs. Ferret.

"Mr. Charlton, do you think you're acting just right—just as you would be done by—in paying attentions to Miss Marlay when you are just out of—of—the—penitentiary?"

Albert was angered by her way of putting it, and came near telling her that it was none of her business. But his conscience was on Mrs. Ferret's side.

"I haven't paid any special attention to Miss Marlay. I called to see her as an old friend." Charlton spoke with some irritation, the more that he knew all the while he was not speaking with candor.

"Well, now, Mr. Charlton, how would you have liked to have your sister marry a man just out of—well, just—just as you are, just out of penitentiary, you know? I have heard remarks already about Miss Marlay—that she had refused a very excellent and talented preacher of the Gospill—you know who I mean—and was about to take up with—well, you know how people talk—with a man just out of the—out of the penitentiary—you know. A jail-bird is what they said. You know people will talk. And Miss Marlay is under my care, and I must do my duty as a Chrischen to her. And I know she thinks a great deal of you, and I don't think it would be right, you know, for you to try to marry her. You know the Scripcherr says that we must do as we'd be done by; and I wouldn't want a daughter of mine to marry a young man just—well—just out of—the—just out of the penitentiary, you know."

"Mrs. Ferret, I think this whole talk impertinent. Miss Marlay is not at all under your care, I have not proposed marriage to her, she is an old friend who was very kind to my mother and to me, and there is no harm in my seeing her when I please."

"Well, Mr. Charlton, I know your temper is bad, and I expected you'd talk insultingly to me, but I've done my duty and cleared my skirts, anyhow, and that's a comfort. A Chrischen must expect to be persecuted in the discharge of duty. You may talk about old friendships, and all that; but there's nothing so dangerous as friendship. Don't I know? Half the marriages that oughtn't to be, come from friendships. Whenever you see a friendship between a young man and a young woman, look out for a wedding. And I don't think you ought to ask Isabel to marry you, and you just out of—just—you know—out of the—the penitentiary."

When Mrs. Ferret had gone, Albert found that while her words had rasped him, they had also made a deep impression on him. He was, then, a jail-bird in the eyes of Metropolisville—of the world. He must not compromise Isa by a single additional visit. He could not trust himself to see her again. The struggle was not fought out easily. But at last he wrote a letter:

"MY DEAR MISS MARLAY: I find that I can not even visit you without causing remarks to be made, which reflect on you. I can not stay here without wishing to enjoy your society, and you can not receive the visits of a 'jail-bird,' as they call me, without disgrace. I owe everything to you, and it would be ungrateful, indeed, in me to be a source of affliction and dishonor to you. I never regretted my disgrace so much as since I talked with you last night. If I could shake that off, I might hope for a great happiness, perhaps.

"I am going to Gray's Village to-morrow. I shall close up my business, and go away somewhere, though I would much rather stay here and live down my disgrace. I shall remember your kindness with a full heart, and if I can ever serve you, all I have shall be yours—I would be wholly yours now, if I could offer myself without dishonoring you, and you would accept me. Good-by, and may God bless you.

"Your most grateful friend, ALBERT CHARLTON."

The words about offering himself, in the next to the last sentence, Albert wrote with hesitation, and then concluded that he would better erase them, as he did not mean to give any place to his feelings. He drew his pen through them, taking pains to leave the sentence entirely legible beneath the canceling stroke. Such tricks does inclination play with the sternest resolves!

185

CHAPTER XXXVII

THE LAST

The letter was deposited at the post-office immediately. Charlton did not dare give his self-denying resolution time to cool.

Isa was not looking for letters, and Mrs. Ferret ventured to hint that the chance of meeting somebody on the street had something to do with her walk. Of course Miss Marlay was insulted. No woman would ever do such a thing. Consciously, at least.

And after reading Charlton's letter, what did Isa do? What could she do? A woman may not move in such a case. Her whole future happiness may drift to wreck by somebody's mistake, and she may not reach a hand to arrest it. What she does must be done by indirection and under disguise. It is a way society has of training women to be candid.

The first feeling which Isa had was a sudden shock of surprise. She was not so much astonished at the revelation of Charlton's feeling as at the discovery of her own. With Albert's abrupt going away, all her heart and hope seemed to be going too. She had believed her interest in Charlton to be disinterested until this moment. It was not until he proposed going away entirely that she came to understand how completely that interest had changed its character.

But what could she do? Nothing at all. She was a woman.

As evening drew on, Charlton felt more and more the bitterness of the self-denial he had imposed upon himself. He inwardly abused Mrs. Ferret for meddling. He began to hope for all sorts of impossible accidents that might release him from his duty in the case. Just after dark he walked out. Of course he did not want to meet Miss Marlay—his mind was made up—he would not walk down Plausaby street—at least not so far as Mrs. Ferret's house. There could be no possible harm in his going half-way there. Love is always going half-way, and then splitting the difference on the remainder. Isa, on her part, remembered a little errand she must attend to at the store. She felt that, after a day of excitement, she needed the air, though indeed she did not want to meet Charlton any more, if he had made up his mind not to see her. And so they walked right up to one another, as lovers do when they have firmly resolved to keep apart.

"Good-evening, Isabel," said Albert. He had not called her

Isabel before. It was a sort of involuntary freedom which he allowed himself—this was to be the very last interview.

"Good-evening—Albert." Isa could not refuse to treat him with sisterly freedom—now that she was going to bid him adieu forever. "You were going away without so much as saying good-by."

"One doesn't like to be the cause of unpleasant remarks about one's best friend," said Charlton.

"But what if your best friend doesn't care a fig for anybody's remarks," said Isabel energetically.

"How?" asked Albert. It was a senseless interrogatory, but Isa's words almost took his breath.

Isa was startled at having said so much, and only replied indistinctly that it didn't matter what people said.

"Yes, but you don't know how long such things might cleave to you. Ten years hence it might be said that you had been the friend of a man who was—in—the penitentiary." Charlton presented objections for the sake of having them refuted.

"And I wouldn't care any more ten years hence than I do now. Were you going to our house? Shall I walk back with you?"

"I don't know." Charlton felt his good resolutions departing. "I started out because I wanted to see the lake where Katy was drowned before I go away. I am ever so glad that I met you, if I do not compromise you. I would rather spend this evening in your company than in any other way in the world—" Albert hadn't meant to say so much, but he couldn't recall it when it was uttered—"but I feel that I should be selfish to bring reproach on you for my own enjoyment."

"All right, then," said Isa, laughing, "I'll take the responsibility. I am going to the lake with you if you don't object."

"You are the bravest woman in the world," said Albert with effusion.

"You forget how brave a man you have shown yourself."

I am afraid this strain of talk was not at all favorable to the strength and persistence of Charlton's resolution, which, indeed, was by this time sadly weakened.

After they had spent an hour upon the knoll looking out upon the lake, and talking of the past, and diligently avoiding all mention of the future, Charlton summoned courage to allude to his departure in a voice more full of love than of resolve.

"Why do you go, Albert?" Isa said, looking down and breaking a weed with the toe of her boot. They had called each other by their Christian names during the whole interview.

"Simply for the sake of your happiness, Isa. It makes me

miserable enough, I am sure." Charlton spoke as pathetically as he could.

"But suppose I tell you that your going will make me as wretched as it can make you. What then?"

"How? It certainly would be unmanly for me to ask you to share my disgrace. A poor way of showing my love. I love you well enough to do anything in the world to make you happy."

Isa looked down a moment and began to speak, but stopped.

"Well, what?" said Albert.

"May I decide what will make me happy? Am I capable of judging?"

Albert looked foolish, and said, "Yes," with some eagerness. He was more than ever willing to have somebody else decide for him.

"Then I tell you, Albert, that if you go away you will sacrifice my happiness along with your own."

* * * * *

It was a real merry party that met at a petit souper at nine o'clock in the evening in the dining-room of the City Hotel some months later. There was Lurton, now pastor in Perritaut, who had just given his blessing on the marriage of his friends, and who sat at the head of the table and said grace. There were Albert and Isabel Charlton, bridegroom and bride. There was Gray, the Hoosier Poet, with a poem of nine verses for the occasion.

"I'm sorry the stage is late," said Albert. "I wanted Jim." One likes to have all of one's best friends on such an occasion.

Just then the coach rattled up to the door, and Albert went out and brought in the Superior Being.

"Now, we are all here," said Charlton. "I had to ask Mrs. Ferret, and I was afraid she'd come."

"Not her!" said Jim.

"Why?"

"She kin do better."

"How?"

"She staid to meet her beloved."

"Who's that?"

"Dave." Jim didn't like to give any more information than would serve to answer a question. He liked to be pumped.

"Dave Sawney?"

"The same. He told me to-day as him and the widder owned claims as 'jined, and they'd made up their minds to jine too. And then he haw-haw'd tell you could a-heerd him a mile. By the way, it's the widder that's let the cat out of the bag."

"What cat out of what bag?" asked Lurton.

"Why, how Mr. Charlton come to go to the State boardin'-house fer takin' a land-warrant he didn' take."

"How did she find out?" said Isa. Her voice seemed to be purer and sweeter than ever—happiness had tuned it.

"By list'nin' at the key-hole," said Jim.

"When? What key-hole?"

"When Mr. Lurton and Miss Marlay—I beg your pard'n, Mrs. Charlton—was a-talkin' about haow to git Mr. Charlton out."

"Be careful," said Lurton. "You shouldn't make such a charge unless you have authority."

Jim looked at Lurton a moment indignantly. "Thunder and lightnin'," he said, "Dave tole me so hisself! Said she tole him. And Dave larfed over it, and thought it 'powerful cute' in her, as he said in his Hoosier lingo;" and Jim accompanied this last remark with a patronizing look at Gray.

"Charlton, what are you thinking about?" asked Lurton when conversation flagged.

"One year ago to-day I was sentenced, and one year ago to-morrow I started to Stillwater."

"Bully!" said Jim. "I beg yer pardon, Mrs. Charlton, I couldn't help it. A body likes to see the wheel turn round right. Ef 'twould on'y put some folks in as well as turn some a-out!"

When Charlton with his bride started in a sleigh the next morning to his new home on his property in the village of "Charlton" a crowd had gathered about the door, moved partly by that curiosity which always interests itself in newly-married people, and partly by an exciting rumor that Charlton was not guilty of the offense for which he had been imprisoned. Mrs. Ferret had told the story to everybody, exacting from each one a pledge of secrecy. Just as Albert started his horses, Whisky Jim, on top of his stage-box, called out to the crowd, "Three cheers, by thunder!" and they were given heartily. It was the popular acquittal.

WORDS AFTERWARDS

Metropolisville is only a memory now. The collapse of the land-bubble and the opening of railroads destroyed it. Most of the buildings were removed to a neighboring railway station. Not only has Metropolisville gone, but the unsettled state of society in which it grew has likewise disappeared—the land-sharks, the claim speculators, the town-proprietors, the trappers, and the stage-drivers have emigrated or have undergone metamorphosis. The wild excitement of '56 is a tradition hardly credible to those who did not feel its fever. But the most evanescent things may impress themselves on human beings, and in the results which they thus produce become immortal. There is a last page to all our works, but to the history of the ever-unfolding human spirit no one will ever write.

THE END

www.ingramcontent.com/pod-product-compliance
Lightning Source LLC
Chambersburg PA
CBHW011504170626
46812CB00008B/2969